"'Red Skies in the Morning' by Nadia Bulkin is ingenious, funny, infuriating, disturbing, scary, heartbreaking. It's a story that only she could write."
—Paul Tremblay, author of *Horror Movie*

"Nadia Bulkin delivers a hauntingly intense novella in which indelible evils and humanity's impending annihilation coalesce in a shadowy world of terror and uncertainty. 'Red Skies in the Morning' is a gripping exploration of the visual, virulent, and visceral horrors that connect us in an increasingly disconnected society, seared onto the page with Bulkin's incandescent and unflinching style."
—Christa Carmen, Bram Stoker Award-winning and Shirley Jackson Award-nominated author of *The Daughters of Block Island*

"Nadia Bulkin's 'Red Skies in the Morning' is so hauntingly beautiful and wicked weird...you can't miss it! Ghosts possessing the living through cursed movies and polaroids, check! Cults dedicated to the spread and worship of said cursed movies, check! Two sisters bleakly entwined in a collapsing world not so different from our own, check! I spend my life searching for reads like this one. You won't be disappointed!"
—Corey Farrenkopf, author of *Living in Cemeteries*

"The work of a genius. Original, arresting—I immediately fell in love with this tech-horror world menaced by psychic disease and Video Man. Bulkin smoothly blends her talent at societal dissection and a tale of strained familial bonds into a unique vision of urban legend as contagion. A truly one-of-a-kind book."
—Hailey Piper, Bram Stoker Award-winning author of *Queen of Teeth*

ISSUES WITH AUTHORITY

NADIA BULKIN

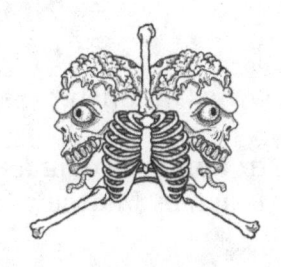

Ghoulish Books
San Antonio, Texas

Issues with Authority
Copyright © 2025 Nadia Bulkin

All Rights Reserved

ISBN: 978-1-963801-12-5

The stories included in this publication are works of fiction. Names, characters, places and incidents are products of the author's imagination or are used fictitiously. Any resemblance to actual events or locales or persons living or dead is entirely coincidental.

Without limiting the rights under copyright reserved above, no part of this publication may be reproduced, stored in or introduced into a retrieval system, or transmitted, in any form, or by any means (electronic, mechanical, photocopying, recording, or otherwise), without the prior written permission of both the copyright owner and the above publisher of this book.

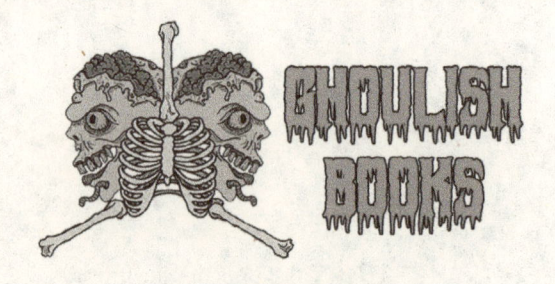

www.Ghoulish.rip

Cover Illustration by Svetlana Radayeva
Cover Design by Matthew Revert

Also by Nadia Bulkin

She Said Destroy

TABLE OF CONTENTS

Cop Car 1

Your Next Best American Girl 61

Red Skies in the Morning 115

COP CAR

1. Carly lends a hand

FOR THE FIRST seven years of Carly Parrish's life, there was no record of her existence anywhere except in her mother's diary. She had been born in a sweat lodge deep among the pine trees of North America's Cascade Range, on the one-year anniversary of her mother's absconsion from her middle-class family to join a cult seeking transcendence on the mortal plane, Peacemakers International. Her mother was twenty-two. Her father was the anointed leader of Peacemakers International, though he never acknowledged Carly as his own. As far as the cult was concerned, paternity—and, indeed, parenthood as a whole—was of no importance. Babies would simply materialize on the Camp Santi commune and be raised more or less collectively, which is to say loosely, and if they died of malnourishment or measles or mountain lions, it was understood to be God's will.

This lackadaisical approach to membership growth was atypical of cults operating in the region at the time, and allowed Peacemakers International to escape the authorities' notice for nearly a decade. And yet this approach was by no means strategic. The cult's leader, Carly's father, Rishi Dev, simply did not care enough to exert that level of control over the direction of his flock. *What will be will be*, he would say when asked to make a decision; when cult members complained of each other or fought with neighboring landowners, he would shrug and proclaim, *it is no concern of mine.*

So Carly spent her early years in a zone of great indifference. Her mother, who was neither equipped for nor inclined toward motherhood, did not write of her often—"she won't look me in the eye," she wrote of Carly the baby, kicking off a two-day flurry of concern for the child's health that ended as suddenly as it began. After all, Alma-Jean was a Level Three Peacemaker by then; she had seven ladders of transcendence to climb. "Melissa's baby Xavier cries all the time," she wrote when Carly was six months old, "praise God that Carly is so quiet." Once Carly was toilet-trained, Alma-Jean's mentions of her in an otherwise well-documented journal dwindled to once or twice per year, and rarely truly concerned Carly. "Rishi Dev praised me for raising such a well-behaved child," for example, or "I will ask Victor, because he owes me a favor, since I've been sending Carly to help him in the kitchen."

Compared to some of the other Peacemaker men at Camp Santi, Victor was one of the safer options to receive a girl-child as an apprentice. He and his wife had joined Peacemakers International together, when the onset of yet another war in the Middle East had filled them with the need to do something with their sadness. But then his wife died after Rishi Dev convinced her that cancer could be cured with silver tincture and alkaline foods, and now Victor—who had taken over his wife's kitchen duties despite having always been a much poorer cook—was ambling from station to station in a fog of grief, forgetting to clean vegetables, letting soups boil over.

Carly, meanwhile, had become very interested in brains. One day she watched a sickly, stumbling deer smash its skull open against a rock, after which it fell in a fit of twitches. When she went to investigate the pink goo leaking from its head as it lay dying, clarity lit like someone had turned on a light in her mind that she hadn't known existed: whatever was in that deer's head, it made the deer

COP CAR

work—and the jumble of pain and confusion radiating from that goo meant the deer wasn't working anymore. Later she opened the skull of a mouse she'd grabbed from beneath the floorboards, and was thrilled to see a quick surge of urgency like a tapestry of lightning flash in her mind, though not her heart: so *this* was the fear that some Peacemakers said ruled the hearts of their enemies. As had happened with the deer, the clarity of the mouse vanished when its heart stopped beating, which was how she learned that this understanding only came from living brains—but what a discovery! Carly had always been a curious child, but had been hamstrung by her own inability to make sense of emotion. This, at least, allowed her to see what people meant by anger, terror, sadness, joy. It took her a few months of practice, staring at animals while on her belly in the dirt, but eventually she learned that she did not need to open a head to see into it: she just had to concentrate hard enough, and the truth would shine right through that bony helmet. People were harder. What Carly wanted most of all was to see inside her own brain, to see how it compared—but since she couldn't do that, she was resigned to poking around the other brains hanging about Camp Santi. Most of them were impermeable—she could stare at them for a week straight and their heads would be just as rocky and hard as they were when she started. But then, there was Victor. Sad Victor. Angry Victor. Daydreaming Victor, and it was these dreams that intrigued Carly the most. They were wild, bloody, exciting; *spongy* in a way that more primal emotions weren't, and when Carly poured a little bit of her own thoughts into the force of her concentration, she could see her colors leak into Victor's fantasies. Like a single drop of vanilla extract sweetening the entire cake.

Firefighters received a call about a fire at a remote property right around dinner time. They managed to quell the blaze only after it swallowed up seventy percent of Camp Santi and killed half its residents, including Alma-

NADIA BULKIN

Jean—Rishi Dev had left her behind while fleeing from his highly flammable quarters. As in all cases of suspected arson, the police followed close behind, corralling the flock of shellshocked, smoke-stained survivors into individual holding pens before they could get their stories straight. Carly, age seven, was one of these survivors. She stood out not only because of her small size, but because of her condition: although her cheeks were smudged with soot, she was not in a state of shock. The transcript is sealed now, but the conversation went like this:

Police Officer: Honey, do you know about the fire?
Carly: Yes.
Police Officer: I need to ask you some questions so we can try to figure out what happened. Is that okay?
Carly: Yes.
Police Officer: Can you tell me what you remember about what happened?
Carly: Victor lit up the grease in his pan and threw it everywhere. The walls caught fire and I ran away so it wouldn't get me.
Police Officer: You saw him do this?
Carly: Yes.
Police Officer: Did he say anything to you before he did this?
Carly: No.
Police Officer: Was he acting strangely?
Carly: Not really.
Police Officer: Do you have any idea why he might have done it?
Carly: Because I told him to.

You can imagine the astonishment that rippled through the police station like a sonic wave after this child—this little girl, small for her age from years of undernourishment—made this statement. The police officer in the room with her was suddenly saddled with the

COP CAR

distinct pressure of being the only deep-sea explorer who could possibly catch hold of a hitherto unknown species of deep-sea fish, and subconsciously dug his heels in at the table, determined to land this quarry.

Police Officer: Why did you tell him to do that, honey?
Carly: He wanted to blow everything up. He just wasn't brave enough. So I helped him.
Police Officer: What do you mean you helped him, how did you help him?
Carly: I said *just do it, do it, do it*, right in his head.
Police Officer: Okay. And how did you know this is what he wanted to do? He told you?
Carly: No. I could see it in his head.

2. Carly keeps her cool

As far as the government was concerned, anomalous assets fell under the purview of a nondescript, exceptionally well-funded department led by Director Ray Neelley. All of the department's expenses were coded "research and development," which was not so much a lie as a heavily redacted version of the truth—half of the department was dedicated to researching psychic powers, and the other half was dedicated to developing them, mostly into weapons.

Carly's case file came in cluttered with so many urgent flags—she was so young, the damage was so great—that Director Neelley stayed late on a Friday to examine it himself. After determining that it was certainly worth a follow-up, he transferred it to the desk of Agent Greg Dunham, a thirteen-year veteran of the agency who he thought might have the patience to communicate with a broken young child. Agent Dunham was in fact still at his desk when Director Neelley walked by in his trench coat and hat, saying, "I've got a live one for you!" An hour later, Agent Dunham was calling his wife Stacy to cancel their weekend winery plans, explaining that he had to travel to Oregon to see a little girl in a foster home.

Agent Dunham was one of the so-called Oxford Boys, often held in contempt by the louder Brass Grunts whose temporary secondments from the military had become permanent—bookish, ambiguously "nervous" in that way human men have often described human women, and thorough. (I say thorough because this was a consistent theme in his performance reviews, not because I saw much evidence of it. Though I'm sure in comparison to the Brass Grunts, he was the picture of diligence. All would agree, I believe, that he was "slow on the draw.")

Carly's foster mother had never been so pleased to see a federal government official at her front door. She explained that the local cops had told her to keep Carly separated from the other children, and that while she typically took their advice with a grain of salt, on account of them being a bunch of ninnies, in this one instance something inside her had told her to listen and she was glad she did. "Because I think she needs way fancier help than I can give her," she said.

"Why do you say that?" Agent Dunham asked. He noticed that they were proceeding unusually slowly up the cramped staircase, prolonging the wretched creaking, and wondered if Mrs. Yablonski had a health condition or if she was just frightened. (It was the latter.)

"When I was making her bed the first night, I tripped over the rug and fell, just about banged my head on the dresser. Nothing to do with her, of course." She was whispering now. "But I look over at her, thinking she might have gotten scared by all this commotion, and she's just looking at me like nothing happened. No surprise. No concern. No emotion or reaction whatsoever."

"I understand she's been through a lot," said Agent Dunham, who wasn't sure this mattered.

Mrs. Yablonski said nothing else as they walked down the hallway to the northernmost room on the second floor.

COP CAR

She could have said more. But she really did want him to take the child off her hands.

They found little Carly sitting at the foot of her bed, shoulders slumped in boredom while a commercial tried selling her on a luxury sedan. It wasn't protocol for Mrs. Yablonski to leave them alone together, so she hovered just outside the open door, biting her nails.

"So, Carly. What have you been doing for fun since you got here?"

She pointed listlessly at the television, where a nature show crew was watching a young puma stalk a lonesome mule deer. Hiding low in the foliage while its ignorant prey foraged for berries, the puma was utterly still save for the occasional slight swivels of the head as the deer moved back and forth. *Even at its young age*, the narrator intoned, *the puma has endless patience for the kill.*

"Impressive, isn't it?" Agent Dunham said, eyes flitting from screen to girl. The puma, he explained, had learned from its mother—how to stalk prey, how to attack, how to kill, how to hide from predators larger and more fearsome than itself.

"What if it has no mother?" Carly asked. "How will it know what it is?"

Agent Dunham thought she was worried about learning vital life skills, becoming a functional adult, now that her mother was dead, and this struck him as reasonable in spite of the fact that her mother would have taught her very little about function or adulthood. "Other adults will teach it," he said, to reassure.

Carly found this unsatisfactory, not only because she had seen no indication that other adults would see a kitten as anything but another meal, but because she was not, in fact, hinting at being worried about learning vital life skills—she was simply wondering, for she was still very earnest then, how she could find out where she sat on the totem pole of predation. This is a perfectly standard—one might even say vital—line of inquiry for mortals, so I have never understood why humans are so put off by it. They seem to find cannibalism to be quite gauche as well, even in the interest of survival—really, I don't know where they'd be if they hadn't mastered tools. I'm sure it was not lost on Carly that the adults she encountered never seemed able to answer her straightforward questions.

"How do you like it here, Carly?"

"It's boring."

"You liked it better at Camp Santi?"

She shrugged again.

"You know how you told Victor to start a fire? Have you ever done anything like that before?"

"Not really."

"Not really? Or no?"

"I tried with Mama, so she wouldn't make me do laundry. It didn't work, though. I couldn't get in. Her head was tough, like gristle. Victor's head was soft, like cheese."

"I see. What about my head? Or Mrs. Yablonski's head?"

Agent Dunham was playing with his life, here. But onboarding at Director Neelley's department included six weeks spent in the desert learning techniques to decrease one's "susceptibility and suggestibility"—clutching the pointy knucklebone of a sheep to ground oneself in reality, for example—and he believed himself to be safe. And he probably would have been safe from the average untrained juvenile psychic, though it was still a risky bet against Carly.

"You? Yours is hard. Like a rock." Carly looked at the door, where Mrs. Yablonski was now shielding her head with her hand—as if that would have stopped Carly. "Hers is, too, but more like wood."

"How would you like to learn how to get inside anyone you'd like?"

He said this at the exact moment that the puma launched itself toward the mule deer—reaching it in two bounds, tackling it, grasping it by the shoulders and finally

COP CAR

breaking its spinal cord by digging its canines into the vertebrae at the base of the deer's skull in no more than five seconds flat—this is what Carly would remember the most, that lightning bolt of understanding that her powers might help her find the answer to her existential question: *Who am I?*

This type of mistake, one cannot blame on Agent Dunham. Carly has always been rather spare with her words, and he was, as they say, "trying his best" to offer what he understood human children to need.

Other types of mistakes, however, are less forgivable for a man of his supposed diligence—for example, his dismissal of neurologist Chuyasu Hara's concerns upon reviewing Carly's brain scans later that month. Where Dr. Hara noted "abnormalities in the structure of the child's brain," Agent Dunham's own brain immediately raced toward the most favorable, most exciting interpretation: that her enlarged striatum and oddly-shaped hippocampus represented a physical explanation for her psychic powers, not a missing moral core.

3. Carly breaks a leg

Stacy Dunham had never wanted children, a deep-seated truth that she had kept concealed within herself until a miscarriage early in her marriage had filled her with more relief than regret. Greg had never felt strongly about children, but he felt strongly about Stacy, and so they'd agreed to go without and craft the life they wanted with only each other in mind. To others, however, Greg pled infertility—his own, Stacy's, or both of theirs. He did not think his colleagues would have understood, and he was right.

All of which is to say—Stacy was not thrilled from the outset about spending the next ten years of her life raising a random seven-year-old girl, especially one that seemed to be mostly feral. Greg tried to craft compromises: he would do all the raising; the child could be sent to live with others after she "stabilized," and that shouldn't take more than a few years; the child would spend as much time as possible in the research facility but she couldn't be asked to sleep there on a military cot, and surely Stacy understood, didn't she? "Sure," Stacy said, in a tone that communicated her displeasure.

In return, Greg Dunham kept his promise: he and Carly spent twelve to fourteen, sometimes even sixteen hours per day at the research facility for the first year of his guardianship. When they returned home, Carly was usually asleep or close to it, and certainly too tired to do anything that would have much of an impact on Stacy; unfortunately, so was Greg.

They were working, that first year, to understand the exact mechanism of Carly's psychic abilities. And yes, I do mean "they." Only Agent Dunham had it written into his MBOs, but Carly needed a deeper understanding of how her gift worked if she had any hope of developing it or controlling it or making any consistent use of it.

The two of them would sit in a room with a soldier. The soldier would be sitting with his or her back to them, wearing a set of noise-cancelling headphones and an assortment of sensors. In front of the soldier would be a tray of cups of various colors. "Try to make him pick up the green cup," Agent Dunham would say to a similarly sensor-laden Carly.

(Carly, who understandably loathed to do anything for no reason, would at first ask "Why?" to which Agent Dunham would answer, "To see if you can do it." After a few tries, Carly accepted this uber-mission as her raison d'être, and stopped asking.)

Carly would make the soldier pick up the green cup. She didn't need to see the cup to do so. *Green cup*, she'd think at him. Asked about it afterwards, the soldier would invariably report a nondescript but overwhelming urge to do so, one that seemed to generate from their own minds even though they had no explanation for it. To reward her success, Agent Dunham would give her a cherry cordial—a bewitching treat the likes of which Carly had never tasted, a shell of creamy chocolate that could be broken to let loose a gush of sweet cherry ooze.

This went on until Carly was able to reliably hack into minds with statistically average demographic markers in under sixty total minutes of exposure. They determined that she could do so indoors, outdoors, through one centimeter of glass and two meters of water. The ease with which she passed these tests made Agent Dunham suspect that she wasn't close to her limits.

But then came concern from the powers-that-be about the socialization of anomalous assets. It was important that they be given opportunities to interact with people who were neither assets nor staff; otherwise how could they be expected to behave normally on missions?

And Stacy, poor Stacy. At first she could compartmentalize, living her life as normal while her husband and his charge were away, and shutting herself in her bedroom at night. But the towheaded child soon began to power through Stacy's sleeping pills. She'd wake from nightmares of Carly skinning rabbits in the backyard and parading their burned bodies through the house on sharpened spears to see shadows of little feet parked silently outside the bedroom door, illuminated by faint moonglow. And she would know: this was not *ferality* she was feeling. Stacy had grown up on a decaying estate littered with animals of all kinds—working dogs, horses, ferrets—and she might have had an easier time with an actual feral child. A feral child might still respond to pantomimed gestures of mammalian caretaking—a stroke of the head, a blanket for warmth—or could at least be relegated to a backyard treehouse to howl at the moon.

I do not think she ever admitted this even to her husband, but here was the truth: Carly frightened her.

Seeing only that Stacy was skittish around the child,

Greg suggested they spend more time together. "Once you get to know her," he said, "you might actually like her. She's very precocious. Very smart."

Stacy did not doubt that Carly possessed either of these traits; these traits were not the problem. The problem was the ease with which Carly would lie about having completed a chore, for example. The way she would start crying on cue if either of them tried to hold her accountable for the lie. The way the tears would stop as soon as there was no longer an audience for them. One time Stacy had actually hid on the other side of a semi-open door, hoping to catch Carly in a performance, only to push the door open and see Carly smiling at her in what appeared to be a mimicry of serenity. Like I said: Carly frightened her.

Still, she humored her husband. She bought a watercolor kit and took Carly out to the backyard, encouraging her to paint flowers or trees or whatever else her heart desired. Carly painted a burning house, its front yard littered with frowning stick figures with Xs for eyes. "I am sorry you had to see that happen to your old home," Stacy tried, but Carly shook her head.

"It's not Camp Santi," she said—at which point Stacy noticed the color of the house, the number of windows on its fiery face.

"I cannot be around her," Stacy said, and so Agent Dunham reluctantly sent Carly away to the Norfolk Academy, a small and secluded boarding school for girls born into a certain level of wealth. He was worried, and so was Director Neelley, about sending her away for five nights a week, but these fears were ameliorated when she passed her first term with zero disciplinary calls home and satisfactory grades.

(Here, again, is another classic Greg Dunham mistake: he misattributed the absence of disciplinary calls to Carly's disciplined behavior, when in fact Carly was simply learning how not to get caught. For example, targeting girls who were already considered odd or poorly behaved, or verbally telling girls one thing while mentally pushing them to do another. Oh yes, she'd heard Agent Dunham's warning to not use her powers at Norfolk since the students and staff there posed so little challenge to her—"just boring, standard-issue people," he called them, and he wasn't wrong per se—but what else was she meant to focus on? Classes were even worse.)

She still returned to the Dunham home on weekends and holidays, visits that became markedly easier after Stacy left for good. Each time he picked her up from among the pines of Norfolk, Agent Dunham found himself wondering what Stacy had been so upset about. Carly was growing into a remarkably even-tempered child—wise beyond her years, he often found himself thinking—who displayed a poise and resilience that would have been unusual for any preteen, but especially one that had come from a neglectful cult. And in a welcome change of pace from Stacy, Carly never seemed to be upset about anything—not difficult classes nor poor grades nor the friends that she didn't seem to be making. If anything, *he* was at first disappointed by her consistently middling academic performance—then he reminded himself that caring about such things had sent him into several mental breakdowns in his teens and twenties and if anything, he ought to admire Carly's ability to care so little. Perhaps he was simply lonely, in the vacuum of a house that Stacy had left behind. But he found himself very much enjoying his drives home with Carly in the passenger seat, listening to Beethoven and the news, pretending that he was her father and she was his child.

For her part, Carly enjoyed school, in the same way that she had enjoyed testing Stacy Dunham. Not only was it more entertaining than the white-walled facility, but she learned a lot about herself. She learned to appreciate bathroom mirrors on crowded mornings, for showing her at last where she appeared to fit into the world—which of her features were considered desirable, which she would need to change. And there was no better mirror than seeing which psychic manifestations of herself, transmitted during class or lunch or sleep, seemed to provoke the greatest level of agitation in those she targeted.

Stacy, for example, was clearly terrified that she was going to go on a murder spree. Lenora with the designer bags was afraid she'd look better in group photos. Miss Freemont the Fine Arts teacher didn't want her to laugh at her. Gary the groundskeeper was scared she could see how much he liked her in a miniskirt. Quintana who did seances in the broom closet thought she already was or soon would be possessed by a demon. Ha ha! Kids say the damnedest things.

4. Carly starts a new job

On her eighteenth birthday, Carly received an entire box of cherry cordials from Agent Dunham that she enjoyed in the privacy of what was now her bedroom in the ancestral Dunham home, and a directive from Director Neelley to "take this show on the road."

Carly was the "show." The "road" was Interstate 20 toward Merrimac, home to the Church of Karmic Renewal, a small doomsday cult wedged into the Southern coastal plain.

Unlike Peacemakers International, the Church of Karmic Renewal did not believe transcendence was possible on the earthly plane. This simple decision had infused them with an air of desperation, of flailing urgency, rendered ever more frantic by Oren Goodyear's strong belief that the United States would soon be annihilated in some type of "supersonic" attack.

The part of the government that employed Director Neelley and Agent Dunham did not care one ounce about the "terrified nutjobs," as Director Neelley described them, who had signed their lives over to the Church of Karmic

COP CAR

Renewal. They had no international connections, no ambition to infiltrate Hollywood or government or the Board of Education, and zero means to execute any sort of national annihilation themselves. They fractured families and brought suffering upon their acolytes, sure, but what religion didn't? As Rishi Dev might say, *it is no concern of mine.*

What *was* of concern to the men who approved Director Neelley's budget was the governor—or should I say *governess*—of the Church's home state, and the incendiary language coming out of her ruby red lips. Depending on one's political perspective she was either a nutjob, an iconoclast, or a fool—regardless, she had started to chitter-chatter about seceding from the Union in order to make better use of the revenue from the state's oil basin, and though the threat was likely idle, the federal government did not appreciate the normalization of separatism. The governess was also unusually popular for a female human politician, likely due to her past as a country music star, and her constituents tended to ignore the destabilizing potential of her rhetoric, lulled by her folksy demeanor and bedazzled by her rhinestone-studded jackets.

(Later events notwithstanding, on this point I do sympathize. Humans are quite stupid, as a rule.)

Carly was assigned to infiltrate the Church of Karmic Renewal because they were one of the few groups that did not seem besotted with the governess, and so represented a unique opportunity to drive a wedge, or so it was hoped, between the governess and her people. The Church's dislike was nothing personal; Oren Goodyear's people were highly unimpressed with secular government of any kind, at any level.

Agent Dunham did not like the idea of putting Carly in another cult.

"What, you're worried she'll accidentally join it?" Director Neelley joked, only half-listening.

NADIA BULKIN

"No," said Agent Dunham, although he actually was. He had read studies about cultic recidivism—her chances weren't good. "I just want her to broaden her experiences."

"Being well-rounded is not a requirement for an operative," said Director Neelley.

I would argue that the much-maligned cult is the natural apex of human organization, but the two men weren't really debating cults, were they? They were debating whether Agent Dunham was treating Carly as a surrogate child.

If the Church of Karmic Renewal followed Peacemakers International's recruitment strategy, Carly could have simply sat down in one of the cult's pizza shops—Noble Peace Pies, they were called—looking young and lost and alone, and waited for a cult member to approach. (This method had a below fifty percent success rate, but it did work with Alma-Jean.) But Oren Goodyear was intensely skeptical of what he called the "sleeping world" and thought it was dangerous to pounce on an unsuspecting "sleeper." He had tried a few times in his youth—a school friend, a coworker, a woman from the DMV whom he'd asked on a date with the sole purpose of teaching her about God—and each time he'd been met with hostility and in the case of the coworker, outright violence. People had to wake up on their own, he said, and only then could they follow the "lamp posts" to the Church.

Carly's first step, then, was to find herself a "lamp post." That is to say, a piece of paper with a cryptic call to worship and some tear-off directions stapled to a reasonably flat surface—the Church of Karmic Renewal was not made of money, after all. Agent Dunham suggested Carly go down the telephone poles of Merrimac's main street, but Carly had a better idea: the local gun store. Taped between a neighborhood gun range's special summer pricing and information about a missing mastiff was a yellow sheet of paper advertising a "Tuesday night dinner and prayer circle" for "concerned truth-seeking

COP CAR

Christians" in a "blue house on Paragon Street." Three of its tabs had been torn off. Carly took the fourth.

On Tuesday evening, Carly got off the 44 bus at the Paragon Street stop and searched for a blue house that looked like it might be hiding a doomsday cult. Only one fit the description: Oren Goodyear's stormy-sky-colored dollhouse with scuffed gingerbread trim, an inheritance from his widowed mother. A man was sitting on the porch, sharpening a hunting knife on a stone. On instinct, she tried to give his brain a quick rap, but he had his head sealed up tight.

"Hi," said Carly. "I'm here for the dinner? With the Church?"

The man on the porch was actually Oren Goodyear himself, which explained why Carly couldn't hack him. She never would be able to, although I never got a chance to help her with it. He didn't smile when he heard her innocent inquiry, didn't jump at the chance to bring a new lost young woman into his fold, because unlike the average cult leader active at the time, Oren had not assembled his following for money or sex but rather because they had been the first and only to take his vision seriously, to believe in his unimpeachable belief. Had he not found them, he would have trudged along as a cult of one (or two, if you count his wife, as that mouse would have followed him to the very gates of Hell).

I am fascinated by this type of human, far more than I am by the average self-centered sinner. They are clearly mis-wired, so obviously out of step with their peers, and yet these self-appointed messiahs believe they are best-positioned to write an all-encompassing doctrine for humanity. Really quite remarkable!

"Go round back," Oren said to Carly, lowering his eyes to his knife. "Kait will show you around."

5. Carly makes a friend

Carly found Kait scooping shit out of the chicken coop. She was in her mid-twenties then—older than Carly technically, though her girlish face and wide-eyed innocence made her look like a virginal martyr. She introduced herself as Kait Lavinia, which she immediately had to explain: "We get to choose our own last names, when we get baptized within the Church. I was nineteen and going through a phase."

Carly didn't know why the woman was turning pink. She was ill-equipped at reading faces, would look for fear in the mouth and so on—a price of her temperament, but I would help her with this later—but even she knew that blushing indicated embarrassment. "I'm jealous," she said. "Wish I could have picked my name." The only thing that "Parrish" called to mind for Carly was burned and bleeding Alma-Jean, her pathetic excuse of a mother.

"Your name's fine. It's nice and normal. Mine is ridiculous."

"Then change it again."

Kait Lavinia looked shocked at the suggestion, at the possibility—nay, realization—that she could just *do that*, just disregard the name she'd joined the Church under like it was a sweater she was flinging off. It had been strange enough to change her name the first time, but it had been positioned to her as a baptism, an indication of her choice to commit to her faith. What Carly was suggesting sounded more like a fulfilled *whim*, an indication of *impulse*—which of course it was. But there was little room in Oren Goodyear's Church for "flights of fancy," as he called them.

After that night's dinner of mashed potatoes, chicken tenders, and a two-hour prayer circle led by Oren Goodyear, Kait walked Carly to the bus stop. "I hope you'll come back for dinner on Friday," she said.

Carly held Kait's gaze in silence, knowing the personal attention—the heat of being seen as her own person instead of one of a faceless community—would unsettle her counterpart. Predictably, Kait started rummaging in her jacket, asking if she needed bus fare, apologizing for not thinking ahead—so Carly grabbed her hand, prompting a shudder, and turned it to reveal a faded pink scar across Kait's wrist.

Kait wrenched her hand free and stretched her jacket sleeve down as far as the denim would allow.

"Is that the phase the Church got you out of?"

Kait chuckled uneasily. "Yeah." When Carly kept staring—kept knocking for an opening—Kait's mouth dropped open under an invisible pressure, a mysterious compulsion to say more. "I'd just had a really bad breakup. Had nowhere to go, couldn't get more hours at work so I couldn't make rent anywhere that wasn't murder rape city. My stepdad hates me, so. Home wasn't an option. I'm lucky Oren let me stay."

"I don't have parents either," Carly said, and Kait allowed herself a private smile. A smile just for her.

Carly did come back for Friday dinner, and for Sunday services after that. Eventually she moved into the house, took the bunk above Kait's in the six-bed "women's dormitory," and signed up for work shifts cooking meals and cleaning floors. During prayer circles she jumped from one bent head to another, tapping like a woodpecker for hollow spots, soft spots, cracked spots that could be opened like an egg with just a few firm taps. They'd twitch and stretch and glance around, the contents of Oren Goodyear's extemporaneous rants dressed as teachings falling to the wayside as they looked for the source of their restlessness and found her, this quiet street waif who never seemed to be on the right page of the Bible.

Most of Oren's commentary focused on the individual sins that stood between the lost people marooned on this imperfect Earth and God's World to Come, which sometimes seemed to be a giant spaceship and sometimes seemed to be a planet and other times was some sort of space blanket, "stretching from star to star." To say that

Oren was making it up as he went along was to downplay the stress of trying to find English words to describe what appeared in his—and only his!—head to be true divinity.

Eventually, however, one of Oren's speeches touched upon "tyrannical government." He was speaking very vaguely, referencing Nero and Ahab and various other leaders he hadn't had the pleasure of knowing, but Carly had heard whispers in the house of "theft by taxation" and "unlawful seizure" and now that she observed his followers nodding vigorously, she saw an opening of a more direct kind.

"Excuse me, Oren?" It was the first time she'd ever spoken in a prayer circle, and Kait gave her a sharp warning nudge—but warnings from the meek meant precious little to Carly. "What are we supposed to do to fight a regime like this? Like, what would God want us to do?"

When I say Carly couldn't get into Oren's head, it wasn't for lack of trying. I don't think he ever felt more than a faint buzz, though, and he probably attributed that buzz to electromagnetic radiation. "He would want us to pray," he said.

More than a few curious heads turned toward Carly after prayer circle that day, but Kait hurried her out of the den before any of them could summon the courage to speak to her. Carly did not go anywhere against her will, but she was amused by the hapless frenzy in Kait's movements and allowed herself to be dragged along. "Oren doesn't like us to get involved in things like that," Kait hissed once they were on the second floor, well outside of hearing distance.

"Even if it's the right thing to do?"

Kait paused. She was feeling a tickle in her brain. "What do you mean, the right thing?"

There was a raw simplicity to Kait's thinking that Carly recognized in herself—a shocking sensation, given that Carly had never seen herself in any person she'd

COP CAR

encountered. "Whatever helps us the most," she answered, trying to guess what Kait would want to hear. Kait gave her an odd look, so she must have guessed wrong. "I mean... doesn't he also want to help people who don't know they can be saved?"

On this last point, Kait was quick to shake her head. "People have to wake up on their own."

It felt like a mind loop, a logical roundabout with no weak spot because its own head matched its tail. It bewildered Carly, but it matched the challenge Agent Dunham had given her—could she break into a mind that had been so thoroughly bricked up?—and she dropped the subject, for now. He'd warned her that the real world was very different from the controls of the facility, and while her predatory instinct had always been to force her way into a target immediately upon locking on, she had the sense to guess that a sledgehammer would not be effective here. Maybe Oren Goodyear was onto something, she thought, about people having to "wake up on their own." Maybe that also included his own congregation.

She did what Oren would have advised her to do: kept her head down and focused on helping others. She rid the house of Bradley Chattanooga, who used his position as Oren's brother-in-law to escape punishment for taking liberties with the house's girls; having no principles and very little sense of self his brain was very pliable, and it was easy enough to convince him his true calling was free solo climbing. She stopped Shawn McDonald's busybody parents from coming to the house and harassing everyone. When Tom "T.J." Jefferson suggested they ban radio as well as television, she drummed up enough opposition that he couldn't get a second, let alone an official vote. Each time she promised the plaintiff that she would "pray on it," and within days her will would be done. Even those members utterly loyal to Oren's endurance-based approach to life would have noticed that Carly's prayers seemed to have a fast track to God.

"When you get baptized officially," Kait asked as they collected eggs from the chicken coop, "what will your new name be?"

Carly had started fantasizing about this long before her current mission. Sometimes when talking to randoms at grocery stores and gas stations—trying on new identities, getting in a little freelance practice—she would say her name was "Carly Suprema" or "Carly Sledgehammer."

"Carly Puma," she said, after her favorite predator.

6. Carly learns a lesson

By the time the governess announced what turned out to be the most controversial policy of her term—a mandatory registration program for certain high-powered firearms following a deadly lovers' tiff at the Chamber of Commerce—Carly's good will within the Church of Karmic Renewal was high enough that her subtle verbal and mental encouragement of a protest against what she was now calling a "tyrannical government" was welcomed by a majority of Church members.

Had the mission not existed, had Carly not existed, Oren Goodyear would have simply stashed the Church's cache of weapons and told his followers to lay low. The group likely would have continued their dinners and prayer circles without incident, unharmed and armed. Alas, the cards were stacked against poor Oren. An anonymous tipster—Agent Dunham, calling from a payphone—alerted local law enforcement to the fact that the Church had dozens of unregistered firearms on Oren Goodyear's property. This prompted a series of mutually-escalatory events: two policemen showing up unannounced on the property; a confrontation on the gingerbread front porch; six policemen returning to the property with a search warrant; a confrontation inside the living room that constituted a refusal to comply—

COP CAR

culminating, finally, in the arrest of several Church members, including Oren Goodyear.

Despite his dislike of paying "ransom to the king," Oren would have wanted his followers to gather enough funds to make the Church members' bail. But without the presence of his steady hand in the house, Carly had an even easier time encouraging his flock to do something bigger. Something bolder. Something that would attract the eyes of the world to what they knew in their hearts was a great injustice. Tom Jefferson, who had quickly started yelling commands in Oren's stead, made eye contact with Carly over the kitchen table and became suddenly convinced that they needed to stage a demonstration at the city jail, demanding the immediate release of the "martyrs."

Carly reported this to Agent Dunham during their regular check-in at the grocery store—Carly had needed to flex her psychic muscles in order to land grocery duty, but it was far too risky to have Agent Dunham sneaking around Paragon Street. He jotted down the details in the cereal aisle, praising her good work, and then reminded her: "They cannot bring their guns."

"That doesn't make sense," Carly whispered. "How are they supposed to make any demands?"

"That's not your problem," he whispered back, pausing to take a breath as a suspicious woman pushed past them with her cart. "Carly, focus. Think. No one is going to be sympathetic if they show up kitted out like a bunch of vigilantes. Remember?"

She remembered the mission objective being long and jumbled and boring—that, she remembered. As much as she enjoyed testing her powers on people, my Carly was never one for strategic gambits. Agent Dunham's attempts to teach her chess only served to annoy her; what was she learning from a silly game's silly rules when in real life she never had to wait her turn? The way Carly saw it, the natural solution to the problem of the governess was to give the Church of Karmic Renewal a clear shot.

NADIA BULKIN

But she didn't want to hear another nonsense strategic lecture from Agent Dunham, so she let it go. A bunch of blah blah blah, she thought. And when the Church of Karmic Renewal made their show of force outside the city jail, they did so peacefully. No guns, no bombs, no gassed-up vehicles. Just Tom Jefferson leading chants through a loudspeaker and Kait distributing pamphlets and Shawn obstructing the sidewalk, and so on. It was all extremely boring and I wouldn't have blamed Carly for falling asleep standing up, but then law enforcement arrived, and the confrontation finally became interesting.

"Folks, I'm gonna need you to disperse!" the counter-loudspeaker bellowed, and so jerked Carly to life. She would tell Agent Dunham later that she needed to make sure law enforcement's response was adequately violent; the truth is that she wanted to know whether she could force a target to break a "rule" that they were objectively better off following. What can I say? She really liked tests.

Stand your ground! She imagined herself an octopus with double—no, triple—the arms, grabbing at as many Church brains as she could and telling them, *Do not comply! Resist, resist, resist!*

And they did. They made like oak trees and rooted themselves to the asphalt. These faces that had so devotedly listened to Oren Goodyear, huddled on whatever chairs they could find, were now enraptured by her. This was Carly's first taste of leadership, as I understand it, and oh, how glorious it was. More decadent than any cherry cordial.

The surge of power and excitement gave Carly momentary wings. She cried out in self-exultation, adrenaline coursing through her blood and racing like sacrilegious Promethean fire to the Church members she was driving—*her* flock, *her* herd—and there, it hit a wall. You must understand: this should not have happened. Carly is a pusher. An accelerant. She should have started a fire that roared across city blocks, burning the whole of

COP CAR

Merrimac, ideally—but she had been told to to keep them non-violent and so had turned them into oak trees, hapless and unmoving, with nowhere to go but down. The Promethean fire had no choice but to blow back to its source and sock Carly square in the gut.

And so, Carly learned an important lesson: that her powers were wasted on anything other than violence. Anything that was not a push toward predation was a tragic misuse of her time.

She was still catching her breath when the state's crush came, as it has come for every human grouping that has tried to challenge a much stronger one: first in the form of shields, and then tear gas, and finally batons, as a drowning and gasping Carly continued to command the falling oak trees as best as she could: *Resist! Resist! Resist . . .*

Agent Dunham extracted Carly before her body could be bloodied like the others.

After he had given her water and buckled her into the front seat of his car, Agent Dunham asked if she was all right. She did not answer or acknowledge him, not even when he added on, "You did well, Car." Without a cherry cordial as a reward, such praise didn't mean much to Carly, anyway. Then, mistaking her sullenness for guilt, he said, "I know it's tough to watch people get hurt like that. But if they'd fought back or brought guns or anything like that it would have been so much worse. People could have died. This was the safest way to do this."

"I was useless," Carly said. "You wasted me."

Perhaps it sounds brutal. But Carly was correct; only Agent Dunham could not see it. When Director Neelley read Agent Dunham's final report about Operation TEAPARTY, even he came to the same conclusion: Carly was not one for gentle missions of persuasion. She would never be their Mata Hari. She was a missile. Not a song.

7. Carly takes a trip

Director Neelley changed the scope and direction of Carly's assignments after Operation TEAPARTY. She drove Robert Doss to kill his wife, destroying his credibility within the U.S. left. She started a steel union riot and then a law enforcement crackdown, creating a rush of both fear and appreciation for the drumming rhythm of the state apparatus. She excelled in these missions, naturally, and was soon nominated for her first international mission, where arguably the ability to sow discord was even more invaluable.

He and Agent Dunham broke the news to her at the white-tablecloth Pincushion steakhouse. Agent Dunham wanted her to feel valued; Director Neelley wanted to practice waxing poetic about the sacredness of the American mission in the world, all that glowing-city-on-a-hill mumbo jumbo, because he had ambitions of holding a position that would require Senate confirmation someday.

It should be no surprise that Carly was unaroused by pleas to patriotic fervor. She would have needed several ungainly human bits and baubles for the concept of nationalism, of an "imagined community" (what a precious phrase that is, perfectly human in its nonsense), to tug on any nerve of hers—a sense of tribal belonging; extreme conditional empathy; bonds of imaginary attachment—and she was blessedly free of all of these.

"Why?" Carly asked after Director Neelley explained the mission of destabilizing a government "crawling with Communists" in the South Pacific, so as to make room for more U.S.-friendly leadership.

"Because it's in our interest," said Director Neelley.

"Why is it in our interest? Will we all die if we don't do it?"

At this point Director Neelley made eye contact with his underling, silently asking: what was wrong with this girl, and could it be fixed? On a scale from "simple" to

COP CAR

"Communist," where did she fall? Agent Dunham, in his nervous way, merely raised his eyebrows in return.

"No, we won't die. We're tougher than that." He made a small snorting sound reminiscent of a muddy even-toed ungulate in rutting season. "But that doesn't mean we're not interested in making sure the world is safe for Americans to move around in. Does that make sense?"

Carly contemplated this between spoonfuls of chocolate ice cream. On the one hand, she saw immediately that it was an incomplete answer (*safety to do what? safety from what?*). On the other hand, Director Neelley's answer did align, however unintentionally, with something Carly had known since she was very small and watching animals kill each other in the Cascades—that the world was predatory. If she imagined each country as a giant effigy, and each conflict as a blow across a fragile straw torso, she could understand world war as the simple pursuit of each state's place in the natural order.

She shrugged. "Sure."

The first order of business when they landed was to find the American pilot Willis Taylor within the annals of the local military prison system and resolve the liability he posed. He was in the midst of attacking commercial ships in order to disrupt the flow of commerce when he was shot down, and though the U.S. Ambassador claimed he was a rebel-employed mercenary who happened to be an American, no one was buying it, and they were having difficulty negotiating his release—a national security hazard, given Taylor had made it clear that he was anxious to get home by any means possible. Agent Dunham presented Carly with a passport under the name of Grace Taylor. "They'll be sympathetic to a family member," he explained. The real sister, back home in Ohio, was being monitored extremely closely.

Willis Taylor had spent roughly ten seconds in a state of bewilderment when he was told his sister had come to visit him—his meek little sister who was too scared to drive to the next town over by herself?—before realizing what jig his government was playing. By the time he was brought to a brightly-lit room that reeked of whatever chemicals they used to clean toilets, he'd fixed his face into an expression of hopeful warmth, ready to listen to whatever offer his "sister" had been sent to give him.

His first thought, when he saw her, was how relieved he was that she wasn't his sister.

"Hi Willis," Carly said, "I'm so glad to see you."

As an actress, she was still a bit stiff back then. Control was very important to the department she worked for, as I understand it. I hadn't yet had the chance to apply the grease she'd need to truly free-wheel, to completely convince her targets of their shared humanity. Fortunately for her, in this case, her co-star was a seasoned performer, accustomed to slipping in and out of various government-commissioned disguises.

"You're telling me," he said, scooting his chair up closer to the metal table between them and locking eyes with Carly. "Shit, I never thought in a million years you'd convince Mom and Dad to let you come, *Gracie*. How are they holding up?"

A little smile formed at the corners of Carly's mouth. It was like being on television, she thought. "They're really worried about you. They were real upset when they heard they weren't gonna get you back anytime soon. You know how they are. Always tryin' to fix what can't be changed. I told them I'm sorry, but this is just the way it's gotta be. We all gotta be strong."

The warmth slid off the pilot's face, like a sunny-side-up egg from a nonstick pan. His eyes twitched within their deadlock. "I have every intention of going home," he said. "I am not going to just—rot—away—in here. You hear me? Sis?"

She heard him, all right. But she wasn't listening. Instead she was hammering a message into his brain, over and over and harder and harder until she could very nearly

COP CAR

see the arc of her psychic force, blazing and golden and the closest she had ever come to seeing the inside of her own brain. She imagined it whirling like a cosmic whip across the table and wrapping around the metaphysical icepick she'd forced into his hungry, frightened underbelly. Imagined pulling it tight. Imagined the message she needed to send to Willis Taylor thundering down that rope without rest:

Kill yourself. Kill yourself. Die. Die. Die.

Afterwards, she took the taxicab Agent Dunham had called for her and met him at the lobby of the Plaza Hotel, where "Grace Taylor" had a "reservation." She found him anxiously pretending to read the Singaporean *Straits Times*, the only English language media offered by the hotel. Telling him the mission had been a success only seemed to marginally reduce his anxiety, and Carly didn't know why.

"Well, at any rate, I think in his right mind he would want this," Agent Dunham muttered—not so much for Carly's sake (she was calmly drinking the chocolate cherry virgin martini he'd ordered her because he hadn't thought to pack any cordials) but for his own.

"Mm, I don't think so," Carly said.

"Or at least know it was the right call to make. Even if he wouldn't have chosen it himself."

Carly kept shaking her head, undeterred by the aggrieved plea in Agent Dunham's eyes. "No, I'm pretty sure he didn't think that, either."

Hope extinguished, Agent Dunham lowered his eyes to the newspaper. "Well, all we need to do now is wait for the phone call."

They got said phone call the following night. From her bedroom, Carly heard Agent Dunham jolt himself awake on the living room futon and stumble toward the telephone in the dark; he hadn't turned on any lights by the time she'd crept up behind him, listening for the end of the conversation. When he finally turned and saw what must have looked to him like a Victorian ghost in a white linen night gown, he cried out to "Jesus Christ" as if that little god of his had answered any of his previous laments.

"He's dead," Carly said. "He is, isn't he?"

Agent Dunham nodded, and though he wanted to tell himself that she was still his little Car, his misunderstood genius, in that moment he felt the truth: she was beyond his grasp. A kite on the wind. A soaring rocket. Much as he tried to resist this reality, to protect the dream of what remained of his family, they were more different than alike. She hovered on a higher plane. "How did you know?"

"I felt the tether go slack." This had actually happened two hours ago, while she was spitting toothpaste froth into the sink, but having never felt a target die she hadn't been sure of what she was feeling at the time. "He didn't fight it as much as I thought he would."

8. *Carly paints it black*

It was the first time she used telergy with the express intent of killing. Agent Dunham felt badly about this milestone—somehow, to him, it had been different when she was merely driving people to throw punches and Molotov cocktails. That was *disruption*, he told himself; this was *assassination*. Personally, I don't see any daylight between the two and neither did Carly—except for one thing, and it was an important thing for Carly's psychic development: Willis Taylor's death taught Carly that she could override a human being's instinct for self-preservation.

All her previous missions had been built on the reliable premise that humans will act to defend themselves, however loosely defined; she might have been tweaking the edges of their instincts, but it was still *instinct* she was playing with, well-worn pedals of the natural order. This was the first time she saw herself operating beyond this order, beyond the human food chain she'd always sought

COP CAR

to find her place in—and of course, it delighted her. I think anyone would be pleased to learn a new skill. No?

Agent Dunham also committed himself to learning. Of course it was much easier for the Oxford Boy to explore the scientific limits of Carly's psychic capabilities than the moral implications of their work. But he was also genuinely struck—as it were—by the potential of what Carly called her "tether."

"How far do you think you can stretch it?" he asked.

Carly wasn't sure, so they spent the rest of the year trying to sort that out. Carly practiced on street vendors and homeless children; Agent Dunham took copious notes. Despite her insistence that her powers were most effective as accelerants of violence, Agent Dunham took pains to keep the experiments harmless, as far as covert missions went: forcing targets to walk in circles or sing songs. Though they never found a way for Carly to slingshot her initial attack beyond spitting distance, they did find that she could stretch her "tether," once she had a hold of someone. While Agent Dunham kept close watch on the target, Carly would withdraw into the smoky distance, effectively extending the purely habitual tether that Agent Dunham had on her. Ten kilometers, she stretched. Fifty kilometers. More.

He sent the results back to headquarters. As the dry season came to a close, they received Carly's next assignment: she was to drive a Communist sympathizer in the military, an Air Force Lieutenant Colonel named Prasetyo, to commit a most dishonorable fragging of a high-ranking anti-Communist general. A list of approved sacrificial lambs had been provided by a "friend on the inside," though for purposes of plausible deniability, the actual selection would need to be done by Carly or Prasetyo himself.

"Why can't you pick the name?" Carly asked, looking through the list.

"Because it can't lead back to us," Agent Dunham said,

and in so doing inadvertently made it clear to Carly that there was an "us" she was not a part of. Did they see her as an outsider, she wondered, or as an object? Either way, his statement provided incontrovertible proof that she was disposable—which would seem to run contrary to every test she had passed, every cherry cordial she'd ever enjoyed. Hadn't Agent Dunham always said how special she was? How uniquely positioned, how brilliant?

He glanced at her, feeling the stone weight of her gaze, and she did wonder in that moment: had he ever feared her? I can say that in those days he did not. She had passed an inner filter of his; he had not been betrayed enough in his life. The fear did not come until later.

Carly made contact with Lieutenant Colonel Prasetyo during a party at the Indian Embassy, where she and Agent Dunham were pretending to be visiting academics (of a leftist lean, of course—here among the non-aligned, they needed to avoid setting off alarms). She and Prasetyo locked eyes in the buffet line, as Carly pretended to fight with the lid of a chafing dish. His mind was not particularly tough to hack, given how preoccupied he was with Cold War spillover in an already contentious national political environment: just a few seconds of shared struggle and she could see how (rightly) suspicious he was about American interference. She planted the nail fast, so fast he attributed it to a snap realization of his own: *the Americans are planning a coup*.

Watching Prasetyo hurry away before he could start panic-sweating into the food made Carly think of a different question to ask Agent Dunham once they were back at their rental house. "How do you need him to do it, exactly?"

It was a strategic question, one that reflected long-term thinking, and she thought Agent Dunham would have been happy to hear her ask it—but its significance seemed lost on him. Its significance seemed to have been lost on headquarters, too. Carly watched him page through the directives he'd been faxed from dark suits on high and

COP CAR

considered how helpless he really was. It was a suspicion she'd had for a while—that for all the cherry cordials he had given her, he had no real power of his own.

"Doesn't say," Agent Dunham said at last, clipping the papers back together. "I don't think it matters, as long as he's implicated." He interpreted her empty expression—incorrectly, as always—as continued confusion, as a need for more instruction from her vaunted mentor. "Just have him do it in whatever way makes the most sense for him. His gun is fine."

Carly held this answer in contempt. She didn't doubt that Agent Dunham believed this, and probably so did everyone else in his department, but to Carly it felt like power left on the table. More wasted impact. I do not think Carly had fully realized, at the tender age of twenty-two, that her body's mortality meant her beautiful brain did not have infinite time. But I will say that her capacity to forgive inefficiency was dwindling rapidly.

Which was why she didn't drop the issue of methodology, even if she had to find the answer herself. "What's the worst way someone can die?" she asked Agent Dunham over a much more humble dinner at the noodle stand around the corner.

He battled through a mouthful of spice before answering: "Burning, probably. Why do you ask?"

"I'm sending Prasetyo some ideas."

Her question would keep him up that night; having been a hypochondriac his entire life, he knew he couldn't blame that particular bout of acid reflux entirely on the noodles. Why had she sounded so cheerful—almost excited?—when discussing such a grim subject? He thought back to Willis Taylor's death and wondered if what he dramatically termed an *assassination* had desensitized her. His poor little bunny! Would a therapist have helped? Should he have vetoed this assignment?

Now that it was too late, in other words, Agent Dunham began to worry.

NADIA BULKIN

9. Carly tries new things

Humans, generally speaking, are not built for demonic possession. Many have learned this at great personal expense. Because humans are also generally not built for postmortem communication, these hard-won lessons have typically been lost. And because humans *are* built to chase ego self-enrichment, these lessons have needed to be taught over and over and over again.

Carly was not the first to wear the mask I lived in. Many others have come before her, by foot and by ship, by auto and airplane, all eager for the chance to wield the gifts I offer. Most have paid great sums to my keepers—Pak Ribut now, and his mother before him, and her father before her, and so on—for the pleasure of having their eyeballs boiled beneath the heat of my splendor. It's not that I am picky; it is hardly a choice on my part. Does a lion choose to crush an ant its paw happens to step on? It's just that their little brains—for one reason or another—cannot handle the glory that I have to give.

If you would like to pity anyone for this sad conundrum, then please: pity me. After all, I have so much glory to give.

Most of my suitors, as I like to call them, have a will to power that far exceeds their capabilities. There is an English saying for avaricious children that I believe describes this bunch well: *their eyes are bigger than their stomach*. For all their resources and connections, all their strategizing and studying, no one seems to have alerted them to the one simple fact that has been true since the beginning of human time: *a human needs psychic powers to survive demonic possession*. Of course, *I* know what will happen to them well before they put my mask on—I know as soon as they enter the room I'm in, emitting as much psychic power as a plastic fork. Pak Ribut does too, but dead men's coins work just as well and it's not his job to

COP CAR

dissuade the misinformed. Anyway, there is no need to feel badly for these big-eyed fools. I like to think that I am giving them, in my own way, the very outcome they truly want, deep in the cavity you call a heart—enveloped by a supernova of energy in equal parts brilliant and terrifying. They might even believe, in their last moments of consciousness, that they are receiving a death befitting a king. Many human cultures burn their most distinguished bodies, after all. I imagine them happy, if perhaps surprised.

On the other hand, about a quarter of my suitors over the millennia have possessed *some* degree of psychic power, but make inappropriate vessels for other reasons. Usually the will is not there. I will also say that most of these have also overestimated their talents, which in their defense is easy to do if you—the royal you, as psychics are few and far between—have never encountered another psychic in the flesh. Easy to get carried away by the astonishment of your brethren when you can guess what number they are thinking of, when you can temporarily sweep them under your hypnotic spell and make them bark like a dog. If they could trade places with me for a moment, and look upon the power and creativity of wonderful human psychics I have known, they would know that their gifts are merely parlor tricks.

Sometimes I will take a psychic if I think there is any hope that they could blossom into something remarkable. Usually, they don't. And then there's nothing more for me to do but slither my way back to my last keeper and return to sleep until the next knock on my door. I have found that it is pitifully rare to meet someone like my prior vessel Trisama who, having risen from absolutely nothing to become an advisor to one of the Majapahit empire's last kings, had used not only his inborn psychic talents but his inborn personal ambition to win many vicious battles on his own before he found me, and won many more after we joined. He was a survivor of the first order, you see, willing to do any manner of things that would horrify a lesser human.

What can I say? I like self-starters. It's as humans like to say: *talent means nothing without hard work.* Correct? No amount of psychic gifts can compensate for a pitiful, undisciplined spirit, an undeveloped will. Some of that is my own laziness, yes, but consider my position. I am no gilded show pony for a two-bit psychic; I am wasted on parlor tricks to charm one's friends. I need to stretch my metaphorical legs and run. And I *will* run, I assure you. I'll run you off a mountainside, run your limbs free of their joints, run you mad until you—the royal you, of course—disembowel your family and write my name in their blood.

And when a psychic suitor gives me no evidence of any ruthlessness, any callousness, any cunning whatsoever? Well, I'd rather not waste time. Mostly theirs, since mine is infinite, but with human lives as short as they are, I like to keep myself available in case the right one comes along. I flame broil these innocent lambs right away.

Oh, and one last complaint before I return to my beloved Carly—I hardly get any sensitives as suitors, even though there's more of them running around than there are psychics. It's such a pity. They're quite a bit tastier than the world's plastic forks and in my personal estimation, have a richer flavor profile than psychics too, full of fear and confusion and general despair (though I acknowledge reasonable demons might differ there). But sensitives like Pak Ribut have their antennae up all the time, scarred by a lifetime of seeing *things* they can neither explain nor do anything about, and those that have survived to adulthood have neither the curiosity nor the megalomania required to go near any *magic mask*. Woe!

All of this explains, I think, why I had been without a long-term human vessel for three centuries—not that I was counting—until I finally made Carly's acquaintance; that is, when I became aware of her, and she, simultaneously, aware of me. And really, we owe our happy rendezvous to

COP CAR

Pak Ribut, because he was the one who saw her potential while she was salivating over cakes in the night market—saw the powerful aura Carly was cruelly kept from seeing for herself, glowing like foxfire among the smoke and hullaballoo—and escorted her to me.

"You like tests," Pak Ribut said. Carly's eyes lit up with that magic feeling of being seen—a feeling she did not often get to experience, at least before she met me. "I have a test for you. Very hard one."

"Really?" Carly took a bite of a mung bean cake. "Never met a test I couldn't pass." She wondered for a second if he was following her casual English, but he seemed to have no trouble understanding what she meant. Fairly quickly, she connected this comprehension of his, this hint at interior sight, to the little buzz she felt when they first made eye contact—she did not believe in coincidences, mostly because Greg Dunham had told her that she was in the business of making them.

Unlike the vast majority of men who she'd spoken with since reaching puberty, Pak Ribut did not pick up the conversational tennis ball she'd dropped on his side of the net. He just stared at her, with an expression of utmost seriousness. He was never much for banter, that one.

Slightly miffed now—miffed that she had to do it, miffed that she cared to do it—Carly asked another question: "What do I get if I pass the test?"

"Everything," Pak Ribut replied, and maybe it was the aftereffects of the buzz or maybe it was the fact he was not so much pushing her toward this test as he was offering it to her, a choice, but Carly believed him.

Many suitors are repelled by my humble abode. I suppose most of them think with great power should come great ornamentation, an indication of the shallow human trappings of their thought. Others aren't used to being in shabby surroundings and feign allergy to dust (that is fine; they have spared themselves a painful death). Others take another look at Pak Ribut and his request that the trial be done one-on-one (on one) and decide this is a murder plot in disguise (ibid). But Carly showed neither fear nor contempt for the small dark room where Pak Ribut kept my mask. Just sat cross-legged on the rattan mats and waited calmly as he lit a few candles and unlocked the wooden box that my mask and I lived in. She adjusted instantly to her environment, because she understood that any human milieu, no matter how opulent or destitute, is little more than the painted wooden backdrops of a theatre stage.

Pak Ribut presented her with the open box, trusting that she would know what to do; and she did. She lifted the painted wooden mask—lifted me—to her face and then pressed me close. Her eyes looked through my black-lined eye holes, momentarily adopting the visage of a Javanese queen. She breathed me in, my sandalwood and sulfur.

Let me be clear: I burn the undeserving. Usually Pak Ribut had to scrape off chunks of charred flesh left behind by this or that screaming idiot—I did not want my mask crusted over with crunchy bits of undeserving humans, no thank you—but not Carly, oh no. Slipping into her pores was like falling into a bed of down, like sliding into a salt bath. She buoyed me. For the first time in centuries, I floated.

She pointed me down the hallway of her life up to this moment, where even the memories she'd forgotten were enshrined. In these testaments she showed me her ambition. Her will. And I, in return, opened the doors to every other hallway that Carly had ever knocked on; Greg Dunham's hallway, Ray Neelley's, Kait Lavinia's, Alma-Jean Parrish's. To her, I revealed it all.

I flooded her veins, wrapped myself around her bones, and left the mask behind. Carly took the empty shell off her dewy, glowing face and handed it back to Pak Ribut to be properly destroyed. We were silent as we left. In the darkness that remained, Pak Ribut bowed his head and smiled.

COP CAR

10. Carly ruins everything!

One of many misconceptions about demonic possession is the idea that the "possessor"—i.e., the demon—takes control of the "possessed." A comforting thought if your interest is in skirting responsibility, I suppose, but I can assure you that it is not so simple. In fact I would argue that "possession" is the wrong word; these relationships are symbiotic more than parasitic. Sometimes I'm the driver; sometimes I'm the passenger. In the very best possessions, we share the wheel.

In the case of this particular politicide, I followed Carly's lead. We were still getting acquainted and she was filled with purpose, so even though I'd rather watch a crusade unfold from a distance—I'm always struck by the depths of "demonology" that humans will conjure on their own—we took our talents to war.

Lieutenant Colonel Prasetyo, first and last of his name, did not use a gun to squash what he genuinely feared was an American-backed coup, but a machete and a razor and what I will call the Dunham special: fire. And he didn't murder one general, but five. Was this overkill? Well, maybe. But as Carly told Prasetyo through the tether, one bullet through one general's head only sends a single message, to a man too dead to act on it. *What message do you want to send to the living?* she asked him.

It turned out he wanted to tell them something they'd remember. So we flooded his mind with the classiest gore—the pristine slice of a royal guillotine blade, the artful snap of a noose against a condemned neck, the rustic elegance of a hillside crucifixion. Gorgeous scenes truly meant to be *seen*.

And Prasetyo's scenes were absolutely seen. Word began to spread just before dawn, when a security guard came across the broken bodies stuffed in a well. Like actors who'd been impatiently waiting backstage, the anti-

Communist contingent of the military—otherwise known as the Army—leapt into action, declaring a state of emergency and beginning the process of chasing down all their known enemies—the Communist Party secretariat; Maoists in the presidential cabinet; Air Force squadrons led by lefty sympathizers. I mentioned war, I know, but it was really more of an avalanche.

In the decades to come, a select few historians would torture themselves with questions none could answer about the politicide: what exactly was Prasetyo's plan? How would he get away with something so shocking? Had he really thought this battle to be winnable?

The answer, of course, is that he had no plan, because Carly had no plan. Carly had extracted herself from his head as soon as he finished dumping the last body into the well and left him shivering and punch-drunk with bloody hands and no getaway car—you can imagine how much this sudden awareness of his predicament terrified the lieutenant colonel who had up to this point thought of himself as a planner. It didn't take long for him to be swept up in the dragnet; he was turned in by his taxi driver.

Although his personal biography would be rewritten afterward to suit the sitting government's politics, Prasetyo had joined the military before becoming a Communist sympathizer. He had joined as a seventeen-year-old during the war for independence, for the same reasons any boy would have: adventure, hatred of imperialists, a desire to prove oneself in the most visceral way. Hatred of imperialists was the one force that continued to drive him well into adulthood, and of all the political parties that had sprung up like weeds in the afterglow of the successful revolution, the Communist Party seemed the most intellectually committed to this sentiment. So that was why he'd become a Communist.

Tribalism took care of the rest. Humans like to sort themselves into groups; they like it almost as much as stacking themselves into pyramids. They are, quite simply,

COP CAR

lost without these structures, entirely uncomfortable with the abyss that otherwise surrounds them. The pyramid positions them in vertical space; the group positions them in horizontal space. Neither does away with the yawning abyss, of course! But both certainly do keep them occupied.

All of which is to say that—what Carly (and I) did to Prasetyo could have been done to any number of mid-ranking military men at the time. They were a minority in the military but certainly not a tiny one, and in the frothing primordial soup that is the newly-post-colonial state, the urgency to make sure one's group wins the future far outstrips the desire for a long, stable career. When change is the only constant, tomorrow's heroes are decided today.

Or something like that.

Considering the popularity of the Communist Party at the time, the Army's goal of definitively winning the future by eradicating the competition was quite ambitious. And there is a world in which they did not succeed—in which the competition had a chance to regroup and a civil war started instead. For the weak-blooded among you who recoil away from the events that did follow, think of it this way: it's possible that not killing a million people would have been "worse." Who can know how many more lives would have been lost in a decades-long conflict fought with double, triple, quadruple the tanks and guns and bombs? Imagine it.

Imagine.

Now imagine that everything ends in a month. The rivers clog with bodies, yes, and detached bespectacled heads roll like soccer balls past elementary schools, but then it ends. It's over. The rivers drain and replenish for the survivors to wash themselves in, the bodies feed the fields, and the nation stitches itself back together just in time to turn the fields into sweatshops into condominiums.

It's better, isn't it?

And it's all thanks to Carly, not that she got a word of thanks for it (or a single cherry cordial). To be fair, she wasn't thinking about anyone's army. She was thinking about the Free Republic Radio tower that she'd passed dozens of times in the back of a cab, and how she didn't know how radio waves would affect her psychic reach. She heard the Army take control of the station and tell all who were listening to take up arms against the Communist coup-plotters—Agent Dunham was listening to the radio in the living room, sucking cigarettes—and decided that their very clear message would be a great one for her to test. She wrapped herself in scarves and climbed out her bedroom window.

When Carly first reached the radio tower—no simple task, as Carly truly had zero sense of risk and I was the one who had to tuck her behind and beneath assorted objects to keep her hidden—the Army's emergency broadcasts were really just urgent pleas: *Please help us kill them all.* But once Carly climbed onto the roof and roped her tether around the antennae, infecting every transmission with her psychic accelerant, those pleas became commands: *Kill them all.*

Now it's true that in wave form, the intense pressure of her yoke was not as concentrated. It was pepper spray instead of a baton. And perhaps would not have been so effective had it been used on a single, individual target—but ordinary humans herd. They metastasize each other's toxin. They follow paths of least resistance. And Carly drove this herd straight into a sea of blood.

The shared euphoria of this commitment to killing was such that it didn't even matter anymore that an American girl was standing with her arms outstretched on the roof of the Free Republic Radio station. I didn't need to give her cover because they didn't see her physical form—they didn't have to. They felt her moving through them. They mistook her for adrenaline. They mistook her for God.

All but one. One middle-aged American man who realized his charge was missing. His vulnerable charge. His dangerous charge. Both feelings seemed to motivate him in equal measure.

COP CAR

"Carly! Stop!"

She didn't stop, of course. Why would she? Why *should* she? Because he'd mistaken their relationship to be one in which she had to obey his orders? So no. She didn't stop.

And he shot her.

Oh, how it upset me! The gall of this small, small man! He would have killed her if I hadn't jerked Carly to the side, allowing the bullet to graze her arm instead. Later he would try to convince himself that this was indeed the outcome he'd intended ("to prevent further damage," callooh callay!), that he *never* could have killed his prodigal daughter—but agents like him don't shoot to wound, and anyway, the startled look on his face said it all.

In the cocktail of pain and shock, the tether broke. Carly clapped her hand over the entry wound and looked at him with eyes betrayed—but I, who had never trusted him, only felt disgust.

11. *Carly goes camping*

I took Carly away as soon as I could; as soon as I could steady her aggrieved pulse and remind her that as for all mortal bodies, her survival should always be the first law. Anger, hurt, confusion—these are just webs meant to hold humans in place, so that a larger predator can take advantage. Carly's immunity to such webs was her strength. I reminded her of that.

We ran, before Agent Dunham could catch her. Carly was too scattered just then to throw human obstacles at him to slow his pursuit, so I threw things—upturned a car, broke a tree, spun a brick in the general direction of his head. He cowered amidst my fury, like the good church boy he'd once been. Though all this was happening in the whirligig of chaos that Carly had kicked off, the way he looked at the car and the tree and the brick did suggest an understanding that they hadn't flown at him by chance.

This was, after all, the man who credited Carly for coincidences.

Looking back, I think that was the moment that broke him, the moment that made him wonder if he'd been worshipping the wrong gods all along.

(Though I don't think he ever let himself become aware of me. Neither his dusty church nor his peer-reviewed research studies had prepared him for the possibility of demons outside of hell. Too gauche.)

I got Carly into the bed of a cargo truck driven by a man who was hellbent on continuing his delivery route into the countryside, checkpoints and states of emergency be damned. The truck was stopped three times on its way out of the city, but I made sure hell traveled with us—onto rougher pavement, into fresher air not yet graced with the smell of copper and rot. I waited until the signs of human settlement grew sufficiently sparse and decrepit, and then pulled her out of the bed.

I took her into the forest to wait out the bloodshed. She was still in too much shock to object. I could have brought her into the realm of the men who'd won the future, yes, hidden her in some wealthy kiai's orchard to feast on papayas and avocados, but to do so would have done her a grave disservice. You see, I understood now that she had spent almost her entire life in the custody of history's winners—that is, the spook factory that went jettisoning across the world bending others' lives to their strategic will. Cherry cordials aside, this upbringing had given her a woefully skewed perception of the human world, entirely too dependent on their self-delusions, and I needed to fix this posthaste.

I gave her tarantulas to eat and a stream to drink from. Truthfully, I would have abandoned her if she'd thrown up a fuss, gone flying back to Pak Ribut and asked him to find me a new mask to hibernate in; she was already more work than I'd first assumed she'd be without also being picky about food. But she wasn't squeamish, reverting back to

COP CAR

her childhood in the Cascadian woods, and I stayed. Stayed to hear her lament what had happened at Free Republic Radio, and what she now believed about herself.

"He always told me I was at the top," she mourned.

Once again, a pyramid. That shape humans cannot seem to stop themselves from repeating, the way ants weave spirals, the way beavers build dams. Dirt pyramids, stone pyramids, glass pyramids—no matter the millennium, no matter the coordinates, there is always one who stands over a few who stand over many. I don't know where they get it from, this pattern. They certainly didn't get it from me, or any of mine.

"But clearly I'm not if they abandoned me like that."

It made me even more disgusted with Agent Dunham, for making her sense of self-worth so dependent on her utility to a state apparatus—but I suppose it made sense for him to impart his values onto his "child." They had worked well enough for him, but he was just a plastic fork. A plastic fork raising an angel.

What they did doesn't matter, I told her. *Nothing they do matters. They're nothing compared to you.*

"They control everything!" she replied. "Look how they're winning now."

In the clearing below our hill, soldiers and teenagers brandishing hand-me-down guns and knives were executing Communists. She was right: the armed men whose message she'd amplified were winning, and would win, for decades to come at least. They would be paraded and awarded and rewarded, like fleas sitting pretty atop the flea ferris wheel, but that was not the message I wanted her to take from this.

Because of you, I reminded her, which at least brought a serrated edge to her gaze.

"And then they threw me out," she muttered, pulling the remains of a cricket head from between her teeth. She was still feeling sorry for herself. "Want to be a winner, not a loser."

I had to resist the urge to howl in laughter. Instead, I

pointed out the next man in line to be shot—unlike many of his shellshocked fellows, he was pleading his case vocally. He was not a Communist, I explained to Carly—nor a trade unionist or an organizer or even a teacher. He was just a man lodged in a bitter dispute with his neighbor over the ownership of a cow, whose neighbor had pointed the finger first. The truth is there is one god that matters, but it is blind, and it is mad, and it steamrolls in random directions through groups and over pyramids in utter disregard to the lies humans tell themselves to feel safe.

The accused man was shot. "There is no safety," Carly said, and swallowed the cricket head.

No, indeed, beloved, I said. *So why play their game? They are wildebeest, all of them, fighting to keep their spot in the herd lest they be cast out and eaten by the darkness. And you are the darkness.*

12. Carly walks the walk

After maggots ate the bodies and a long national silence descended upon the archipelago like a low-hanging raincloud, Carly decided she wanted to return to the United States. I pointed her toward someone who could help—not some rubber-stamper at her Embassy, but a slight and fashionably-dressed man sitting in one of the ratty lounge chairs at the old Club Omega, so popular with shoestring expats and enterprising con artists before it was unceremoniously burned to a crisp several years later. I'll admit, now, that there were easier ways to get her a passport—sneaking it out of the possession of an intoxicated lookalike at a youth hostel, for example—but I suppose I wanted to give her a challenge befitting of her powers. She was not some common pickpocket. She was an apex predator, a giantess straddling the Earth. Besides, following the incident at Free Republic Radio, I wanted to boost her confidence.

COP CAR

For this man too envisioned himself a world-killer—and what better way for Carly to know where she stood than to slay another giant?

Like many thousands of others, he was wanted by police in Bangkok and Calcutta (under different names and with different faces) for suspected passport fraud and drug possession; unlike all but a handful of others at the time, he had also murdered five tourists in order to acquire said passports, said drugs, and other things he wanted. He spoke excellent English and passable French, could pass for any age from twenty-five to forty-five (he was actually forty-one), and looked like he could have come from anywhere—a fact he used to his advantage when sliding in and out of various human "skins." Costumes, I should say. I suppose I also hoped Carly could learn from him.

She sat in her own ratty lounge chair, near an open window, and waited for him to come to her—which he did, after she threw him a quick shy smile. When he welcomed in that smile, he also welcomed in the image of herself she'd tucked within it: a lonely tourist, new to the city, unsure of how she'd ended up in the Omega and what she was supposed to do now. An ingenue in desperate need of a guide. He approached her, bought her a drink, and struck up a conversation.

They discussed their favorite beaches and least favorite tropical diseases (Japanese encephalitis for him, rabies for her). Then, for a few minutes, they watched the flow of human and vehicular traffic—the speed with which people, young and old, would jump from doorless minivans and into a sea of oncoming cars; the remarkable ability of supposedly fixed objects like wheels and engines and torsos to melt into ever-shrinking space—until Carly said, "People are fleeting."

The man looked at her. "You mean fragile?" He assumed that she, the ingenue, was thinking about the cruel prognosis of accidents in a developing city—about children ripped limb by limb from parents, about hospitals overflowing with infection instead of saline—and it made him smile, to imagine how unfamiliar she must be with malice.

"That too, but no, I mean, fleeting. They jump in and out of each other's lives so easily, never think of each other again. Maybe some of them take a bite off each other in passing. Leave a mark, a scratch. But even these marks fade. They move on. Until in the end, they die alone."

She was toying with him here, leaving little clues—do you notice, the way she says "they" instead of "we"?—but this was a man singularly consumed by his mission, too blind to realize that it was entirely possible for his quarry to have a mission of her own.

"But I am different," she said, and now as she turned her chin to face him, gone was the fluttering butterfly gaze of before; no, her eyes had weight now. Heavy not with sleep but with granite, pressing in on the soft mental underbelly that he hadn't shown to anyone since he was a child, spongy spots of loneliness and rejection that he had tried to conceal with his hardened disregard for the people he met as an adult. "I am a cop car. Once I have you, you cannot be free of me."

She got in. She sank her metaphorical hands and then her psychic teeth into the meat of his life—saw the diamonds he coveted, the villa he dreamed of, the light slip out of his victims' eyes as he strangled them on hotel carpets, on bathroom tiles, on beach sand—and his lower jaw dropped open. He normally desired only dominion over others. He normally knew survival was the first rule. But he curled into Carly's touch. He wanted to not be free of her, to be held in her clutches if it meant being held.

That is how you can tell a predator from a superpredator.

Slowly, I said, because she needed him to not be scared, not yet. *Gently*.

Little by little, she tightened the tether as he led her back to his hotel. She kept her grip tender, just tight enough that he wouldn't be able to wriggle free in a moment of clarity without snapping his brain stem. He wasn't frightened as they passed through shadows on Jakarta's small broken streets; he felt seen. Understood. He saw them sitting on a beach beneath a blanket—he a child, craving and reaching toward her sparkling skin, her windswept hair—burying their toes deeper and deeper into the wave-soaked sand.

"I need passage," he thought she said. No, that wasn't right. She was saying: "I need a passport."

Then they were standing in his room. She was still shimmering as if by moonlight, still smiling, and he moved toward the safe where he kept the passports and watched his hands spin the dial—he could not think of the combination, but thankfully his hands remembered—so that he could help her. She thanked him, sat him on the bed, and then they were on the beach again, though now he was looking up at the stars and she was piling wet sand on top of his body, packing it in close and tight like a blanket. Like a hug. Heavy, heavy. Heavy with sleep.

"Stay still," she was saying, though night had come and he couldn't see her anymore. "Keep you safe."

13. *Carly comes home*

My Carly could have become anyone. With our talents combined she could have crossed any border, entered any door. She could have become a president's wife, could have won awards for her artistry or appearance or both, could have inherited a fortune or three. Many human vessels and would-be vessels I have known, whether for one season or fifty, have sought these prizes exclusively. I understand they bring satisfaction on the mortal plane, which is all these creatures have.

But she knew, as I do, that all of these delights, these *creature comforts* if you will, are mere shadow play. Those gilded trophies and the cases they sit in are just well-polished pebbles, meant for occupying the fancy of the world's meat as it is slowly, surely spent. Would it not have debased Carly, to spend her time on such silliness?

And yet I was still surprised when she chose to return to Merrimac and to the still-floundering Church of Karmic Renewal, specifically. There seemed to be nothing at all remarkable about this town, or this little collection of tormented, mosquito-bitten people.

"They got away from me," she said, and then I understood. This was personal.

We found the Church in tatters. Oren Goodyear was in prison following a (rather poor) attempted assassination on the secessionist governess, who had since declined to run for another term of office—leaving the Church shuddering and mobilized with nowhere to aim its cannon fire. In Oren's absence, Tom Jefferson had taken on the mantle of leadership, though can one call it leadership when you oversee a decline in every sense? Membership had dropped. The website was down, as were the lamp posts. Morale was certainly in decline. And following the assassination attempt, state surveillance was constant. Certainly an ironic turn of events for a formerly apolitical church, but history is littered with the bones of humans who believe they can predict—let alone control—the future.

With Oren Goodyear gone and his property seized, the Church had relocated its headquarters to Tom Jefferson's land. When he was younger and trying to court women, he'd called it a "farm," but he'd since given up on this pursuit and fitted the premises with the barbed wire fencing and security cameras it was made for. The lack of lamp posts was no deterrence to Carly—I could simply point her in the right direction, and make sure she walked up to the property when Kait Lavinia was alone outside, feeding a lone aging hound. Kait's excitement upon seeing Carly passed immediately to the dog, who jumped up with a whooping bark that Kait quickly and ineffectively tried

COP CAR

to quiet. Left to her own devices, the dog would have roused everyone in the house. Yet one pantomimed muzzle pinch from Carly and the dog dropped like a sack of sleeping potatoes without so much as a whimper.

Kait hurried to the fence, breathless in her excitement. "That was amazing, how did you do that?"

Carly shrugged. "I don't know. I got a way with animals."

She was evoking, here, Kait's love of four-legged beasts and her deep-seated belief that animals could distinguish between "Godly" people and "Evil" doers. (I do so love these supposed "tells," they make humans that much easier to fool.)

Kait grinned, clearly happy to be mystified, and grabbed Carly's hand through the fence. "I prayed you would come back. T.J.'s been telling people you were some kind of informant, but I knew that was B.S."

Carly sighed and tucked a strand of hair behind her ear, trying to look demure. "I was afraid of that. Is that what everybody thinks?"

"No. No, no, no. Most people just don't know what to think."

Ironically, Kait had just summed up the crux of the human experience, and why they fall so quickly into pyramid formations. How desperately they long to be led! How comforting the sheep find the shepherd, even as he leads them unto slaughter!

"I'm sure if we explained . . . " Kait was going on, but Carly waved that away. If you're explaining, as humans like to say, you're losing. Carly nodded instead at the ramshackle ranch house, its doors barred and its windows blinded. It looked like it had been stitched together in a battlefield hospital. "This is a lot different from Oren's place. How do you like it?"

Kait grunted in disdain. Carly smiled, happy to see how much quicker to rebel Kait had become. "I hate it. T.J.'s even worse than Oren. We're so focused on *hiding out* and

-51-

laying low that we're not doing any of the work at all. And I keep thinking about what you said, like, is this what God would want His chosen people to be doing? What's the good of being awake when we're not doing anything with our time?" She glanced back at the house, at the never-sleeping security cameras, and as if reminded of the line she was supposed to be toeing, acknowledged, "And I get it. We're definitely being watched. They're always dropping by the house, looking for this-that-and-the-other violation to get us on. Digging through our trash. Following us to the grocery store. They even called Pete and Lily at their jobs, trying to get them fired. And it worked with Pete! It's sick. It's like they're trying to *push* us, closer and closer to the brink."

For a minute, Carly and I pondered the pickle that the Church had found itself in. If she was thinking with her mortal head, Carly would have abandoned this operation as hopeless—abandoned the Church of Karmic Renewal to their fate and found another pond to dominate. But all this talk of federal agents, the visceral way Kait had said the word *push*, had her thinking big. And I loved the confidence. "What if I call them off?" Carly suggested.

Kait looked confused, and perhaps a little afraid that Carly was a double agent after all. "By cutting a deal? T.J. would never go for . . . "

"No deals. None necessary. Feds are people, too, Kait. They're all just people."

It would have been ironic coming from Carly even before she met me; it was downright sinister of her to say with a demon on board, and the slyness of her smile almost gave away the joke. But Kait was so taken with Carly, had so thoroughly bought in to her vision of earthbound glory, that she could not see the wolf's eyes beneath the lamb's skin. And to that I say: oh well.

COP CAR

14. Carly saves the day

By human standards, the sensible move would have been to find the counterterrorists overseeing surveillance of the Church of Karmic Renewal and to break those men and women upon the wheel of Carly's brain. But the sensible bores us, which is why Carly was never one for Agent Dunham's version of "strategy." We also wouldn't have found peeling back layers of bureaucracy to find a random rusty cannon that had had the misfortune of being selected to point at this particular target to be very enjoyable—and what's the point of doing anything if you're not having any fun?

"There's someone else I want," Carly said, popping open the can of cherry cola she'd cajoled a motel clerk into buying for her. "A different kind of jackal."

Georgia Neelley, the only child of Director Ray Neelley, had the sort of baby-soft soul that resulted from a lifetime perched on the pinnacle of the human pyramid—which meant nothing to me, except that it did make her an especially vulnerable target. Uncalloused. Raw. Carly could carve her up like butter. Our only real challenge was to keep her from melting down too quickly; after all, we needed her father to see what we had done, the sculpture we had made of her organically-fed, yoga-trained ballerina body.

I suspect Georgia would have tried to befriend Carly had they ever met, like a doe cuddling up to a rifle. But they never did, aside from some passing smiles at the coffee shop that they both frequented, around the corner from Georgia's pre-war one-bedroom apartment.

Georgia was there to do her class readings, and chat with friends, and agonize over text messages unreceived from boys—festival-going heirs to multi-national companies, mostly, Georgia had a certain type—who had other options than the daughter of a government employee, no matter how high-ranking. (One thing I will say for human pyramids: they come in all shapes and sizes.) Carly was there to send a message to the fear-producing nodes of Georgia's brain: there was something wrong with her leg.

It started with an itch. Persistent, distracting. She would scratch herself bloody in the middle of the night. The scab, then, refused to heal properly—to her eyes it was swollen, infected, leaking black pus—how could the doctors not see? The purple tendrils snaking from the wound, growing longer and darker by the day, confirmed to Georgia not that she was maiming herself but that the rot was deep—and that if she didn't fix it, if she didn't *cut it out*, it would be everywhere.

Oh, the Neelleys fought to correct her wrongthink. She was put in therapy (in-patient and out), hospitals, the best total-body holistic retreats the New World had to offer. But they were no match for Carly's claws, embedded so deep that she could needle that wound—not the one struggling to heal on Georgia's leg, but the one throbbing in Georgia's brain—even from a distance of many miles.

(Incidentally, this is my favorite type of joke: Director Neelley only had himself to blame for the failure of his money and status to protect his daughter. After all, he was the one who specifically authorized Agent Dunham to develop Carly's remote attack abilities when he learned about the concept of the "tether," knowing the state could not airdrop an American girl in front of every enemy.)

One day, Mr. and Mrs. Neelley were consulting with Georgia's doctors about the poor girl's prognosis when Mrs. Neelley looked at a photograph of the wound and exclaimed, "Good lord! It looks like a tea kettle!" The doctors and her husband crowded in and saw to their shock that she was right: Georgia had been picking her wound into the shape of a slightly squashed circle with what looked like a c-shaped handle and a snake-shaped spout: a tea kettle. A tea kettle for Operation TEAPARTY.

Director Neelley got the message. He forced all

COP CAR

investigations of the Church to be brought to a halt, reclassifying the organization as a non-target as far as the federal government was concerned. Of course, by then there was no treatment on Earth that could have saved Georgia's leg.

That is the true fruit of Carly's attacks, you see, the true magic of her cruelty—long after she lets go, they go on, and on, and on! She studies her targets, looks for the weak spots tucked in the folds of their brains like the crème beneath the brûlée, and drives her hammer there. Which is to say: Georgia was always over-conscious of her body. Not just the standard calorie-counting that her mother got her started on, but a microscopic focus on the size of her pores, the duration of her menstrual cramps, how her breathing changed as she slept. *Body = temple*, she would write in her journal, where she fastidiously logged every glass of water consumed and every minor ache endured. And yet the more she focused on her health, the less healthy she became, at least if her worries were to be believed. Her parents encouraged her to take all the sabbaticals she needed, which was why she hadn't yet graduated college and was still spending hours poring over class readings at Atomic Coffee, where Carly found her.

Carly had fully let go of Georgia by the time Georgia tore fully into her leg, looking for infected nerves to tear out. In so doing, she introduced new (real) bacteria into the wound that quickly ate away at the traumatized tissue—when the doctors decided amputation was the only option that would save Georgia from the necrosis that settled in, her parents wept in horror while Georgia wept with relief, thrilled to be finally separated from what now felt like an undead alien limb.

The aftermath of the Georgia Neelley incident, verified by a chat with her building's talkative doorman and several of Georgia's friends, did not unfold entirely as Carly expected. It was not that Tom Jefferson was not awed of Carly's power—rather, he could not in his heart fathom the possibility that his God had touched down in the body of this woman he did not feel to be devout, and this had left him with the terrifying conclusion that Carly's "divine intervention" was in fact powered by something else. He decried her before his followers, called hers the work of the Devil, said she had been sent to them as a test of their faith. Could they endure in hardship, he asked, or would they be drawn to this false light?

A test! You can imagine how Carly's heart laughed at this phrase.

But on the outside she was stoic, and after assuring them that she was only trying to be helpful, graciously left T.J.'s property and began walking west on Interstate 20. Kait followed soon after, just as soon as she finished unleashing a torrent of righteous rage upon Tom Jefferson, and then followed Pete Wolf who having been let go now had nothing left to lose, Shawn McDonald who felt Carly to be authentically radiant, Ron and Michelle Patience who had always found Tom Jefferson to be a poor substitute for Oren Goodyear, Lily Hatchet who was tired of hiding in the dark, and the Zion family who feared the church's seclusion was sliding the group toward mass suicide—and when Oren's wife Ella Goodyear came out of her self-imposed exile to join a church she felt "could bring Oren's vision to life," the Church of Karmic Renewal effectively transferred ownership, in spirit if not in name.

15. *Carly returns a favor*

As for Agent Greg Dunham, first and last of his name, he waited and waited *and waited* for Carly to hunt him down, claiming conspicuous tables in expat cafes in post-colonial backwaters around the world; when she didn't, he went hunting for her. It took him months of scouring crime logs, but once he read rumors of "hypnotist burglars" in the area surrounding Merrimac, he realized she had rejoined—nay, seized—the Church of Karmic Renewal.

COP CAR

He found Carly's Church camping in the abandoned state fairgrounds west of Harpstar, some twenty miles west of Merrimac. He tried to watch them from a reasonable distance; I suppose he was trying to be stealthy. But several Church members' eyes and ears had been reshaped into a constant state of high paranoia and these members quickly noticed an unfamiliar car driven by an unfamiliar man following Church members traveling to and from the gas station, the grocery store. They boxed him in on a desolate stretch of road and commandeered both unfamiliar car and unfamiliar man to the fairgrounds.

They brought him struggling, conscious and grunting and resisting, into the camper where Carly was waiting, sitting on a recliner with her knees up like the small child she'd been when he first brought her out of the wilderness and into civilization—such as it is. He stopped his flailing when he saw her, and instead assumed a posture of exaggerated prostration. Putting on a bit of a show to be sure, but he really had been afraid that the cultists would kill him without taking him to Carly. "Thank God," he said, an expression of gratitude that withered and died upon the tarp-covered carpet, "thank God."

"If you've come here to kill me," Carly said, "your preparations have been poor."

"No. No, no, no, I would never, Carly. You have to believe me." But Agent Dunham had lost the privilege of trust when he betrayed her at Free Republic Radio. "Carly—Car—I just wanted to talk to you. Can we talk, please? In private?"

"We can talk here," Carly said, and that was the end of that.

Agent Dunham forced a swallow. "Okay. That's fine. In that case. I have a favor to ask you."

The fact that he had come seeking not a traditional deal but a *favor*, offering nothing to Carly in return, is an indication of his delusional grandiosity. What had he done for Carly that she could not have done for herself, really?

Surely all the wrong roads he led her down that I'd had to pull her back from had cancelled out the food he'd bought her, the vaccinations he made sure she got. Or did he expect her to live in a perpetual state of indebtedness to him? Looking back, I'm sure he did. I'm sure that was why he looked so insincere on his knees, his figurative hat in his figurative hand: he couldn't keep the expectation out of his eyes. He was if nothing else a man who thought in pyramids, and if there is a more pyramidal human structure than the parent-child relationship, I don't know it.

Carly did not respond. She wasn't even looking at him—she was fiddling with her Rubik's cube. She was trying to hit a new personal speed record.

"I'm sick, Carly. Cancer. It's spread and . . . there's nothing doctors can do about it."

At this, Carly paused her twisting and looked at him. "And you want me to . . . what? Round up all the world's best medical researchers and force them to work twenty-four hours a day trying to find a cure?"

A twitch crossed his face as if he was entertaining the thought—but then he blushed and shook his head, recognizing I suppose the selfishness of such a request. "No. I'd like you to kill me."

"Oh? Don't you have a gun?"

"I left the agency," he said, and the wretchedness of his life since Carly departed it rolled out before us. How his day-to-day existence had become the equivalent of a hollowed-out tree trunk, by all appearances still standing but rotting on the inside; dead where it mattered. And how very tired he had been.

"Suicide is free," Carly said, "There's a Southern Railway track a few miles north. Why don't you just head over there and take a nap? The freight from Virginia comes at five thirty."

"I want . . . " Breath caught like a choked hiccup in his throat—it had been a very long time since he had expressed any kind of desire of his own, any selfish want that hadn't

COP CAR

first been authorized by federal edict. It must have felt quite frightening to him.

"Yes? Tell me." Carly already knew what he wanted and why, of course. But she was determined to make him say it. To make him acknowledge the truth. After all the tests he put her through, the definitive results of which he didn't end up respecting very much at all, he owed her that much. She swiveled her legs and sat upright in the recliner, so he might fool himself into feeling that much more connected to her.

"I want to feel what your power feels like. Just once, before I die. I've studied telergy for—for longer than you've been alive, Car. I've seen what it does to people. And I've always been curious, but ... but afraid. And now I'm afraid ... that because I've always been so focused on protecting myself from it, I may have deprived myself of one of the most sublime experiences known to man. And yours was ... yours was always the most sublime. You know that. I know that."

Carly smiled like he'd just awarded her the fanciest, richest cherry cordial.

It was a worthy compliment. But this man was not even his own master.

"How would you like to go?" She took on the hunched posture of a waitress taking an order. "Would you like to ... hang yourself a noose? Slit yourself a Glasgow smile? Tear yourself to shreds? Or maybe slam your head into a wall until your tough little skull cracks open like a chocolate egg?"

The plastic fork shrugged and smiled helplessly. "Whatever you think is best."

I do wonder if a little part of Carly—something malleable, maybe a tendon—would have granted him his wish if he had actually, finally, asserted himself here. Told her something that demonstrated just a little bit of agency instead of a relentless submission to the will of others. As it was, he remained as bland and empty as he'd ever been. She'd been wrong, when she first prodded the consistency of his mind at the age of seven: his head was no rock. It wasn't even chalk. He was just drywall. Punchable, yes. And as he himself would have told her, many years ago, posing no challenge at all to her.

"You don't deserve that privilege, Greg."

So at last, Agent Dunham became afraid of Carly. Not of the power that he would never experience. Of her now undeniable cruelty. After all their years together it should not have surprised him—after all, she had never made any attempt to hide it—but until the very end, he would cling to the thought that maybe Carly was experiencing a mental break, or a brain tumor, or someone else's influence. Anything to keep himself from facing the truth: that this was Carly, the child he loved, unadulterated. Carly at her clearest.

(And for the record: I may have a great deal of pride, but I would never claim responsibility for turning Carly into the marvel she has become. I am far too lazy to put that much work into a mortal. Nay, the gap I fill with Carly is small. I freed her, and that is all.)

Without another word, Carly returned her attention to her Rubik's cube. Technically she didn't command what happened next; Carly did not believe in pyramids, a point that her parishioners loved to tout, but her tether wrapped like ribbons from her maypole around each of their prefrontal cortices. She was not exactly guiltless. She was a part of them, even though they could never claim to be a part of her.

Kait was the first to act, grabbing a baseball bat and whacking Agent Dunham in the head with it. The blow effectively finished him, but parishioners of all ages and genders joined in thereafter, kicking and stomping the dying man and laughing at the gurgling sounds he made. He reached out between their ankles for Carly, hoping at least not to die alone—but she was busy. Busy putting fifty-four colors into their proper place.

Right, down, right, down. Up.

YOUR NEXT BEST AMERICAN GIRL

1. *The Woman Behind the Mask*

VERONICA LEANED TOWARD the full-length mirror to check the status of the blackheads on her nose; leaving the salicylic acid on overnight was definitely helping dissolve them. Then she turned to eyeball the thickness of her body's profile—she was doing a juice cleanse in the hopes of not needing to suck in her stomach so hard at Miss Pioneer Spirit this weekend—but before she could roll her gaze down to her stomach, it snagged on something else. Something far more alarming.

Three round red sores on her right arm, each about an inch wide, snuggled so close together that they almost looked like the bite of a three-fanged monster. Or a crimson set of insect eyes.

She stared at them for so long that they started to stare back.

She touched one of the sores with a cringe, hoping it wouldn't be wet. And it wasn't—it was worse. Half-gummy, half-crusted. Like something that had been left inside an oven for too long. Completely disgusting.

The bed, she thought. Something had bit her in bed. Veronica grabbed her jumble of bedsheets, wondering if she had the will to smash a poodle-sized spider, but when she tore the sheets away there was nothing—no sign of any animal incursion, and when she scanned the rest of her body, no other sores, either.

Her mother Irene cringed when she showed her. And then, as Irene was wont to do, she immediately turned away and decided it wasn't her problem.

"I bet it's because you're so busy," Irene said. "Stress is bad for the skin, you know."

Sometimes Veronica wondered if she'd be happier living in the campus dorms, bonding with girls who knew nothing about pageants over froyo and pizza. She could almost imagine herself, sometimes, as a normal twenty-one-year-old. But every dollar they saved on room and board costs went straight back into financing her dream of being crowned Miss Americana. First, the entry fees for the local preliminaries—she couldn't assume she'd win the first one she entered, so that line item needed extra. Second, the entry fee for Miss Heartland Americana—fingers crossed that she made it that far. Third, wardrobe. Fourth, beauty supplies and treatments. Fifth, hotel and gas. Not everybody had a suburban megachurch to sponsor them like Addison Dove. Some people had to make sacrifices.

"You know what you need?" Irene said. "To *relax*. Take another one of your steam baths."

That was not, in fact, what she needed. Miss Pioneer Spirit was in four days. She needed to not look like she was growing *berries* out of her arm.

She took the grossest pictures of the sores she could and texted them to Dr. Gillies. *Need these gone by Saturday!!!* Three exclamation marks because it had taken her three weeks of begging to get him to approve chemical peels for her acne scars, a routine treatment that every other girl competing for Miss Americana was undoubtedly getting monthly. She'd probably be relegated to the Ms. division before he approved baby Botox for her forehead.

Then she headed to campus, putting on the latest episode of the *Pageant World* podcast hosted by former Miss Americana and current pageant coach Tanya O'Dell.

YOUR NEXT BEST AMERICAN GIRL

The episode was called "Five Mindset Hacks to Win Your Next Pageant," and she willed it to be a positive omen for this weekend's contest. You couldn't punch your ticket to Miss Heartland Americana by winning Miss Pioneer Spirit—you could get a ton of *other* prizes, though, courtesy of its big ag sponsors—but you could see how much you needed to panic. A good showing at Miss Pioneer Spirit meant your outfits were good and your talent routine was solid, and you'd probably snatch a ticket by winning one of the early local preliminaries. A bad showing at Miss Pioneer Spirit meant you had less than two weeks to re-sculpt yourself into the form of a queen.

"The first hack is: don't let fear rule your heart. It's okay to be nervous! But don't make decisions because you're scared. The girls that play it safe? They might place in the top ten. But they'll never win. Because nobody will remember them."

Dr. Gillies phoned in a prescription for a steroid cream by lunchtime, promising the redness would go down "immediately." But when she ripped the bag open in the convenience store parking lot and lathered the cream on her arm's unholy trifecta, the only thing she felt was a sizzling, stinging pain.

"The pain means it's working," she muttered, curling her toes into the soles of her shoes and through those shoes into the carpet floor of her car. "The pain means it's going away."

⟫⟫⟫⟪⟪⟪

Backstage at Miss Pioneer Spirit, a pretty blonde in a magenta power suit was talking to Addison, making big cartoonish gestures with her long pink nails. Last year's Miss Heartland Americana, Jenna Bublik. She'd gotten tanner, and fillers, since she won the title.

Veronica and Nayeli squinted at what looked from a distance like a game of charades, trying to interpret the advice that Addison's parents had paid Jenna to give their daughter. Was it—tilt your chin up really high? Widen your eyes so the judges could see the whites all the way around? Make werewolf claws out of your hands? Act demon-possessed? Whatever it was, Addison was nodding thoughtfully.

"Maybe she's saying to growl at the judges," Veronica suggested. "*Grrrrr*."

Nayeli chuckled at first, but then her voice dropped and she muttered, "Hey, Jenna would know."

Veronica glanced at her best friend. Nayeli was picking at the fringes dangling from her red-white-and-blue dress, a somewhat desperate attempt to cater to Miss Pioneer Spirit's all-American theme. Veronica thought she'd probably crossed the line into kitsch, given she was also playing "America the Beautiful" on the violin, but Nayeli's sister said she had to "compensate" here in the heartland. "Gotta keep up with all the gringas," as she put it, staring meaningfully at blonde Veronica.

"Whatever," she said, trying to lighten the mood, "Jenna wasn't even top ten at Miss Americana anyway."

"Ooh, I'm *Veronica*, I don't need *Jenna* because I have *Lucrece*."

Veronica rolled her eyes while a small smile crept onto her lips. Not too big a smile, though, because while Lucrece had indeed placed second runner-up at Miss Americana, it had been twenty years ago. In those days, Miss Americana had been about composure and restraint and grace like a diamond under pressure—and when it came to evening gown, Lucrece's sense of posture was still undefeated. She knew how to exude the glamour of an art deco silhouette, the precise shape of a perfume bottle. It was why they got along so well, she and Lucrece. They shared an understanding of beauty.

But sometimes Veronica did worry that Lucrece was too conservative. She didn't think girls ought to be getting plastic surgery. She was skeptical of the freelance photographers who hung around pageants, offering to add

YOUR NEXT BEST AMERICAN GIRL

photos to girls' portfolios. She didn't follow any start-up hair and makeup brands that were always looking for brand ambassadors. She understood that Lucrece had had some bad experiences in the aftermath of her Miss Americana run—she hadn't shared details, but Veronica assumed it involved one or more creepy men—but she also didn't want to play it safe, as Tanya O'Dell said.

"I bet she's saying," Veronica said, nestling what was thankfully her unblemished arm against Nayeli's shoulder, "to not let fear rule your heart."

"Aww . . . " Nayeli rolled her eyes. "Dork."

"Just one final question, Veronica—how'd you get that bandage on your arm?"

The sores on her right arm had not gone away. In fact, Dr. Gillies' treatment only seemed to make them angrier, redder, more horrifically bulbous than they already were. One in-person visit and two telehealth appointments had not helped clarify the crisis. "Give it time," he said at first, and then, "We don't want to make them more irritated." Like they were in a hostage situation, and he was too much of a coward to go in guns blazing.

All of which meant that Veronica had been forced to drive around the city, buying every type of adhesive bandage she could find. FlexStretch and HydroSafe and PermaStay and the like. "What about this one? Can you see this one?" she'd repeatedly asked Irene, who'd glance up from her phone, squint at Veronica's tricep, and say, "Well, yes . . . " Desperate, she'd tried to pick the one that would look the least obtrusive against her skin. Evidently, she had failed.

"Um . . . " Under the stage lights, Veronica's mind flitted like a housefly from one outdoor activity to another—a world of mud and gasoline that she had never known, but had overheard boys and girls chatter about during passing periods at Wanahoo High. She needed something that would balance out her clean-cut, paper doll image. Something that would appeal to the downhome country judges of Miss Pioneer Spirit. One of them, the wife of the Forger Foods CEO, blinked her long eyelashes in exaggerated expectation.

"I was riding an ATV through the woods and scraped my arm against some bushes," Veronica said, forcing a ghostly giggle. "Sometimes I can be a bit clumsy."

The judges chuckled. Mrs. Forger Foods CEO raised her painted eyebrows. At least they couldn't knock her for being over-rehearsed this time.

Addison was just behind the stage, having the last tresses of her chestnut hair delicately curled by her mother. As Veronica passed them, trying not to trip over the taped-down electrical cables, Addison gave her a smile so fake it would have curdled milk. "I didn't know you rode ATVs, Dairy Queen," she purred. "That's *cool*." Addison's mother giggled, "Addy, don't be mean."

Obviously, it wasn't cool. And obviously, Addison's mother wanted her to be mean. Addison's mother had probably given the bitch the idea to put glue on Veronica's headband at Junior Miss Bliss a few years ago. It was insane that Addison hadn't been banned from every pageant in the region after that. She "didn't know the glue was so strong," apparently. What a joke. But then, pageantry was just a twisted simulacrum of real life. The harshest sort of light, the kind that burned away comforting lies like "high school isn't forever" and "sooner or later, everyone grows up."

It was then, after Addison's snide comment, that the itching started. No, itching was too gentle of a word for the eruption on her arm. More like a pulsing. A pounding. By the time the judges were ready to announce the winners and all the contestants teetered back up on stage, Veronica had to grind her teeth together to push the desire to scratch her arm bloody to the back aisles of her consciousness.

Stephanie Agar won Miss Congeniality. Jada Poppy

YOUR NEXT BEST AMERICAN GIRL

won Miss Photogenic. Krista Spoot won Second Runner-Up. Excitement at the possibility of an improbable victory temporarily overtook the itch and she glanced across the stage, hoping to exchange an encouraging smile with Nayeli. But it was Addison who she caught looking at her, eyes narrow with scorn. It only lasted a second before Addison swiveled her head away and gave the audience a big lupine grin.

"Our first runner-up . . . "

Not me, not me, not me

"Contestant number eleven, Veronica Muenster!"

Damn. But Lucrece had trained her for these moments, and Veronica swallowed the disappointment so fast it gave her heartburn. She clamped on her perfectly-calibrated gracious loser smile, accepted the little plastic trophy as if it was a presidential medal of honor, and golf-clapped when Addison was announced as the winner. Again.

But at some point during the ritual of crowning—maybe it was when the sash slipped over Addison's shoulder?—her dam of control broke. In one swift fall from grace, Veronica passed the award to her right hand so she could claw her left into the latex covering her sores and *dig*. Dig deep into that cluster of *wrong* just begging to be corrected. She imagined her fingernails scraping muscle, grazing bone, ripping tendons open and apart. Imagined her fingers pushing past all the damaged tissue, all the way through to the other side of her arm where the air and her skin would be clean and free. What a dream.

The pain that radiated from her arm was so satisfying—like a firm pluck of her most sensitive nerve endings—that she actually let out a small noise, of obscenity and delight.

>>>><<<<

Veronica and Nayeli pried off their tippy-top heels on their way back to the dressing room, groaning as the plastic separated from their swollen, contorted feet. Veronica had expected her arm to be bleeding from all the scratching she'd done on stage, but her fingernails had only collected a gory red crust. Nayeli's eyes were black with mascara smudge, victims of her bad habit of wiping when she felt tears coming on.

"You'd think they would like patriotic Latina bullshit," Nayeli huffed. She was referring to Winnie Hu, last year's Miss West Coast Americana who'd done a baton twirling routine in a stars and stripes mini dress. "I guess that's only good for *some* brown people."

Some girl they barely knew was crying in the corner of the dressing room, but otherwise, they were alone. While Nayeli went to tear herself out of her dress, Veronica glanced at the area that had been Addison's station. One of her monogrammed tote bags had been left, mouth open, in the chair she'd been sitting in. Veronica glanced over her shoulder to check that Nayeli still had her back turned. What did the police always say when they confiscated stuff without a warrant? That it was lying in "plain sight"? Veronica snuck up on the bag and peeked in.

There was body spray (Eternal Joy, whatever that smelled like). Painkillers (extra strength). Bronzer (Jenna's idea, probably). And one pale blue tube that looked oddly, horribly familiar. Everything that Veronica got specially formulated from Dr. Gillies was branded like that—had Addison somehow *stolen* her moisturizer? In a white-hot state of incredulous rage, she reached into the bag and grabbed it.

"Vee," Nayeli called. "Are you done changing?"

It was indeed from Dr. Gillies. But it was prescribed for Addison. There were ingredients on there that she recognized from her own supposedly secret formula, high-value ingredients that she'd paid a premium for—if, in fact, she was actually getting any of those ingredients. She hadn't seen any sores sprouting on Addison's perfectly sun-kissed skin, after all. Of course, no one would dare shaft the great Addison Dove, already an ambassador to five brands. But

YOUR NEXT BEST AMERICAN GIRL

Veronica the Dairy Queen, sponsored by none? A cheap knock-off would do. Just mix some petroleum jelly with some parabens and call it a fucking day.

A furious roar arose from her right arm and she sank three of her nails, still coated with a paste of bloody dead skin cells, into the bandage. She was trying to push each nail into a sore, as if preparing to rip off her arm and throw it down a bowling lane.

"Are you snooping?" Nayeli asked, suddenly digging her chin into Veronica's shoulder and prying at the fingers holding the moisturizer. "What is that?"

"Nothing." Veronica threw the bottle back into the bag. "Some crap."

⁂

She waited until she was in the car to pry off the bandage and check the damage she'd done to herself. Her fears were confirmed when she saw *five* little sores bubbling away in the heat of the bandage, not *three*. Two more tiny lakes of fire. Two more little uprisings. And then she jolted forward, the seatbelt hitting her throat, as Irene hit the brake. "Oh God," Irene was saying, "now what's that guy doing?"

A disheveled-looking man in an ill-fitting suit was standing in the middle of the parking lot with a bullhorn, steadfastly ignoring everyone else's nasty looks. "Little children, keep yourselves from idols!" he was yelling, "Get on your knees and repent, you women of Zion! Beg for forgiveness for your vanity!"

When Addison emerged from the convention center at the nucleus of a lively human swarm, the protesting man picked up his heels and started weaving between cars to get closer to her. As if he was called, moth-like, by her sun-sparkling crown. He wasn't moving very fast, and every step he took was met by vigorous minivan honking, but he still carried with him a vague sense of threat, an urgency that seemed combustible, unstable.

"Miss, you take that crown off your head!" he

commanded Addison, one hand outstretched and pointing at her scalp as if he meant to rip it off himself. Addison froze. Her mother screamed. The protesting man was ten feet away from them, now. "That crown is not yours! Give it back to our Almighty God or risk eternal damnation!"

A man in a fleece pullover who Veronica remembered to be Addison's dad went barreling up to the protesting man, his face contorted purple in anger, and punched him in the head. Veronica couldn't quite tell what Addison's father was saying, after the protesting man fell on his ass and just lay there—*sick freak*, maybe.

"I hope you don't expect me to start beating people up for you," Irene muttered as she took her foot off the brake, "if you ever start collecting fans like that."

※※※

Over the next week, Veronica tried to put the fact that Dr. Gillies was also Addison's doctor out of her mind. She had to fill out her entry forms for Miss Summerall—the first and most prestigious Miss Heartland Americana preliminary, and one that Addison was more likely than not to win, given how decisively she'd won Miss Pioneer Spirit.

Lucrece would have smacked her on the hand if she'd heard her say that. "There are no done deals," Lucrece would say, "What do they say in sport? You have to play the game."

A notification on her phone drew her away from the question of why she should win Miss Summerall: Miss Pioneer Spirit had tagged her in two photos. One was a group shot with all the contestants—her eye went straight to beaming Addison with her five-inch princess tiara in the center of the stage—and the other was a solo shot of her receiving her runner-up trophy. Thankfully, it was taken before her little itching incident.

Veronica zoomed in on her face and opened her notebook. Her eyes looked especially asymmetrical in the

YOUR NEXT BEST AMERICAN GIRL

photo—could eyeliner compensate for that? Better brow threading? It was a poor angle on her nose. And her teeth needed another round of whitening. When she first started pageantry at age twelve, it would have killed her to write so harshly about herself. Now it was an addiction. Because every flaw she could dissect now was a possible future point in her favor.

Lucrece had taught her that: control every point you can. Veronica knew she was no great beauty. "Weirdo," they called her in school, because her eyes were disproportionately large and her sense of fashion was about five decades out-of-date and she never understood their jokes. But Lucrece had shown her that a billion little tweaks could transform a sparrow into a swan.

And then there was the bandage. She zoomed in on that, too. Was there a bit of red peeking through? The sores seemed to be pushing against the latex, just enough to cast the smallest of lumpy shadows. God—they made her want to vomit. She zoomed back out in a useless attempt to get away from them, and noticed two new comments on the photo.

This girl is such a crown-chaser lol, the first comment read. *Kinda sad.*

Never gonna happen, read the second. *#TeamAddison*

An unholy itch rose out of her arm again. She was wearing a tank top to try to give it air, but air wasn't helping much. She slapped her hand against the itch to try to numb the fire—only to realize that she was pawing at the wrong arm. Her left arm. With her heart plunging up into her throat, Veronica twisted toward the mirror.

More sores. Her left arm, this time. For a second she thought she'd gone crazy, until she realized that these holes were farther down her arm than the first set. She stepped in front of her full-length mirror and rotated both arms forward. Hunching. Yes, two clusters. Both sides now.

As if he'd been summoned, her phone dinged with a text from Dr. Gillies. *Hi Veronica*, it read, *how's the arm doing?*

NADIA BULKIN

Was he mocking her? How much was Addison's family paying him?

How much poison might have seeped into her skin since she first met him?

Every tube, every jar, every bottle filled with serum—none of it could ever touch her skin again. She raced downstairs to grab one of the large black kitchen garbage bags and a pair of cleaning gloves, then back upstairs to throw each container into an impromptu quarantine. She really belted them, too. The better to get the rage out, since she would never be able to go to Dr. Gillies' office and throw them in his face, see how he liked *growths* coming out of his cheeks—could she? No. It would be beyond disqualifying. They had disqualified Samara Farro from Miss New England Americana for posting a "fuck you" sticker on her school's social feed.

"Oh my..." Irene had followed her upstairs and now poked her head in the doorway. "What on Earth are you doing?"

"We need to find a new dermatologist," Veronica said. "I want a second opinion."

2. The Woman and the Secret

Her second opinion, from a dermatologist whose website promised a full arsenal of state-of-the-art technology to support his patients' skin care goals, was as bad as the first. Actually, It was worse. "Have you heard of dermatillomania?" he asked.

Veronica shook her head, but she didn't like the sound of that "mania." Her skin felt manic, all right, but didn't doctors only use mania to describe what happened in people's heads?

"It's an obsessive skin-picking disease."

Veronica narrowed her eyes. "I don't pick my skin."

Even though she had a roaring hunger, just then, to run her fingers over her face and feel for new bumps,

YOUR NEXT BEST AMERICAN GIRL

ridges, indentations. Her left hand, the one that had served as an agent of her disgrace at Miss Pioneer Spirit, twitched with a desire that she immediately and tightly clasped. No. She did not pick her skin.

Dr. McIndoe pursed his lips together, barely trying to hold back his skepticism. "Do you think there's any chance you're doing it in your sleep?"

Incredulous, Veronica held up her hands—the hands that she took painstaking care not to pick at, not to dehydrate, not to even *use* if she'd had a fresh manicure. "Wouldn't my nails be all bloody if I was doing that?"

Because he apparently didn't have a comeback to that, Dr. McIndoe turned to Irene. "Mom," he said, as if she was his mother, as if it was her name, "what do you think?"

"Well." Irene took a deep inhale, bending back to scrutinize Veronica from an angle, the way she'd squint at a sloppily-assembled holiday window display. "I mean, I don't have eyes on her all the time. But there was that little . . . " Irene did a jazz hands shake, " . . . *episode* you had during Miss Pioneer Spirit . . . "

Instantly, her entire carpet of skin began to tingle. "It was itchy from the bandage!"

Irene looked plaintively at Dr. McIndoe. He was her type, Veronica thought. A silver-tongued, silver-haired charmer who knew how to lean theatrically against the counter as if auditioning for the role of "handsome doctor" on a daytime soap. "She just went to *town* on those sores on her right arm. It was terrible."

Goddamn Irene. Veronica could see Dr. McIndoe nodding sympathetically, firming up his opinion, so she had to jump in: "No, no—okay, fine—I scratched it that *one time,* and I agree, I shouldn't have, it only made it worse." Even if it had felt so good. "But doctor, I promise you, I woke up with these . . . whatever these are, these wounds. In fact, I have reason to believe . . . " She took a deep, centering breath. "I have reason to believe that I may have been poisoned."

"I understand your concern," Dr. McIndoe claimed, falsely, "but the thing is, Veronica, I don't see any sign of any toxin or environmental contaminant whatsoever."

She didn't know how that was relevant—didn't toxins wash out? Wasn't he supposed to be a doctor? "Did you look at the bottles I brought you?" She could see him breathing in, preparing an answer that she could already tell would not inspire confidence. "Like, *really* look at them, send them to a lab to do a full chemical analysis and everything?"

"I've reviewed the ingredient list," he said. "And there's nothing unusual about the formula. It's almost exactly what I would have prescribed myself."

For a moment Veronica imagined a great gathering of dermatologist mercenaries, Dr. Gillies and Dr. McIndoe included, looming over a list of pageant contestants who had or had not paid them off. Imagined them crossing out her name. "I'm not asking you about what it says on the stickers that are printed on the side. I'm asking you about what they actually contain."

For a few minutes they stared at each other, she and the dermatologist. "I'll send them to a lab," he said at last, "but only if you promise to start wearing gloves at night."

⇶⇷

On the eve of Miss Summerall, Veronica lay on her bed and fantasized about cauterizing her skin. Putting a heated knife to those awful little colonies on her arms and burning them alive, Old Testament-style. "The Wrath of God," she'd call it.

She was supposed to be relaxing, the better to whittle away her supposed demonic inner urge to scratch away her skin. Irene was far too enthusiastic about the treatment plan—lighting her a lavender candle, making her chamomile tea, helping her slide on her dermatillomania gloves—it was the most mothering she'd done in years. "Now don't you take those off before your alarm goes off

YOUR NEXT BEST AMERICAN GIRL

tomorrow morning," Irene said, wagging her finger. "Promise me."

It made Veronica wonder if she was the butt of a universal joke.

Just inside the open closet door was the peach sleeveless gown that she'd hoped to wear at Miss Summerall. That plan, like the skin around her sores, was dead. Her sores were too many, by now, to cover up with bandages. Her limbs looked like stony coral, pale landscapes riddled with tiny red hills that were too many to count—she'd given up a few days ago—but almost lovely in their natural symmetry. Almost.

Lucrece thought she should go without bandages and just show her skin, "warts and all!", but Veronica assumed she was drunk. There was no loveliness in her scabies-limbs. Instead, she was wearing a long-sleeved navy dress that she'd bought when Felicity Nigella went viral for competing in a full coverage velour gown a few years back. Of course, that gown had matched Felicity's platform—it was a statement about the risk posed by Earth's increasingly extreme weather, or something. She wondered where Felicity was now. Chained to a tree or throwing blood at a government official, probably.

Maybe she could change her platform to awareness of dermatological disaster. The oversexualization of women's arms.

And hope that the navy dress's hip-high slit and the six-inch silver heels she'd be wearing would make up for the lack of skin up top.

Lack of skin. She would love to not have skin. Just a smooth expanse of muscle, strong and stretchy and streamlined. Shining bloody crimson beneath the lights, in perfect contrast to a white dress. And completely devoid of scabs. Because it wasn't even the redness of her sores that bothered her now. Redness could be from anything—a mosquito bite from bicycling through the twilight, an allergic reaction to a shrimp cocktail. It was their *crust*, these obscene mesas of dead, dry skin that made her arms look like they were growing scales. A bastardization of the kind of silky skin a pageant queen—an all-American girl—was supposed to have.

Redness could be covered, disguised, neutralized. But crust could not.

Maybe she could rip the scabs off. The skin was dead, after all. It shouldn't hurt. There was no need for the blunt edge of a nail; all she had to do was grab and pull. She could keep her promise to Irene and keep her gloves on—not that it mattered much. And who knows, under the thickest slabs of magma-like crust, maybe her skin would be new and healed and baby-smooth. Maybe this skin disease was actually a revolutionary exfoliation ritual. Maybe it would all be worth it, in the end. She took a deep breath.

She was wrong. It hurt. The scabs stretched instead of breaking. *But we're part of you!* they seemed to sing, clinging to her arm under duress until her vision went white with pain. Ultimately, the determination that Lucrece said was her strongest quality won out. The scabs fought hard, but she tore harder.

Unfortunately, the skin beneath wasn't healed. The sores were still there, looking like perfect circles of refrigerated cherry jam. But at least now they were flat. At least now she could run a butter knife down her arm and not feel a bump.

If she'd been friends with the goth girls at Wanahoo High, they probably would have told her to burn the scabs in a banishing spell. But she hadn't been friends with anyone—and she was afraid to inhale whatever fumes the scabs might release. So she took them out to the yard, to the weeds that had taken over Irene's long-lost flowerbed, and buried them instead.

"And stay there," she said, trying not to feel strangely sad.

YOUR NEXT BEST AMERICAN GIRL

A gaggle of girls were gathered around Addison in the Miss Summerall dressing room, breathlessly congratulating her on—what? Her new glamour headshots? The five thousand dollars and rhinestone cowboy hat that she got for winning Miss Pioneer Spirit? Oh, something about a new brand ambassadorship. Another jewelry company? A hair product MLM? No, Angel Dancewear. They made . . . leotards? Veronica wouldn't know. Veronica couldn't dance.

When Veronica first started competing in pageants, she had wanted her talent to be dance. She envisioned herself doing the Charleston in a black flapper dress like a young Ginger Rogers, or pirouetting in a white tulle crinoline like Cyd Charisse. But her body would not cooperate. It could stand up straight and it could hold a pose, but it absolutely could not, would not flow. Every movement staggered and stuttered, as if she was more metal than flesh.

Like so many other graces that had fallen from Heaven since they first started competing against each other as teens, it was Addison who turned into the dancer. Addison's repertoire seemed to consist mostly of jumping and rolling across the floor, kicking her legs, arching her back while pointing her toes—her routines reminded Veronica, cruelly, of a show dog's tricks. But Addison was the one getting leotards for free.

Addison. Addison, who had forced her to wear a wig to school because they couldn't get the headband off at Junior Miss Bliss without shearing a two-inch-wide strip of hair from all around her head. She used to torture herself with questions of what she could have possibly done to deserve such cruelty, before Lucrece told her that if you spent enough time in the pageant world, you could trick yourself into thinking that the people on stage were just dolls. Murderous, thoughtless, carnivorous dolls.

"Um, excuse me." Veronica hurried over to a harried-looking volunteer with a clipboard and a bright yellow Miss Summerall shirt. "Is there another dressing room?" She was thinking of her fragile legs in that winter gown, of that slice of skin she had to keep pristine for the judges. She was imagining Addison pouncing on her and spraying her with a new poison courtesy of Dr. Gillies, making her entire body burst into red pustules like a river of cranberries.

The volunteer let out an awkward laugh of horrified disbelief. "No, there's just the one."

"Do you have an extra bathroom or something?"

With that she had broken a cardinal sin of pageantry: don't piss off the volunteers. She knew it because this one folded her arms over her chest and let her voice slip from cheery to nasal. "I'm sorry, what exactly is the issue here?"

"I'd just appreciate my privacy."

"That isn't how it works, princess."

By then the other girls had stopped their chatter, their fawning over Addison. They took a break from their dressing, from their pinning and smearing, to watch Veronica lose her mind. She thought she heard someone whisper Addison's favorite nickname for her: "Dairy Queen." She definitely heard someone—Stephanie? —say "psycho."

"Literally, put me in a closet, I don't care. Just don't. Put me. Here. Not with. Her."

The other girls could not contain themselves. The giggles burst the way girls' giggles always did, with cruelty and disbelief. Veronica tried to steel herself. As Lucrece always said, there was no point concerning herself with the behavior of the other girls. She was not here to make friends. Except then she saw Nayeli, getting her dress sewn on by her cousin in the far corner of the dressing room. Nayeli was looking at her in concern. In silence.

"Seriously?" the volunteer swung her clipboard so recklessly she nearly hit Veronica in the face. "Fine. There's

YOUR NEXT BEST AMERICAN GIRL

a broom closet right around the corner. If you can fit yourself in there, you're welcome to it."

Veronica gathered up her bags and turned her back on the dressing room, muttering a "thank you" to the volunteer that was lost beneath the chorus of giggles and willing herself not to look at Nayeli. It was a relief to close the door on them, even though the hallway seemed to be swaying, dimming, collapsing on itself.

Twenty paces away, the broom closet that would serve as her private dressing room had barely enough space to stand in and didn't seem to have been dusted in years, but at least she was alone. It smelled like a mixture of bleach and mold, but at least in here she'd be safe.

It was just after she shut herself inside it, before she found the lightbulb pull chain, that she saw the other girls covering their teeth as they whispered sordid stories about the madness of poor Veronica. That she saw Addison laughing, open-mouthed.

>>>><<<<

Addison won Miss Summerall. Big surprise. *May as well just give her the Miss Heartland crown*, she texted Lucrece from the seclusion of the broom closet. *Well, you certainly won't get it with that attitude*, Lucrece replied.

She wanted to snipe back at her that it wasn't her *attitude* holding her back, it was her fucking diseased skin. Christ, after she struck her second pose during the evening dress presentation, she'd taken a glance down at the slit in her dress and watched a new hole burst in her leg. That calf had been perfectly fine one second and then a red pinprick grew—like a drop of food coloring spreading in water—into a perfectly round, raw, dime-sized sore. By the time she got back to her broom closet, an equally awful twin had sprouted right next to it.

I'm dying, she thought. I'm falling apart.

Nayeli stopped by her closet, holding a small trophy commemorating her second runner-up finish. Veronica looked at it in a hunger that filled her mouth with saliva; she didn't know her scores yet, only that she hadn't made the top ten. Considering there were only twenty-four total contestants, she hadn't done this poorly at a pageant since she was sixteen.

"Why are you wearing that dress, silly?" Nayeli's quivering fingers reached toward one of Veronica's skin-tight sleeves, zeroing in like a heat-seeking missile on a hidden patch of sores—as if she could see them through the velvet. Were they oozing? Did they smell? Veronica sharply batted her hand away. "I mean, you knew there was no way they'd like it, right? Maybe if it was Miss Amish Country or something."

"Just felt like it," she muttered. "Thought it would be unique." She threw a glance she hoped was withering at Nayeli. "Thanks for backing me up earlier, by the way."

"Backing up what? You freaking out and stuffing yourself in a closet for no reason? I have to compete too, you know."

She thought Nayeli was angry—but instead she was giggling in a carefree, careless way that made Veronica feel invisible, that made Veronica question every pageant they'd spent together, every inside joke. Nayeli was going on about the rest of the weekend, her plan to sneak off to see Temo, but Veronica had tuned her out so thoroughly that she didn't see her leave.

Her phone shuddered. She had a brief, horrible fantasy about being disinvited from next week's Miss Wickham pageant on the grounds of decomposing—but no, it was a message from Dr. McIndoe. *Lab results from your old prescriptions came back normal*, he wrote. *Attaching them here so you can read them yourself.* She tried looking through the document he'd sent, but after a minute decided to stop kidding herself. It wasn't Dr. Gillies, nor anything he'd sold her. Nothing his office had prescribed had ever touched her leg, and yet. Look.

The door swung open, lighting up the broom closet in

YOUR NEXT BEST AMERICAN GIRL

a sea of yellow. Veronica's first instinct, aside from shielding her eyes, was to hide her holey leg from view.

Jesus Christ. Well, Addison, to be specific. She was still holding her bouquet of orange roses, still wearing her peacock tiara. She looked so perfect, so still, so ensconced in shadows that her angelic angles looked even more dramatically statuesque, that Veronica wondered if her sores were now causing her to hallucinate. Maybe Addison was here to kill her. In some ways, that would be a relief. She could be remembered as the victim of a zealot, instead of forgotten as a competitor of no consequence, an anonymous failed pageant girl.

"Sorry," Addison said, "I tried knocking."

"Oh. Well. Congrats on your win," Veronica mumbled. "Well deserved."

"Thanks." Addison's voice was flatter, duller than she'd ever heard it. She found herself thinking back to those extra-strength painkillers in Addison's tote bag. "Um, look, I just wanted to say . . . " Addison sighed, her roses drooping in her arms, "that I hope you get the help you need."

※※※※

That night Veronica peeled off the navy dress one sleeve at a time, terrified and resentful and . . . strangely excited to see what her sores had done while she wasn't looking. It wasn't that she savored this new daily ritual, exactly, but there was a richness in its horror that was hypnotic, almost intoxicating.

Lucrece said the dress had just functioned as a giant bandage around her body, calling attention to the fact that she was ashamed of something. No one likes an insecure pageant queen, Lucrece said—but whatever happened to disguising one's flaws? Didn't Lucrece also preach the gospel of "control every point you can"?

"A flaw is in the eye of the beholder" was how Lucrece had replied to that. It didn't make much sense to

Veronica—the "control every point you can" doctrine required an objective assessment of how you lined up against the judges' criteria. Flaws were flaws. A dress that was half-an-inch too short. Eye shadow that was a touch too sparkly. A belly that stuck out. Teeth that were crooked. There was no precedent, no, but wasn't it safe to assume that most judging panels would subtract points for skin that looked riddled with a flesh-eating disease?

The sores being faded was too much to hope for. All she'd done was dab them with antibiotic ointment this morning and cross her fingers that the sores wouldn't sprout more crusted scabs that she'd have to pull off. And lo and behold, they hadn't!

But they had done something else. They had . . . sunken. Recessed. Cratered into her arm so that she could slide the pad of her finger into their indentations. As if they were committed to joining her, forever. As if to remind her that they had risen from her own swamp of a body, from the earth that was her skin.

3. *The Woman That Was*

"The first reason that you might have lost your last pageant is that you just don't have 'the look.' What's 'the look'? Well, it's whatever *look* the pageant is looking for."

Veronica was experimenting with ways to "plug" the indented sores in her skin while listening to "Five Reasons You Lost Your Last Pageant" on *Pageant World*. Lucrece had told her that if she wore another long-sleeved dress, she might as well not show up to Miss Wickham—but Veronica knew that if she showed up as is, they might not even let her into the convention center.

Her first instinct was to smear them with thick layers of liquid concealer—like filling a pothole with asphalt, she figured—but it never seemed to fill the holes up to the surface. Like her skin kept absorbing the concealer before

YOUR NEXT BEST AMERICAN GIRL

it could harden. Like the indents were actually getting *deeper* by the moment—was that possible? She sighed, watching the concealer drip from the craters. "No Limits," as the Miss Americana website said. No limits to her body's absurdity.

"The second reason that you might have lost your last pageant is that you're what we call a pageant patty—you're too stiff, too nervous, and the judges think you're a robot."

She tried a bit of adhesive putty that she'd used to put up her posters of Audrey Hepburn and Princess Grace—posters that she should have been putting up on the walls of a dorm room, but *never mind*—but it refused to stick to her skin. It was frustrating, but a little slice of her actually felt weirdly proud. Proud of her skin for so decisively neutralizing the putty. For defying her attempts to bring it to heel.

"The third reason that you might have lost your last pageant is that you used too many clichés in your interview. You weren't creative enough in your answers."

So then she tried toothpaste, which nestled into the gaps without much protest. She covered the minty freshness with foundation and she could pretend, if she squinted, like she was once again the person she used to be.

"The fourth reason that you might have lost your last pageant is—well, this is a tough one, maybe the toughest one to fix. But it's possible you aren't surrounded by the right people."

She thought of Nayeli, who'd been distant since Miss Summerall. *Just busy*, Nayeli said. Her best friend. Her only friend.

She pulled up Nayeli's profile and zoomed in on every picture Nayeli had taken with Addison, even the ones that Veronica herself was in. Scrutinized the level of affection in every comment between them, the number of heart and fire emojis. When Nayeli was distracted on her phone, was she really texting Temo? Or was she reporting back to

Addison, so they could share laughs at the expense of Veronica the Dairy Queen?

Or maybe it had nothing to do with Addison at all. Nayeli's posts had always blurred the lines between cryptic and inspirational—Veronica had seen her reading books on the power of attraction—but recently her language had bordered on belligerent. Things like, "don't ever let them see you coming" with a knife emoji. Or "if you want it as bad as you say you do, then you'll let nothing stop you, NOTHING." Maybe Addison wasn't so much a co-conspirator as she was next. The thought of Addison the Perfect covered in dents like a hail-hit car made her snort, until she remembered that for this theory to be true, her every happy memory with Nayeli had to be a lie.

She started looking through Nayeli's hundreds of mutuals, looking for people who might know something about skin diseases. Bioweapons. There was somebody named Dr. Kimura, whose expertise was "natural" medicine. There was somebody named Jason, who worked at a pharmaceutical company. There was a personalized cosmetic start-up called Cleave that could have mixed a poison into a small, easy-to-carry delivery package—lip balm, maybe. Something that could be smeared around the rim of a water bottle. Something that could be loaned to a target with friendly ease.

Veronica forced herself to look away. Had Nayeli ever actually liked her? Or had she just tolerated her desperate overtures for friendship because they were so often stuck next to each other in line, *Muenster* coming right after *Mora* in the alphabet? On her limbs, the toothpaste started to sting.

"The fifth reason that you might have lost your last pageant is that you actually want it too much. Sounds crazy, I know! But when you want something that bad, it can totally warp your perspective. You develop this tunnel vision, where the only thing you can see is the crown, and everything else goes dark."

YOUR NEXT BEST AMERICAN GIRL

>>>><<<<

Veronica sat huddled with her knees up to her chest in a corner of the dressing room provided to the Miss Wickham contestants, trying not to make eye contact with anyone. While the other girls twirled in half-zipped gowns, spinning their hair around their wrists to display their delicate wing-like scapulae, Veronica hid inside her trench coat while Lucrece fixed her makeup. Not just for privacy, but for warmth. As her holes had deepened—down to three centimeters, now—her body seemed to have lost some of its ability to retain heat.

When she saw Nayeli with her family, Veronica actually felt her stomach flip. She bent her head, hoping she wouldn't be noticed as they set up Nayeli's battle station. Half an hour later, Nayeli hurried over with an energy drink-fueled smile, motioning for her to take off her headphones—and Veronica sternly shook her head. *What's wrong?* she saw but didn't hear Nayeli say. Veronica averted her eyes, so she wouldn't see Nayeli say anything more.

The pageant staff cleared the dressing room for competitors only, so Lucrece had to go—but thankfully, so did most everyone else. "You're radiant," Lucrece said, smoothing her hair. "Just be confident. The judges will see your beauty, trust me."

She still kept her trench coat on as long as she could, finally wiggling out of it just before she stepped out of the shadows of stage-right. She swore she could feel the toothpaste wiggling in her holes with every rattling step she took. She found herself holding her breath to try to keep it sucked in.

"Here's our first question," the main judge asked her once she reached center stage. "What makes you different from the other girls competing for the Miss Wickham title?"

NADIA BULKIN

An easy question, thank God, one that Lucrece drilled her on every time they met. "Well, before I answer that, I just want to say that I think all the girls here are incredible and amazing competitors . . . " But then she trailed off, because Lucrece had also drilled into her head that she had to make frequent gentle eye contact with the judges, and the judges were currently furrowing their eyebrows at her in alarm.

In a moment, she realized what had happened. The stage lights were hot, and the toothpaste was melting. Seeping through the foundation and dribbling down her arms in thick, creamy chunks. It looked like she was leaking vanilla custard.

One of the judges—a beautiful man in his thirties—abruptly gagged into his handkerchief and had to excuse himself, though he only made it a few carpeted yards before he had to lean his head into one of the giant hotel trash cans and unleash a series of loud retches that echoed across the ballroom: women into their tote bags, men into their elbows, children and babies anywhere.

The main judge cleared her throat. "Anyway. Please continue, contestant number five."

The only thing she could think to want was the trench coat she'd left on the floor of stage-right. She felt naked as she stumbled around the back of the stage, moving as quickly as she could with her hands over her sores, but not quickly enough to dodge the whispers of a couple girls she passed along the way: *"Swiss Cheese."*

>>><<<

Veronica stared into the dressing room mirror, summoning the will to use the energy she was saving from sitting down to squeeze new pea-sized dots of toothpaste into the weeping holes of her body. To fix in the span of half an hour what she had spent two hours meticulously crafting this morning.

A sharp gasp rose up from the clothing rack behind

YOUR NEXT BEST AMERICAN GIRL

her. Nayeli had come back to the dressing room, apparently to get a roll of hem tape. Her cousin did all her tailoring; sometimes her outfits fell apart. "Oh my God," she said, "what happened to your arm?"

"I don't know," Veronica replied, honestly. "What do you think?"

Nayeli didn't answer. She only yelped: "You're bleeding!"

"No." In some ways, that would be simpler. Stigmata. Blood loss. She would faint; without medical intervention she would die. She could stop. This could end. "I'm not."

Nayeli knelt down next to her, clasping her hands in prayer. "Did somebody hurt you?" she whispered, and because she couldn't tear her eyes away from the cluster of cavities in the crook of her left arm, she seemed to be asking them the question.

"I don't know," Veronica said again, because the sores weren't going to speak. "My new doctor says I'm doing it to myself. But you'd think if I was going to pick my skin, I'd choose a spot that wouldn't show all the time. Like my stomach, you know."

"Excuse me, is he high? Why the fuck would you do this shit to yourself?"

It was a relief, she had to be honest, to hear someone else say what she was thinking. "Because I'm under so much stress," she said, sarcastically. "But hey, it means one less competitor for you though, right?"

Nayeli sniffled. "Bitch, shut up. You know I wouldn't want to compete without you."

Nayeli was the first person who wasn't a board-certified dermatologist who she allowed to touch any of her sores. Irene had expressed no desire to; she'd said no to Lucrece. Nayeli touched her gingerly at first, too cautious to really pack the toothpaste in—but within a minute, she toughened up. At one point, she even licked her finger before wiping away an extra bit of paste to level off a hole. It touched Veronica, Nayeli's dedication to her repair.

NADIA BULKIN

Veronica could see Nayeli's hand flying up to wipe her heavy lashes—it was as if the girl could feel tears preemptively itching at her ducts—and quickly grabbed her wrist. "Don't touch your eyes," she muttered. "They're perfect."

"Aren't you upset?" Nayeli asked.

She stared into the mirror, into the empty porcelain plate of her face. "Yeah. I guess so." She squinted, giving tears permission to flow if they wanted. They didn't. Her heart was a boulder. No, too organic. Too likely to chip. Her heart was plastic, and would not disintegrate for a hundred years, even though her flesh now found it so easy to falter. "I mean, yes, I am."

Nayeli glanced at the clock; she had to go, she said. "See you out there for talent," she whispered.

But when it came time for Veronica to emerge from the dressing room, she could not make herself go. She couldn't do it to herself—poor melting *Swiss Cheese*—and it hardly seemed fair to subject the judges to another nauseating viewing of her corrupted body, either. She stood, took two practice strides, and felt her eyes crossing, her head lolling. The only thing that made her feel safely tethered to planet Earth was dragging two overloaded clothing racks back to her corner of the dressing room and making herself a little cage. A little protective shell, for her *and* the rest of the world.

After twenty beautiful minutes of reprieve, the door swung open and after a flurry of steel heel taps she'd recognize anywhere, Lucrece pulled apart the dresses serving as her curtains and stuck her head beneath the top bar of the clothing rack. "What are you doing? What's wrong?"

"I'm not going back on stage like this."

"Why not? It's not like it's going to get any worse!"

Was she joking? Could she not see? She could not possibly be paying Lucrece enough to lie to this level. "Because there's no point. Literally! There are not enough points I could win by doing anything else to make up for the fact that I look like a melting candle. I can't *win*."

YOUR NEXT BEST AMERICAN GIRL

"Is getting a plastic crown the only thing that matters to you?" Lucrece hissed, baring her teeth. "Because if you really need one, I can buy you one off the internet for ten dollars. I thought you wanted to be a future leader of America, a role model for young women? Not all the little girls who'll be watching you in the audience can win plastic crowns, but they can see you walk out there with courage and pride!"

Burning shame welled inside Veronica's throat. But no courage, and no pride.

"Now come on. I told the judges you were throwing up and they agreed to let you go last. So go get yourself out there." Lucrece pointed to the door, and beyond it the site of her humiliation: the stage. Veronica wondered if she had dripped onto its hardwood floor. If they'd had to clean up before letting the next contestant walk on, put up a sign that said Caution: Slippery When Wet. "Now."

Veronica clenched the chair. "No."

At which point Lucrece stormed off, angrier than Veronica had ever seen her in their five years of working together. The dresses in their plastic veils fell back into place with a soft rustle, and though her heart was aching, Veronica could once again breathe.

Veronica stayed long enough to hear them announce the winner. *"Your new Miss Wickham . . . contestant number eight, Nayeli Mora!"* She smiled at that before slipping out the back door in her carefully-buttoned trench coat, hurrying to get out before anyone saw her precisely coiffed hair and realized that she was out of place, on the run, a coward.

⟫⟫⟫⟨⟨⟨

When she got home, Irene was waiting in the dark in her hideous old robe, curled around the hideous old table lamp. "Oh, thank God," she said, when Veronica told her what had happened at Miss Wickham.

Thank God?

"Honey, look at you."

Yes, she had done plenty of that. She had spent all day looking at herself. She'd bet her bottom dollar that in the past month she'd spent more time scrutinizing herself in the mirror than Irene had spent looking at her at all.

"You need to get whatever is going on with your skin under control before you go to any more pageants. I mean, I don't even know what you hope to accomplish at this point."

Irene had no understanding of the grit that had to steel up the spine of a pageant queen. She had been a cheerleader in high school. And not a competitive one. Just a run-of-the-mill pom-pom tosser who got on the team because she was blonde and thin and friends with the right queen bees. She'd never faced the judgment of anyone except the men she'd married.

"I'm just trying to protect you, sweetheart. I know how upset you get when you lose."

"It's not about *losing*," she snapped, a bit too ferociously to make her point. "It's about the fact there's only three preliminaries left and if I don't win one of them, I can't even go to Miss Heartland, let alone get a shot at Miss Americana!"

"There's always next year," Irene mumbled, unfussed by Veronica's fury. She was slumped over toward the lamp now, eyes closed but lips somehow still mumbling. "Miss Americana isn't going away."

But her flesh was, wasn't it? Next year she might be nothing but bone. Next year she might not have enough skin and hair left on her skull to hold a crown.

4. The Woman in White

Veronica did not turn on the ceiling light on the day of the Miss Maddox pageant, even though there was no daylight at six a.m. in the guest room. She crawled to her clothes by the wobbly light of her phone instead. It was better for her, these days, to get dressed in the dark. She did not want to risk seeing any signs of red blisters creeping up her neck, because she did not know how deep those lesions could drill once they reached the cratering stage.

She had moved to the guest room (small, never used) in an attempt to circumvent a possible infestation in her own bedroom. An infestation of what, she wasn't sure. But the fact that the lesions had continued to deepen even after she tried every DIY hack to healthier skin—stopped every dermatological treatment except soap and water, paused the juice cleanse and switched to a diet of omega-3 and vitamin C, bought an air purifier—had made her think about rodents nibbling her sores at night. Invisible insects rooting in the holes.

It was during this self-imposed quarantine that the sores had finally eaten all the way through her limbs. The first time she managed to stick her fingers through her arm, bringing her thumb and middle finger to meet inside what should have been solid flesh as if to turn herself into a human daisy chain, she went woozy and passed out. It took her another month to be able to look at herself in a mirror without needing to lie down and close her eyes and pretend to be someone else.

By the time she came to her senses—by the time she remembered herself—Miss Maddox was the only local preliminary left. She'd begged Lucrece to help her prepare for it. No, not prepare: there was no time to simply prepare. There was only winning, now, and losing. There was no other way to Miss Americana. *Only if you promise to be fearless*, Lucrece said, *and to wear your skin with pride.*

What this meant, in practice, was no more long-sleeved dresses. No bandages, no toothpaste. Veronica had considered learning how to graft skin from hidden parts of her body onto her holes—she might come out looking like a rag doll, but surely that was better than looking moth-eaten—but Lucrece's ultimatum took that option out, too. That was probably for the best. Veronica did not trust her ability to thread a needle now, let alone perform field surgery.

She slowly dragged herself and her bags down the stairs, where Irene ambushed her. It was strange, to see Irene dressed so early. "I talked to the doctor," Irene said. "He says you need to go to the hospital right away. So let's go."

There was this girl, Kayla, who she and Nayeli used to drink sugary juice boxes with on the carpets of shitty hotels across the region. Kayla's mother took her out of pageants when she was thirteen because, apparently, Kayla was very sick. Kayla had postural orthostatic tachycardia syndrome. Kayla had chronic fatigue syndrome. Kayla had chronic Lyme. Kayla had to travel to see a specialist. Kayla needed surgery to get a port installed in her body. On the pageant circuit, everyone was sure of the real reason for all of Kayla's illnesses: Kayla's mother didn't want her to compete in pageants anymore.

Sometimes she and Nayeli would distract themselves from their nerves while waiting for results to be announced by drinking energy drinks and speculating: what had happened to Kayla? Was her mother keeping her bedridden? Had her mother put her in hospice? Was she dead?

Kayla had been thirteen. And Veronica was twenty-one. "I'm not going to the hospital," she said, tugging the bags down the last step of the staircase. "I have the pageant today."

"You have holes in your body, Ronnie, they could be infected."

Ronnie. Her baby name. Was she a baby now? A baby for her mother to mind?

"I'm going to the pageant. Lucrece is picking me up."

"No. Veronica. Stop. I know you don't look in the mirror anymore, but you look worse than ever. As your mother, I'm telling you to stop."

YOUR NEXT BEST AMERICAN GIRL

The only thing she needed to stop, Veronica thought, was letting fear rule her heart.

She tried pushing past Irene. Irene tried stopping her. She tried to resist. And Irene's thumb slipped into a hole on her right arm. The sensation plucked some string inside her that made her nearly faint while Irene recoiled, her face twisted into an expression Veronica couldn't read. Was it disgust? Amazement? And then a determination that she had never before seen on her mother's face overcame that expression, and Irene grabbed her by those very holes. As if she was prepared to pull Veronica's arms off, to make her stay.

And maybe Irene would have finally won a fight against her—had Lucrece not started banging on the door. The top of her head was bobbing in and out of visibility through the transom window above the door—she must have been jumping. "Hello!" she was yelling. "Veronica, we have to get going! Hello!"

"Fucking Christ," Irene muttered, squinting as Lucrece's banging got to the headache that always seemed to be lurking just beneath her skull. She left Veronica on the floor while she marched to the door and opened it. Not wide enough for even Lucrece to slip her way in; just wide enough for Veronica to see a sliver of her savior. "Sorry you had to come all this way, but she isn't going to be taking part in any more competitions."

"I know you've been worried about Veronica," Lucrece said, "and I've been worried too. But she's got her pep back now. Let's support her, shall we?"

"What do you mean, got her pep back?" Irene pulled the door open another few inches, enough to display Veronica struggling to sit up on the floor. "She's sick, extremely *sick*, look at what she's done to herself! You can literally stick a fork *through* her!"

Shame. Horror, even. But mostly shame at a body that was being consumed by an invisible mouth, a body that was not so much a body as a condemned house. She glanced up at the woman who'd been her gut-check for the past five years, and when Lucrece smiled at her without flinching, Veronica could have cried. "She wants to compete, let her compete," Lucrece said. "She's a grown woman."

"No, she's not, she's a child!" Legal age. Twenty-one. "And she is mentally ill—oh!"

Lucrece had shoved her shoulder against the door and scraped her way into the house. When she descended upon Veronica, gently asking her if she could stand, all Veronica really wanted to do was collapse against her. But Lucrece had been right, when she was banging on the door earlier— they had to get going. They got her up awkwardly, Veronica panting with effort and digging her nails into Lucrece's leather jacket. Lucrece's designer sunglasses tumbled off her head with a clatter—"leave it," she said, "it's nothing."

Yes, all this was nothing. The stage was everything. Lucrece grabbed the garment bag with one hand as the two of them struggled out the door with all the grace of a pair of contestants in a three-legged race, Lucrece calling back at Irene to "bring out her makeup bag, please?"

Yet when Veronica twisted her neck around, Irene was just scowling on the welcome mat, her arms folded tightly as if to keep them from accidentally doing something useful.

She decided to appeal to Irene's newfound maternal instinct. *"Mom!"*

Nothing changed on Irene's face. But she did grab the cosmetic case and drop it on the stoop with a disturbing rattle before slamming the door. Hopefully Irene hadn't broken a mirror.

Veronica slipped into the backseat of Lucrece's car— their getaway car—while Lucrece went back to collect the cosmetic case. She crawled in, slithered across the leather, put her head down. There was no sense exerting herself by trying to sit up on the drive to Maddox. She needed to save her strength for the competition.

YOUR NEXT BEST AMERICAN GIRL

>>>><<<<

A tornado had blown through Maddox several weeks before the pageant. FEMA trailers were set up on the outskirts of town for families whose houses had been flattened; some residential blocks looked like they'd been spat out of a giant woodchipper. The town council had considered canceling the pageant altogether, but ultimately decided that maintaining this tradition would symbolize the town's defiance in the face of destruction. "Maddox Strong," the banner above Main Street read.

The truth was that Miss Maddox had never been a premier preliminary for Miss Americana, landing at the end of the local competition season as it did. It was for the dregs, the stragglers, the girls who hadn't already secured their place in the regional competition; the last refuge of the crown-chasers who didn't know when the world was telling them no. No Miss Maddox had ever won Miss Heartland Americana, "but there's no reason why you can't be the first," as Lucrece said.

The convention hall had been destroyed, so they were holding the competition on a baseball field, with contestants prepping in locker rooms and under the bleachers, prancing toe-first to keep their heels from getting stuck in the soil. Preteen boys leaned over the fence across the road, gawking and laughing and making jerking-off gestures. Normally at least a couple girls from Maddox proper would be taking part—a fun little "why not" before finishing up the school year—but this year, those girls were needed at home.

All that meant there were only six contestants in Miss Maddox. Only five girls to beat. One of whom was staring at Veronica while her mother sprayed her hair with something that could punch a hole in the ozone. "What is up with that girl's skin?" her little competitor said. Her mother glanced Veronica's way, squinting as she sized her up. "Don't stare," she told her daughter, who kept on staring nonetheless, "she probably got hurt in the tornado."

Lucrece came to her little corner of the bleachers after scouting the competition and said, "They're nothing. They're just . . . livestock. Crispy hair, glitter shadow. Easy peasy, for you."

But nothing felt easy to Veronica, anymore. "You can see through my body," she said, and Lucrece hurried to stoop to her as if in prayer—in prayer to Veronica in her satin white dress that pooled around her folded legs as if to trap her in a frozen pond.

"Yes," Lucrece said, nodding with excitement. "That's the beauty, don't you see?"

Miss Maddox was late kicking off. They had issues setting up the stage. Rehearsal took a while, because several of the girls had never competed in an official Miss Americana preliminary before. One judge was a no-show until two hours past the designated start time, when he turned up drunk. So it was night by the time the talent portion started. Veronica was second to last in the line-up, and one of the judges seemed to be asleep when she tottered up on stage.

"Hello," she said. "My name's Veronica Muenster, and I'm going to be singing 'His Eye Is on the Sparrow'."

The drunk judge leaned forward. "Go ahead, sweetheart. Please."

"Why should I feel discouraged?" She could feel the stadium lights shining through her body, warm and buoyant and comforting. Until she saw the gold flooding from her body, she had not realized how flat and dull she'd been before the holes. How much she, and everyone else, had simply swallowed light. "Why should the shadows come?"

She heard one of the judges—the one who'd fallen asleep—mumble, "Oh God," as if they were afraid. And they would be right to be. Because Veronica was not a sparrow transformed into a swan. She was a black hole transformed into a star.

YOUR NEXT BEST AMERICAN GIRL

"Why should my heart be lonely, and long for heaven and home?"

The night was quiet, so quiet that she could hear the thinness of her voice. She did not have a voice for radio; she was not cut out to be a singer. She was cut out to be an idol. Stolen, smashed, worshipped.

"I sing because I'm happy, I sing because I'm free, for his eye is on the sparrow, and I know he watches me."

She exhaled away from the microphone, waiting. At first all she heard was the violent thudding of her heart, thrashing like a worm on a summer sidewalk against her ribs.

But then the drunk judge stood up, pushing his folding chair over into the dirt, and started to applaud.

>>>><<<<

Nayeli called that night. A video call that Veronica was glad to be able to answer in pitch darkness since Irene had apparently gone to bed early. "Congrats, Miss Maddox," she said. "Thank God you'll be at regionals. I would have killed myself if I couldn't bitch to anyone."

"Thanks. Are they calling me Miss Paddocks yet?"

Nayeli's lip dropped dramatically in one corner. "Um..."

"So, yes."

"You know what, don't worry about it. There's been a lot of weird comments."

A knot pulled tight in Veronica's stomach, even though she wasn't surprised, exactly. She did, after all, look weird. No, not weird—*remarkable,* Lucrece would call it. One of the mindset hacks that Tanya O'Dell had mentioned on that one episode of *Pageant World* was "use nice words to describe yourself: you're not short, you're petite; you're not snippy, you're sassy." *I'm not weird, I'm remarkable. I'm not covered in holes, I'm adorned with them.*

"Anyway, the reason I called you—other than to say congratulations, of course—is that I think I found something. I've been watching these trypophobia videos..."

"What videos?"

"Oh, it's like. Fear of clustered holes. Lotus seedheads. Yeast holes. There's these toads that, like, carry their eggs on their backs so when they hatch it looks like all these little holes on their bodies bursting open and . . . " A full-body shudder moved through Nayeli, whipping her spine like a towel. "I'm actually pretty sure that I have it, this trypophobia thing."

Because you saw me? Veronica wondered. *Because you touched me?*

"It's not an actual condition, dumbass." The surly voice belonged to Temo, who was hovering somewhere just beyond the frame of Nayeli's camera. She was in her bedroom, so he must have snuck in. "It's just people being freaks on the internet, trying to gross each other out. Pretending to be grossed out for clout. Just like you're doing right now."

Gross. The word hung in the air like the stench of spoiled food. *So gross.*

"It is absolutely real, because I absolutely have it," Nayeli snapped back. "You saw me almost throw up last night looking at the cow gut picture."

"Yeah, cuz it's cow guts! It's the same way you get grossed out when you see a smashed up squirrel on the highway. Or a dog that's got the mange. You're reacting the way your brain has trained you to react to a sign of disease. Like oh, fuck, get away from me!"

Nayeli rolled her eyes. "That is not it at all. It's got something to do with high-contrast spatial frequencies that some people are just extra sensitive to."

"It's perfectly normal. You're not special."

"Then why won't you look at these pictures, if being scared of them is so *normal*?"

"Because you aren't actually scared of them, you're *obsessed* with them."

Nayeli turned her attention back to the phone. "This boy, I swear to God. Anyway. I was watching this one video compilation of clustered holes in nature and I saw this one plant that . . . well, look at the picture I sent you."

Veronica opened the message that had just come in from Nayeli. The long leaves of a plant marked with perfectly round holes, as if someone had gone at it with a paper punch. Staring through the empty spaces where leaf matter should be, Veronica's stomach did a somersault—and all of her own clustered holes began to tingle at once.

"Doesn't that look like what's going on with you?"

"What is that? What's wrong with it?"

"Hang on, I saved it. Okay, it's called shot hole disease. *Coryneum blight*. It's a fungus, I guess, that attacks . . . stone fruit trees? Like cherries and peaches and shit like that."

"Shot hole." For some reason she thought of golf courses, the kind owned by men that sponsored beauty pageants and owned cherry orchards. "Is that like shit hole?"

"No, it's shot hole like a BB gun shot." Nayeli cocked her fingers for emphasis. "God, of course you've never fired one of those."

"Wait, so it infects the tree and leaves these holes in it?"

"Yeah, it says it starts off with . . . lesions and then they dry up and fall away and leave these round . . . holes. 'The holes can appear anywhere on the plant but are most prominent on the leaves'." Nayeli looked nervous, as if she was afraid of causing offense, but Veronica was thinking about herself as a plant, how her arms would be her leaves, reaching for the world. "Do you think you might have . . . touched a tree that had this, or something? Or breathed around it? I'm pretty sure you can get fungal infections by inhaling them."

Off-screen, Temo objected. "Dude, diseases don't jump from plants to people like that."

"Oh, look who's suddenly Mr. Botany over there."

Never mind about any of that, Veronica thought. That

was a question she'd have all the time in the world to answer, after she cleaned up the damage that this disease had wrought on her heretofore carefully-preserved body and won all that she could win. "How do you get rid of it?"

"It just says . . . " Nayeli sighed. She had to wet her lips a couple times before finishing her sentence. "To cut off the parts of the plant that are diseased."

"Oh." She imagined throwing her arm down in front of a buzz saw, pulling a tourniquet tight with her teeth. Much like firing a BB gun and riding an ATV, woodworking was not a world she was familiar with. "What happens if you don't? If you just leave it alone?"

It took Nayeli a minute to answer. She could see Nayeli's scrolling phone screen reflected in her glasses and knew if it was taking her this long to speak, she wasn't finding anything good. Finally, Nayeli shook her head and whispered, "I think it just spreads."

<hr>

So there was nothing else to do but figure out how she'd gotten sick. She'd been sick for so long, by then, that it was not so difficult to imagine the possibility that her wounds would never heal. Occasionally her thoughts hovered on the precipice of a more frightening truth—that the holes would grow and multiply until her body simply disappeared—but she couldn't stay on that cliffside for very long. She would lose her will to search for her killer, if she did. If only those girls who'd called her Swiss cheese could see her now that she'd truly earned the name—now that her limbs were hole-punched, shot through, now that the first of the bulbous red wounds were spreading to her chest.

And they *would* see her again. She had guaranteed it by winning Miss Maddox. They would all see her again at Miss Heartland Americana, unless the holes overtook the flesh first.

She sorted through her closet, holding each item and

trusting her body to know when she'd found something important. Mostly, all she felt was a flat sadness, the memory of the healthy body she used to have. When she didn't find anything in her bedroom, she crawled to the bathroom she shared with Irene. And it was there, in the cabinet under the sink, that she found the thing that made her holes throb: a bottle of essential oil. It was for baths, supposedly. She'd used it a couple times, although she couldn't remember exactly where she got it—it looked like one of those home-packaged bottles that witchy women sold at farmer's markets with the claim that the contents had been blessed by the harvest moon or some shit.

What had Nayeli said? *I'm pretty sure you can get fungal infections by inhaling them.*

"Truth & Beauty," the label read, in what looked almost like handwriting. She unscrewed the cap to take a whiff, and as soon as the scent hit her—a slightly musty mix of sandalwood and clary sage—she remembered the difficulty she'd had with the dropper, the relief she felt when even two drops managed to pool out and fill the entire bath.

And she remembered Irene giving her the bottle. Pushing her to "take another one of your steam baths" the week before Miss Pioneer Spirit. Wanting her to "relax," supposedly.

Irene was still groggy from her nighttime sedative when she came slouching down the stairs the next morning. Maybe she'd taken a double dose, because she looked like hell. "Oh," she said when she saw Veronica. "Did you win your pageant?"

"Yes. No thanks to you. Did you know that this thing would kill me?"

Irene paused at the bottom of the stairs. "That's why I tried to take you to the hospital."

"But there's no cure. Right?" She had to keep her heart steady, her hope flattened. Her body wasn't strong enough to endure an emotional crash. "You know there isn't a cure."

Irene squinted at her, blinded by the sunlight streaming into the living room. "Know? What the hell are you talking about, *know*. God knows I'm always the last one to *know* anything about you these days. You're never here. You never talk to me."

The whine in Irene's voice as she lumbered toward the kitchen made Veronica and her holes recoil with disgust. That didn't seem truthful out of Irene, and it certainly wasn't beautiful. "What do we have to talk about? What groceries to buy? The latest weird bullshit you saw online? Or maybe you just want to keep me stuck here in this house with you, so you don't have to look at my life, and the fact that I might someday get the fuck away from here. Maybe you're just jealous of your own daughter."

Irene's chin was wobbling, but her eyes were solid steel beams boring across the room, refusing to let Veronica's gaze go. "I want, so much, to be jealous of you, honey. I really wish I was. But all I feel is sad. No, you know what, it's worse than that. It's pity."

"Oh, here we go. You're sad. You feel sorry. No, you don't get to act sad. You did this."

"No, I . . . wait, do you think this is *my* fault? What, because I'm the one that first signed you up for a pageant? Jesus, Ronnie. You know, maybe you're right. Maybe this is all my fault."

There was a time when Irene had been the one coaching Veronica, quizzing her with sample on-stage interview questions, finding the best ninety seconds of singing to showcase, showing her how to stand, how to smile, how to walk. Irene would stuff her mouth with bobby pins while putting up Veronica's hair; she would give her the starting pitch for her Do-Re-Mis. There was a time when Irene had seemed to relish her role as "pageant Mom."

And then, one weekend, it all fell apart. They were late getting on the road and there was a screw-up with the entry forms and something had gotten left behind—she couldn't even remember what, anymore—and they'd ended up screaming at each other in the dressing room. Irene stormed off, telling Veronica she could finish her own hair, even though she knew, didn't she, that Veronica did not have the hang of up-dos? Veronica spent fifteen minutes in an escalating panic, trying to spear and spray her hair into order, until a kind woman put a gentle hand on her shoulder and told her she'd look better with her hair down. "Crispy buns are overrated," she had said, winking. "My name's Lucrece, by the way."

"You know, the only reason I signed you up for Miss Junior Fucking Pioneer Spirit in the first place was because I wanted you to feel beautiful. Because I was tired of you coming home from school all sad because your friends were going to the mall without you, or some boy made fun of you. Because clearly, you didn't believe me when I told you that all you needed was just confidence. A nice smile. People. Like. Positive. People."

But Veronica had never been interested in winning Miss Congeniality. That was what Irene never understood about her daughter.

"I wanted you to go back to school with your chin held high, that's all. But you never . . ." Irene cocked her head, as if finally guessing the answer to a riddle, "you never even heard that message, did you? All those crowns and sashes and little plastic trophies you've got in your bedroom and you never actually got the message. You still can't even smile right, my God!"

"I'm not talking about any of that . . . fucking ancient history! I'm talking about the bath oil you gave me! Truth & Beauty! The stuff that did this to me!"

For a good few ticks of the family's heirloom clock, Irene furrowed her eyebrows at Veronica. And then, finally, the cobwebs cleared, and she spoke. "Oh, that?" she said. "That wasn't me. Lucrece left that for you."

NADIA BULKIN

5. *The Woman Clothed with the Sun*

A small housefly was hitching a ride on the window of the bus. Its fragile legs wobbled as its wings fluttered, hapless, in the wind. Veronica wondered if it was terrified, clinging on for dear life like that. Or was it happy to be flying faster, higher, farther than it ever had before?

Lucrece's office was in a small brick building near the city's oldest mall. As the bus rolled up to the Holmes and 48th street stop—and the fly gamely crawled out of view—Veronica stared at the boarded-up windows of what had once been the mall's largest department store, where she and Lucrece had searched for her first pair of six-inch nude patent heels. After they found them, Lucrece had her do a little runway walk in front of the middle-aged men and children sitting on benches waiting for their women, just to get her used to the feeling of eyes on her. "Be the most exciting thing they'll see today," she said. "Change their view of what beauty is, bend their standard toward you."

How old had she been then? Sixteen?

Inside Suite 180 of 4750 Holmes, she found Lucrece sitting at her desk, staring at a window that opened onto a brick wall. She turned when she heard Veronica slide into the room, leaning against the wall for support, and put on a pensive smile. "Hello, darling. You must be very angry with me."

Anger was an interesting way to describe the feeling in her heart. It felt too small for the damage that had been done to her, and yet too big for the will she carried to resist further harm, to condemn Lucrece, to demand revenge.

"I just want you to fix it," she sighed. "Honestly. I won't tell anybody. I won't report you. I just want you to make it right."

The sadness in Lucrece's eyes scared her more than the holes. Control every point you can, Lucrece always said, to make up for the things you can't possibly change, the things you simply have to bear. "There's no fixing it. The

YOUR NEXT BEST AMERICAN GIRL

blight in the bath oil creates a . . . permanent alteration to your appearance. But darling, darling—there's nothing to fix! You are more compelling, more attractive now than you've ever been!"

It made Veronica want to laugh. "What the fuck does that say about your coaching, if *this* is me at my best?"

"That I know how much you want it. That I know the fire in your heart. You're such a hard worker, Veronica. I would have considered it a personal failure if I had not given you this ultimate advantage."

"You're insane." Insane. Crazy. What had Addison's friends called her? Psycho. A psycho coach for a psycho contestant. The scream inside made her want to dig her nails into the netting of skin she had left, pull it off like mozzarella. *Swiss Cheese.*

And Lucrece really did laugh. "Maybe, yes. I've been in this business for thirty years. It does drive you batty, watching girls flatten themselves into little cookie cutter shapes with their smiles stapled on and their goo-goo eyes glued open. All so the men who run the show can watch the little parade go by and say, 'ooh, that one. That's the one I want.' And the ridiculous bit is, they're just buying variations of the same model. Like shopping for groceries!"

"So what is this, some kind of fuck-you to society?" It hurt, to think of herself as a walking affront, an insult on legs. "Because I didn't sign up for . . . "

"No, darling, it's a reminder of what beauty actually is. Beauty is truth. It's clarity. Vulnerability. Beauty doesn't block out the light, don't you see? Beauty is the light shining through the human soul. Like it shone through you last night, when you were crowned Miss Maddox." She reached her hand out to stroke Veronica's cheek. "I knew the judges would see it, if you just let them see you for who you really are." Veronica twitched at the suggestion that these holes—this blight, as Lucrece called it—was who she *really was*, and Lucrece jerked back her hand, biting her lip. "If we could all be so lucky, to be accepted in our truth."

"Maybe you should have done this to yourself, if you wanted to be—"

"No. No, no, no. I couldn't have done it. My dear, nobody would have seen me."

Veronica had spent so much of the competition season in a state of resistance—resisting what was happening to her body, resisting others' attempts to explain it, resisting death—that the urge to kick back against Lucrece had been practically instinctive. But now she felt her eyebrows twist in understanding, because Lucrece was right. Lucrece was objectively beautiful, far more so than Veronica would ever be. Her Miss Americana run had catapulted her, for a time, into glossy jewelry ads in rich women's lifestyle magazines. But she was too old, now.

"Here." Lucrece held up her phone to a picture of Veronica, crowned, on that baseball field in Maddox. The lights shone through her as if she was a glass Christmas ornament. "You are viral."

What Veronica heard was: *you are a virus*.

"Look at this girl. Elle. Look how she's made herself over today." Lucrece pulled another picture onto the screen. A girl in her bathroom had used gore makeup to give herself wounds that looked, with the right lighting, exactly like Veronica's. *Miss Americana*, she'd captioned it, complete with a tiara emoji. It had over one hundred thousand likes. "And she's not even the real thing. She's just a cheap imitation on a screen. A flatterer. But you see how they respond."

The fake stoic look on Elle the Influencer's face—like a high school musical star trying to act—only made Veronica angrier. She smacked the phone out of Lucrece's hand and it went tumbling to the floor. Lucrece didn't even look to see where it landed. "Who cares? That's fucking stage makeup. They're probably impressed she can make herself look like a monster."

"Have you even looked at your own socials, Veronica?"

Reluctantly, Veronica pulled out her own phone and

YOUR NEXT BEST AMERICAN GIRL

took it off "do not disturb." Her follower notifications were the first thing she noticed. There were so many—her follower count must have quadrupled since she last checked it on the drive to Maddox—that she first thought that she'd been hacked. And then she noticed the number of unread messages.

I can't describe it, but I truly have never seen a woman as beautiful as you.

Please never go out in public where small children can see you. You are a disgrace.

God smiles upon you and your beautiful soul <3

BURN YOUR CROWN BITCH

We don't deserve you, queen. Future Miss Americana.

I would kill myself if I looked as awful as you

She read that one aloud to Lucrece. "It says I'm awful," she said, in case Lucrece didn't understand.

But Lucrece seemed neither able nor willing to understand the weight of that word, the way it pummeled everything Veronica had tried to protect about herself. The *at-least-people-think-I'm-pretty,* the *at-least-I-scored-better-than-them.* Instead of collapsing, Lucrece's smile broadened.

"Yes exactly! Awful!" Somehow coming from her smiling Revloned lips—Crushed Rubies, the shade was called—the word didn't feel quite so heavy. "Didn't they teach you what awful means in English class?"

Veronica narrowed her eyes. She shook her head.

"Awe-ful. Inspiring great awe. That's what it means. Deserving great respect. It means you are . . . " Lucrece dropped to her knees, her wince only barely visible even as the sound of bone hitting tile filled the room, "majestic."

⫸⫷

The day before Miss Heartland Americana, Lucrece arranged a meeting with Hebe's North American marketing team to discuss the possibility of a brand ambassadorship. They were tucked away from the rest of the pageant, on the second floor of the Continental Hotel in a room filled with artisanal bottled waters, which Lucrece said was a good sign.

"They want to snatch you up," she said. With white shift dresses selling for thousands of dollars in European capitals, Hebe would be a much more prestigious sponsor than Forger Foods. Hardly even comparable to Angel Dancewear. Hebe had all sorts of ideas for groundbreaking photo shoots: threading gold chains through her limbs instead of over them; hanging baubles from the holes in her flesh for Christmas. All under doctor supervision, they assured her. Veronica had never heard the words "open doors" so many times.

But she didn't like the way the brand director was looking at her. With greed. She couldn't pinpoint, exactly, what the greed hungered for—except that it left her feeling sure that he collected trophies. Two-headed calves. Cat mummies. Shrunken heads.

Veronica turned her head toward the window so she wouldn't have to look at him. Peering down at the street, she saw that the religious nutso who'd yelled at Addison to "take off your crown" at Miss Pioneer Spirit was across from the hotel. He'd brought his bullhorn again.

If she was Addison's father's daughter, the Hebe guy wouldn't have dared look at her that way. He would have known that he'd have ended up knocked out cold. But she wasn't Addison's father's daughter, and Irene wasn't here to stick up for her. She was at home, tending to the strange, pale little plants that had grown out of the scabs Veronica had planted. Watering them, sprinkling them with plant food, giving them little umbrellas when she was afraid the sun would be too much for them. Being a good mother.

After the meeting ended, she slipped away from Lucrece and the man from Hebe before he could get close enough to touch her. She rode the escalator down to the lobby to put more distance between them and then kept walking, leaning against planters and columns, imagining

YOUR NEXT BEST AMERICAN GIRL

getting on the first truck that would let her lay down in its bed before remembering the crown. How badly she wanted the crown.

Could she hire bellhops to protect her? No. What about security guards? She saw some loitering outside, past the sliding doors. She had to put on her jacket to get the motion sensor to detect her, then stumbled into the heat.

The security guards were laughing at the protesting man across the street. Calling him a loser, a hater, saying he was fucked in the head to hate beauty pageants so much. "Surprised they don't call the cops," one said, even though he wasn't breaking any laws. They were too weak to protect her, Veronica decided. Not enough conviction. Not enough passion. Too willing to pass the buck.

But then there was the protesting man. The nutso. "Why dress yourself in scarlet and put on jewels of gold?" he was yelling on the curb of the carwash. "You adorn yourself in vain! Your lovers despise you! They want to kill you!" He might have the strength of character necessary to defend a girl in need.

She teetered across the street, even though Lucrece wouldn't want her to expend any more energy than she absolutely had to, and uncrossed her jacketed arms as she approached the man. He immediately averted his eyes and started yelling words like "begone!" and "devil!", like a priest warding off a vampire.

Unfortunately for him, these words had no impact on her. "Look at me," she said, rolling her shoulder, and then her arm, out of its sleeve. Her muscles were weak. It took a while. After she was done, it took the last reserves of her depleted energy to stand there, swaying like one of those floppy inflatable balloon-people that got staked down at car dealerships, letting the sun and the smoke and all the acrid scents of uncollected garbage seep through the prism of her body.

It started with his silence. Then the silent mouth began to tremble, like he was about to cry, and the silent neck leaned backward while the silent shoulders drooped. It was as if the blight had suddenly released him from all the rules he had spent his life following, all the braces that had held him upright, and now he was custard. He was jelly.

And then she too was released by her body, crumpling like a puppet whose strings had been cut. From a distance it probably looked like she'd fainted, but her eyes were wide open on the sidewalk, staring at the man. He had followed her down, dropping his bullhorn and flattening himself against the hot grainy asphalt so that he need not look down at her, apparently. His chapped lips kept parting, then closing, then parting again—as if he wanted to say something.

"You can speak," she told him, and his jaw dropped open. So she was rebuilding him.

"Angel," he whispered, "you have no flaw."

Veronica smiled. You could take the man out of his church, but you couldn't take the church out of the man.

"Take me back to the hotel," she said.

He immediately leapt up to do so, wrapping her up in her jacket so as not to touch her skin directly. It wasn't disgust, she could see that. It was reverence. Lucrece had told her that the blight had a power that couldn't be predicted, one that might manifest very differently for different audiences—it urged the Hebe brand director to possess, while it called this man to serve. Which was how Veronica learned that beauty was subjective, after all.

>>><<<

On the first day of competition, people thronged around the woman who held light in her body—contestants and their relatives, the army of volunteers and vendors who staffed Miss Heartland Americana, respected members of the pageant's board of directors. It wasn't hate in their eyes, no. They were curious, craning their necks, touching the spots on their own bodies where Veronica's holed body carried light. Not even her competitors could hate the gilded being whose steps they now followed, awe-struck.

YOUR NEXT BEST AMERICAN GIRL

But there was a pressure in their proximity that put what little skin Veronica had left on high alert. Theirs was a hunger that refused to share.

The protesting man—now no longer protesting—pushed them all back with the zeal of a man who had seen God. He didn't care who he shoved. When a middle-aged volunteer woman ran up to try to get a photo with Veronica, he grabbed her by the collar and threw her like a wrecking ball into a throng of people. Veronica only had a second to glance back at the mass of upturned bodies before Lucrece hurried her down the hallway, because they needed to get to the dressing room by five p.m. Now that Lucrece was solely responsible for makeup and it took Veronica twice as long to get in and out of her clothes, they needed all the time they could get. Having holes where uninterrupted muscle and bone should be had given Veronica a debilitating fear of tearing.

Her fellow Miss Heartland Americana contestants were all in on the latest beauty trend. Who knows how it had started. One girl saw another girl try it, and get a thousand "likes" of validation. One girl clicked on a trending hashtag. One girl heard about it from her coach, or her mother, or her dermatologist. One girl listened to the latest episode of *Pageant World*: "Five Ways to Pull Off This Summer's Boldest Look."

Boldest. Sickest. Most Blighted.

And these girls weren't dotting on red and black eyeliner, they weren't applying paper-mâché prosthetics. They were changing themselves for good, burning and carving clustered holes into their bodies while rehearsing their interview answers: "I always had a voice, but the crown will give me a microphone . . . " "I didn't choose my platform, my platform chose me . . . " "As Miss Heartland Americana, I will . . . "

That was the thing about pageant girls, the one true thing after all other pillars fell into doubt. They always committed, to whatever they did.

NADIA BULKIN

Girls were using whatever they could get their hands on—a lot of cigarettes bummed off the security guards, a lot of needles from their sewing kits, but Addison, of course, had access to the best: a hot knife, plugged into the wall in place of her curling iron.

Amid this chaos, Veronica alone was still. Lucrece was vigorously teasing her hair into a bouffant. Every so often Veronica would ask if there were any signs of blight on her head—because surely she would die, wouldn't she, if a BB-sized hole opened up through her skull?—and Lucrece would say, "no, no, no" in a tone that Veronica didn't quite believe. The truth, she supposed, would be revealed soon enough. It was a lot like blight, in that way.

To avoid looking in the mirror for too long—she found it gave her migraines—Veronica scrolled, only semiconsciously, through the notifications on her phone. Most of the posts she was tagged in were pictures of a blonde woman she barely recognized as herself—some of them blurry paparazzi-style shots, some of them watermarked pageant photos. But there were also a few strangers who apparently wanted to feel her gaze through the internet. Strange, for someone to desire *her* to look upon *them*. Among these strangers was a middle-aged woman in a Miss Heartland volunteer shirt, proudly tilting her face to the camera to better display the bruises and scrapes she'd gotten falling through the crowd. *So happy to have met the lovely Veronica*, she'd written. *And look at my gorgeous souvenirs!*

"It's the woman who wanted a picture with me," Veronica said. "She's hurt."

"Aren't we all," Lucrece said, frowning as she gingerly pulled a boar bristle brush over the crown of Veronica's head. "Eat your energy bar. It's fifty grams of protein."

Somewhere in the dressing room, Addison was screaming. Veronica would recognize that voice anywhere. That mouth, open and teeming with orthodontically-perfected teeth.

YOUR NEXT BEST AMERICAN GIRL

>>><<<

The Venus Ballroom was packed, and vibrating with anticipation. There had to be a thousand hearts pitter-pattering, two thousand lungs hyperventilating in Veronica's direction. A few stray camera flashes went off as Veronica entered stage left, but a soft murmur of the microphone quickly reminded the audience that there was to be no flash photography.

Her blighted legs felt so light that they almost seemed made of cotton candy. Save for brief flashes of electric pain when she had to hoist each heel up and forward, she might have felt like she was gliding. Or sinking. Or falling. Fortunately, Lucrece had sewn ribs of sturdy coat hanger wire into the sides of her dress that were helping her stay upright, so all she had to worry about was pushing her cotton candy legs toward the central X.

She knew when she'd reached it because a thousand throats gasped as the lights lined up behind her blighted body. "My name is Veronica Muenster," she said, leaning ever so slightly toward the mic. "I'm going to be singing 'Abide with Me'."

Such a melancholy song would never scoop up the talent points needed to win Miss Heartland, which was why Lucrece had pushed her to repeat "His Eye Is on the Sparrow." It had been her lucky charm at Maddox, after all. But Veronica had felt strongly that this occasion called for a different vibe. "I don't want to sing about someone else watching over me," she told Lucrece, "while I'm the one watching over them."

Besides, winning was no longer the objective, was it? Winning was superfluous to their mission of the blight. Winning was child's play.

"Where is death's sting? Where, grave, thy victory?"

As soon as she started singing, holes burst in the judges. Only one of them cried out in pain; the others swallowed the force of the injury, out of their deep respect for Veronica the Majestic. Blight burst apart their ear lobes and turned flesh into flags, fluttering on the faint breeze of the air conditioning.

A confetti-sized piece of human meat that had spun off a judge found the air current and floated sleepily toward the stage. Veronica watched as it veered off to the right of her head, rolling her eyes until they hurt so she wouldn't have to turn her head—and saw Nayeli standing in the wings, eyes brimming with love. Her heart twinged a bit when she saw blood dripping from Nayeli's arm—was she digging holes? No. Nayeli would never risk her manicure if she didn't have to. She was using a pair of nail scissors. Boring them into her arm over and over, like a poorly-aimed corkscrew.

"I triumph still," Veronica sang, reaching forward as if to hold the ballroom, this small snow globe of a world, in her tattered arms, "if thou abide with me."

RED SKIES IN THE MORNING

1. Day Zero

MARLY D.'S PRESS CONFERENCE was being held outside the hospital instead of the police department, even though there was no medicine, no surgery, no treatment anywhere in the world that could save Marly—and Marly knew it. "I'm just so sorry for my parents," she said, heaving tears into her sleeve as said parents—two stoic-looking senior citizens wrapped in weatherproof outerwear—dutifully propped her up on either side. "They don't deserve to watch me die like this."

Maybe in the old days, the pain of watching a child die would count as something remarkable. For Marly D.'s parents, the *like this* was the part that really mattered, the blade that truly stung. Hers would not be a quiet death in a hospital bed, soothed to eternal rest with painkillers and loved ones' kisses. No doctor would be able to tell Mr. and Mrs. D. that "she's at peace now" or "Marly's sleeping" or "your girl's with God"—not with a straight face, anyway.

Instead, an entity would tear its way out of Marly. It would be violent. Bloody. Inside, organs would be crushed. Outside, skin would tear. A screaming thing, a fundamentally dead thing, would emerge from between her ribs, breaking bones as it climbed and struggled, made its first and final ascent toward the open air. It would die, the entity. It could not have what it wanted (life). But Marly would die first. Maybe she would be bisected. Maybe she would be decapitated. Almost certainly, she would be exsanguinated. Demolished. Implosion first, and then explosion. It would be fast. Too fast to stop. But not so fast that she wouldn't feel it.

The feed switched to the Channel 5 reporter on the assignment. "The video is described as depicting a children's ballet dance recital, taking place inside what appears to be a school auditorium and recorded from a distance of approximately twenty feet away. The recording is just over four minutes long. Authorities are urging anyone who has any information about this paracontagion to stop what you're doing, pick up the phone, and call the police right now."

"I wonder if they're gonna opt for euthanasia," Selene said.

Hannah cocked her eyebrow in question, and Selene suddenly became conscious of what a fucked-up thing to say it was around her younger sister. It had been ten years and they were all adults now, but she still couldn't shake their mother's voice, urgently commanding her to *keep it together for Hannah*. That was what their mother's death had been like—a feverish rattling off of makeshift parenting instructions as time slipped away. "It's a bad death, is all. I'm sure they're still hoping they'll find the tape and give her a path out."

Hannah's quizzical look—not horrified, but seemingly amused at Selene's slip of the mind—persisted for another ten seconds, and then she went back to scrolling on her phone. "You should see what they're saying about this woman."

"Who's 'they'?"

"People. Online."

Selene snorted. "Right. Them."

"They're like, oh, she's such an idiot, why didn't she just close her eyes instead of watching . . . "

Selene's attention snapped up from the dark lull of her

RED SKIES IN THE MORNING

coffee. What an audacious thing to say, considering the terrible ways people had died in the early days of paracontagions—upper-floor residents called to an abandoned camcorder in the basement laundry of their apartment building, retail workers called to a fluttering letter in a shuttered mall across the street. The messaging from government officials had been consistent from the outset: shutting one's eyes, even refusing to leave the house, was not an effective mitigation method. "I swear to God. Really?"

"I know, I know," Hannah sang back, prompting a *thank God* grunt from Selene. "But you know there are people who think you can up your resistance by like, meditating and eating eggs. Or saying magic words when you feel a paracontagion pulling on you. Kanda . . . estrata . . . " She put up her hand to preempt Selene's protest, but Selene was mostly peeved by the carelessness in Hannah's tone, a flippancy about the process of paracontagion mitigation that she didn't like. "Sorry. This comment is actually worse, I think: *that zombie totally deserves it.*"

"Marly D.? Why? Also what the hell's a zombie?"

"An undead creature."

It was too early for this. "Hannah."

"They're talking about people who don't add value to society. People who just blindly plod along in their empty little lives, brainless, basic, boring. Zombies. Zeroes. I guess they think this Marly lady's so terminally boring that she deserves to die."

Selene slammed coffee grounds into the trash. "That sounds pretty damn subjective."

"Oh, it's *totally* subjective. I mean, I don't think anyone's a zombie."

That was just like Hannah, Selene thought, looking at her younger sister with a fondness she didn't always have time for. And she didn't have time to spell it out now, either. "Well, you have fun with that. I gotta go. West has been on our ass lately about not keeping cases waiting."

"'Kay." Hannah worked mid shifts at a clothing store she hated, and wouldn't have to go in for a couple hours yet. "Happy paperclipping."

Selene wormed her way into her coat, awkwardly grabbing her tote bag before the sleeves were even completely on. "See you tonight," she called toward the general vicinity of the couch, receiving a faint "Bye" in return as she was pulling the door closed behind her.

⁂

Despite the run she broke into several times over the course of her commute, Selene ended up late to her first appointment anyway. The trains were delayed due to a "person on the tracks" who'd already been cleaned up but was still causing back-up, and then she couldn't find her ID despite dumping the contents of her tote bag all over the lobby, which meant she had to call Frank to walk her in. And unfortunately, the person waiting for her beneath the abstract, unobjectionable office art was Mr. Ryosuke Kudo, who she didn't have a path for yet. Fuck.

"Sir. I promise you. We are working on it. We will find someone to watch your paracontagion." She hated to call it *his,* even though it was technically correct: the paracontagion was currently bonded to him, and would remain so bonded until someone else came into the office and watched the video it was housed in.

"There's only two more days."

"Yes, I understand. Two more days after . . . " she quickly checked the bright red numbers on her computer screen. "Seven o'clock tonight. The system's a bit busy right now so connections are a little tight, but, it's okay. Our goal today is to take care of the folks whose chains are expiring tomorrow. I'm sure by . . . oh, tomorrow afternoon we'll have someone lined up to be your path."

"What if there's nobody?"

The fear in their voices never failed to tickle even the parts of her brain she thought had turned to steel. It was

RED SKIES IN THE MORNING

obvious how much terror consumed the incidentals like Mr. Kudo, who had volunteered to help a neighbor but now found himself in a hall of closed doors, with no one to reciprocate the favor. Some of her regulars, the "professionals" who used pathing compensation as side income and came in as frequently as the law allowed, tried to hide the fear, joking even as their remaining hours whittled down into something sharp and shank-like. But she eventually realized that even they were mostly staying sedated to endure the anxiety of not knowing with absolute certainty that the system would provide them a path. *Jesus take the wheel,* one of her regulars always said. *If Jesus rams me into a tree then I'll be the first to tell him thank you.*

"There's five hundred thousand people in this city." The weight of that number spread, icy, across Selene's desk and around Mr. Kudo's throat. Five hundred thousand strangers walking obliviously across the grate he lay beneath. She had never asked for details about his family, but she knew his emergency contact was his landlord. *Everybody has somebody, don't they?* People said that all the time—when declining to volunteer to path, when passing on their paracontagion to someone else, when changing the subject—but Selene didn't think it was true. Frankly, she'd seen too many people for whom it wasn't true. That was why pathing offices existed. Finding "somebodys" for people who didn't have anybody was exactly what she was paid to do.

What she said instead was the same thing she said to Mr. Kudo now: "There's always somebody." If nothing else worked—if they couldn't get a hold of anybody on the volunteer list and no walk-ins arrived and a last-minute urgent request for volunteers solicited no one—then they would go to the city jail. "I've never lost anyone, and I don't intend to start now."

Would that be reassuring? She hoped so. The old man nodded.

There had to be more she could do. There was always more. "What kind of symptoms are you having? Hallucinations?" Another nod, more cautious this time. "Okay. Visual or audio or both?"

"Mostly I . . . feel her? I don't see her face. I don't hear her voice. But I can tell she's there."

Selene glanced at the computer screen—who was "she," again?—and saw a jumble of words that she couldn't make perfect sense of at a split-second's notice, except—

Mr. Kudo kept talking: "She lives in red light."

She fought off the chill that seeped out of his mouth by confirming vigorously to herself that yes, that tracked—there were a lot of "she"s jumping out of the screen, and an approximately equal number of "red"s. Really, she was furiously treading water at the surface of the pool so she wouldn't have to look down beneath. "Okay," she said, "That's normal for this paracontagion."

"It feels like she comes closer every day. At first it was just . . . the traffic light turns red and I feel like someone is staring at me. Like the red light is a window and she's looking through it at me. It went very fast. And I thought, well, that's not so bad. I can get through this week. But then the lights at the office started turning red too. Only for me, only when I was alone. And she was . . . stronger, you know? This morning the light in my . . . my bathroom was red and I could feel her . . . standing on the other side of the door. And pushing against my ribs. Heavy."

What she could offer suddenly felt so small, so inconsequential, so insufficient for propping up this man's woe. But it was all she could do. "Here's a four-day prescription for a mind relaxant. It won't make the hallucinations go away but it tends to make the experience feel less severe. You can fill it at your regular pharmacy."

He stared, befuddled, at the piece of paper she'd handed to him. "But it's only two days left."

"Sometimes the . . . symptoms can last for a couple days after the attachment's been broken."

RED SKIES IN THE MORNING

She didn't know why she felt the need to add it—maybe the abyssal depth of the terror in Mr. Kudo's eyes?—but out it came, before she could hold it in: "It's not time to worry yet. I'll tell you when we get to that point."

After Mr. Kudo left, she saw another shape move into her doorway. Frank, spooning up the last of his breakfast yogurt. "You're still saying it."

"Saying what?"

"We. When *we* get to that point."

Selene wanted to protest that "we" was accurate—the government had put together a PSA campaign called We're In This Together when they launched the pathing program—but she knew that in the private spirit if not the public letter of government policy, Frank was correct. Privately, pathing agents received federal guidance that while they needed to exhaust every approved option for creating a pathway for each of their exposed cases before their seven days expired, they were not to attach themselves—emotionally, psychologically—to any single case. Privately, every paracontagion path began and ended alone.

"Okay. Here's a proper we. Do *we* think St. Eloi got any new volunteer paths since last week?"

"Define volunteer." The city council had given the St. Eloi halfway house a grant to funnel recovering addicts toward the T Street pathing office, but neither St. Eloi nor the volunteers were particularly eager about the arrangement, and often needed to be persuaded with additional perks. "Anyway, West isn't authorizing any emergency aid packages, so don't even ask."

"I have twenty bucks," she offered, and although money was of course still exchanged across various paracontagion paths, whether through official government compensation or under-the-table handshakes, something about sliding a vulnerable person an untraceable twenty-dollar bill to be sent to hell for seven days still made her feel vaguely sick.

NADIA BULKIN

Frank shook his head. "Don't. Call your regulars. Someone will come. Someone always does."

→→→»«←←←

Jim knocked on her door after he knew they were both off work. He had a new bottle of wine for them to try. It was the reason she'd never volunteer for the overnight shift at T Street, even if Hannah eventually moved out: she wanted to maintain the ability to drink in the dark.

She grabbed two glasses and they went to the roof. Jim would never be so presumptuous as to invite her into his apartment, and she had Hannah to worry about. Not that Hannah would have given a shit, and it was Selene's money that paid the rent anyway. But as her friends used to joke, she'd effectively graduated college and become a single mom. Did she resent those comments? Yes. Were they wrong? No. She wasn't about to bring a guy home when Hannah was doing homework in the living room. Hannah deserved to have the adolescence their mother would have given her.

Not that Jim was *a guy,* in that particular sense. He was a nice enough man who happened to be her neighbor, or rather a nice enough neighbor who happened to be a man. He was not *a guy.*

A brilliant wash of deepening magenta streaked across the sky that evening, and Jim whistled in appreciation.

"Red skies at night," Selene said, "sailors delight."

Jim cocked his eyebrow at her.

"Red skies in the morning," she continued, "sailors take warning."

"Well look at you, little miss farmer's almanac," said Jim, even though she had never lived outside of the city, and she was definitely not a little miss anymore.

"My mother taught me that one. Easiest way to tell whether you've got bad weather coming."

Her thoughts threatened to veer toward her mother—her own fault, really, for looking at the sky—but Jim

RED SKIES IN THE MORNING

mercifully redirected them toward a safer subject: the serial killer stalking the city. "Where do you think Video Man's getting all these paracontagions? I mean, there's no way he's just going around finding them in the wild with some kind of . . . dowsing rod."

"It's gotta be the black market, right?"

Jim gave her a hapless, melted-face look. She worked at the pathing office and he worked for an insurance company. Neither of them knew jack-shit about black markets.

"How many people has he killed by now, Video Man?"

"Let's see. There was the librarian lady." Jim stuck out his thumb. "The guy who exploded in Northern Market, who never reported anything."

"Marly D."

"Well, she's not dead yet."

Selene rolled her eyes. Despite what she'd told Hannah that morning, the police were clearly not going to find the video shell of the paracontagion that Marly had been exposed to. Life simply did not work out that way. "She's basically dead."

"What about the homeless person they found at Prospero Park a couple months ago? I mean, that was a paracontagion thing, right?" He was wincing as he said it; the man's head had been blown apart from within, at least if the local news was to be believed.

Selene shifted so she was facing the sky instead of Jim or the bottle or her empty glass. "I don't know if they ever linked that one to Video Man."

"All right, so sticking with confirmed known victims, that's three people. Are paracontagions really that cheap on the black market?" Selene burst out laughing, prompting Jim to egg her on: "Seriously! Wouldn't they be like a million dollars each?"

"No way. More like nine hundred ninety-nine. Before taxes."

"I don't think there are taxes on the black market."

"Shut up," she said, giving him a soft, playful shove, because she'd already finished one glass.

He made a big show of rolling over, and when he got himself right-side up noted, "I guess it depends on the cost of goods at the paracontagion factory, huh?"

She knew that he was—mostly—trying to be funny, and she smiled in acknowledgment of that attempt, but she'd never felt totally comfortable joking about paracontagions on anything but a purely practical level. Hannah loved speculating about the meaning and origin of paracontagions, even without the assistance of mood-altering substances. But Selene didn't like where those thoughts took her brain.

Jim, bless him, did not pick up on her drop in energy and decided to push further into the abyss. "You know my favorite theory? They're being sent—get this—from the future." Jim pantomimed his brains being blown out his ears. "Or a parallel dimension. I like that one too."

"What, like they're trying to stitch up a bad timeline, or something?"

Jim laughed. "I mean, I was thinking terrorists. But okay. That works too."

Selene did wonder why her head went straight to annihilation by decree. Too much Hannah, she figured. Too much Hannah-logic. She remembered Frank saying it had to be hard to bring home dates when she lived with her little sister, but really, her biggest problem was the toll Hannah-logic took on her mental health. Literally, on her ability to live: to make coffee, go to work, tend to people's pending catastrophes, come home, zone out, sleep.

The red sky had gone down by the time Jim asked, "Do you ever think about having children?"

That was a change of subject. "Huh?"

"I just mean . . . can you imagine how terrifying it would be to be a parent these days? My brother has one and he's got a tracker on her but he still follows her everywhere, scopes out every place she goes before she gets

RED SKIES IN THE MORNING

there. I guess he figures if there's a paracontagion there, it'll get him first? It's crazy. He's crazy. She's going to get fed up with it. I think he regrets it, honestly."

Thankfully, Selene had not felt pressure to partake in such precautions; Hannah had been eighteen when paracontagions were discovered. "Being so paranoid?" she suggested.

"Having his daughter," Jim mumbled, lifting the glass to his lips. "She was born a few years before they found the first batch. He couldn't be happier at first, and now . . . "

Selene heard his voice fading, and she chose to let that topic fall. To answer Jim's original question, she did not think about having children. She did not in fact plan much further ahead than the next week, the next month. Hannah always told her not to let her hold her back from the world. She'd say things like, "if you want to hike across the Appalachians" or "if you want to go back to school" or "if you want a night out to yourself," but Selene didn't want any of those things. She didn't know what she wanted, other than for Hannah to be okay.

>>><<<

Hannah wasn't home by the time Selene said goodbye to Jim after they descended the stairwell at nine. It was a bit curious—Hannah's shift was supposed to end at eight, and she hadn't said anything about meeting friends after. Wobbling just a little bit, Selene popped a tiny frozen lasagna in the microwave and took advantage of Hannah's absence by turning the television to something Hannah would never choose herself: a game show based entirely on chance.

When she still wasn't home by ten, Selene contemplated calling, but decided on a text upon reminding herself that Hannah was twenty-three: *you headed home soon?* Something neutral. Not pushy. There was no response, but an hour later the message was "read," so she let it go and went to bed.

She could only hope that Hannah hadn't gotten waylaid trying to save—or God forbid adopt—a kitten, or an OD. Hopefully she was out there having fun, being impulsive, making questionable choices, maybe breaking a little rule or two.

2. Day One

Her head was still ringing when her second alarm went off.

She had overslept, she realized, because the apartment was quiet. Ordinarily Hannah would be clattering dishes in the kitchen with the 7 a.m. news blaring—Hannah had to be the only twenty-three-year-old who enjoyed local news—no matter how late she'd gotten in the night before. There was a franticness to Hannah's attempts to carpe diem by getting the best possible start to the day, a certain manic desperation; Selene thought she was setting herself up for inevitable disappointment, but maybe she was just annoyed by the barrage of early noise when Hannah didn't even have a nine-to-five.

And today, it was quiet.

"Hannah?" She knocked on Hannah's door, pressed her ear up next to the particle board that passed for wood. "You home?" She bit her lip, looking around the empty kitchen, hearing their mother's voice humming *you have to watch Hannah,* and then added, "I'm coming in, okay?"

Hannah wasn't home. Her oversized coat wasn't on its hook. Her phone wasn't charging on her nightstand. Selene checked her own phone again just in case she'd missed a message from Hannah the first time she looked, but there was nothing.

The rational part of Selene's brain wanted to fire off excuses immediately: Hannah was an adult with her own life and her own friends and if she decided she was better off staying with them for the night than taking a gamble on a safe post-midnight train ride, then good for her, actually.

RED SKIES IN THE MORNING

But the lizard part of her brain that ran on instinctual fear drilled deeper, sending a message that roared louder than all others: *this isn't like Hannah*.

⫷⫸

The cop in charge of logging missing persons reports did not appear overly disturbed by Hannah's disappearance. He was listening, sort of, or at least nodding at all the right moments. But when Selene stopped talking and looked at him in slack-jawed expectation, he clamped his lips together and said, "Well, best I can tell you is to be patient for now. And keep calling. Keep checking the hospitals, too. Sometimes people need to sober up before they realize they're fuckin' bleeding out and can't stitch up their own ass."

He must have seen her face twist in indignation because he added, "She's at that age. The shit we see kids doing nowadays . . . lady, you really don't wanna know. Frankly, being gone overnight is nothing. If we ran after every twenty-three-year-old who disappeared every once in a while . . . " He turned his hands upward. As if calling on God.

"No, this isn't . . . " Selene pressed her hands to her eyes, "I could give less of a fuck if she's partying or using or having an orgy." If only that was her problem. It would be so much easier if Hannah was the kind of bad girl that pop songs were written about. "I'm worried about the possibility that she doesn't *want* to be missing. There is a . . . " She paused, scared to speak it out loud in the police station, so she lowered her chin and her voice: "There is a *serial killer* running around this city with black market paracontagions. You follow me?"

The cop stared at her with the same sort of fatigue that she herself probably projected when Hannah talked about the possibility that the real incidence rate of paracontagions was rising faster than the pathing system could keep up with. Slow-burning apocalypse, Hannah called it. One time Selene had actually exploded at her: *what do you want me to do about it?* The answer, of course, was nothing. "I'm just stating reality," Hannah had said, matter-of-factly.

"I'm not going to confirm or deny or even acknowledge the existence of a *serial killer,*" the cop said, though she noticed that he hissed those words as well. "Look, let me ask you this. Was anything missing from the house this morning, other than your sister?"

"Just the stuff she went to work with last night. Her coat, her wallet, her phone . . . "

"Not a toothbrush? Extra change of clothes? Jewelry? Maybe *your* jewelry?"

"Like I said. Just the stuff she went to work with." Though in truth, her "check" had been little more than a half-blind rampage. "Will you please at least file the report?"

"I'm doing it right now," he said, and obediently pulled out his keyboard. He started taking down the details they'd need to identify a stranger, or a corpse: height, weight, age, hair color, eye color, full name. Piercings? Tattoos? Birth marks? Had she been exposed to a paracontagion recently? "Any other siblings? Any other family?"

And Selene just kept shaking her head. She found herself wanting to ramble, to explain—their parents were loners from cold, bedraggled clans, and the sort of events that should have brought relatives out of the woodwork with money or love, like their father dying when Hannah was four and their mother dying when Hannah was eleven, had prompted nothing but silence. She stopped herself. She too was a loner. She too was cold, bedraggled. Hannah alone had glowed, ever since she was little, with hope and possibility.

"Do you have kids?" she asked, remembering the conversation with Jim.

"In this world?" The cop scoffed. "Hell no."

⇶⇶⇶⇶⇶

RED SKIES IN THE MORNING

The one concrete thing the cop told her to do was the same thing he might say to someone who'd lost an earring, or a pet: retrace its last known steps in the hope of finding it lying loose on the ground. She took the train downtown, getting off at each station along the way to scour the benches lined with sleeping people, and upon getting out at Pool Street, methodically crossed water-logged streets to reach the store where Hannah worked.

Hannah's sleepy-eyed coworkers made long drawling "oh" sounds when Selene explained who she was and why she was there. It was unclear whether they had actually realized that Hannah hadn't shown up for her shift that day, but they promised they would let the manager know. They affirmed that she left at the same time as everyone else, although no one had seen what direction she'd left in for certain. There were always suspicious characters hawking their wares and ideologies on Pool Street, but no one out of the ordinary, they said. One coworker said that Hannah had been quiet yesterday, but another added that Hannah never talked much anyway.

After turning to leave, Selene was struck by the store display she'd had her back to. She was used to the paracontagion sweatshirts—closer to the entrance, teens with iced coffees sorted through hoodies that read *always on day six* and *when I die young* and *it gets worse*. She wasn't used to the zombies. Well, not zombies. *Zombie-hunting*. A zombie in the crosshairs of a rifle; a zombie chewing through a red and white no sign. Selene thought back to her conversation with Hannah on Monday morning and hoped this was just an aesthetic and not a show of support for a serial killer, but what passed for humor had become quite strange in recent years.

"The zombie thing," Selene asked the one coworker who was still standing there, absently folding jeans. "What is that about?"

The coworker grinned, revealing a little ball of white gum between her teeth. "People are tired of all the brainless leeches taking up space in the world, I guess."

NADIA BULKIN

>>>><<<<

Selene didn't know where to go from there. So she got back on the train and went to work.

West told her to go home, of course, but she begged to stay; she didn't know what else to do, and hopefully putting out fires would keep her busy while she waited for something to change. Ironically, Monday's crises had largely abated. Her new ID card was ready and waiting on her desk, an overnight delivery from federal headquarters. A good Samaritan had come in and relieved Ryosuke Kudo of his paracontagion. Only two cases had been added to her caseload.

Which left her making clumsy calls for next week's cases, pretending to worried coworkers that she was much more certain than she really was that Hannah would turn up soon, and doing a thing she hated: waiting. *Hate to wait,* Selene used to say as a little girl, demanding immediate progression to whatever was next, even if it was tonsil surgery. *I absolutely hate to wait!*

She flipped her phone onto its face, flipped it back over, set it to ring, set it to silent, took it to the bathroom, stared at it until her eyes watered in the hopes that the force of her desire would be enough to overpower this slide toward a story as old and sad as a muddy grave:

Young Woman, Missing.

Which was still better than Young Woman, Dead.

Near the end of her shift, she tried to delay going home by checking the news for an update on Marly D. What popped up were stories about a would-be copycat killer who'd been arrested the night before—some dead-eyed dude who decided to take a page out of Video Man's playbook and tried to force a black market paracontagion on an ex-girlfriend, but got shot in the leg by her new boyfriend in the process. Talk about same shit, different day.

RED SKIES IN THE MORNING

"Any word?" West asked on his way out the door, and so brought her crashing back to Hannah, who she had no word from. No word from Hannah. No word from the cops. No word from a kidnapper, if she had in fact been kidnapped. Although she wasn't really expecting to hear from a kidnapper. Video Man wasn't abducting people—he was blitzing them. Stunning them for a momentary attack and then letting them go. If he had attacked Hannah then she was probably just wandering around out there. Confused. In shock. Psychically shackled to a monster.

"No," she answered her boss.

She thought she saw Hannah no less than five times on her commute home that day. Four of those times she strained to get a better view before ruling out the stranger; once she was flooded with such adrenaline that she grabbed a girl with a coat that looked like Hannah, whipping her around and then apologizing when a face that was not-Hannah—so not-Hannah that Selene actually found herself repulsed, even though the girl met every objective standard of beauty—turned around in rightful indignation.

Feeling sheepish as the train pulled into the next station, Selene sat down next to a lump of a man who rolled away from her, probably having witnessed her assault an innocent bystander.

She had to be sensible, she reminded herself. She had to be rational. Careening around like a cannonball would only make her sloppy. Think. Think. Think. What would Hannah do if she'd been pushed out of a moving car in the early hours of the morning on the outskirts of the city, freshly infected? It crushed Selene to think that calling her wouldn't be number one on Hannah's to-do list, but God only knew what strange decisions Hannah-logic might compel.

To hell with Hannah-logic. What the hell could anyone do?

Would Hannah try to save herself? It wasn't technically

possible without access to the paracontagion shell, and if they didn't have Video-Man then they wouldn't have his videotapes—but there were grifters out there. Liars. Frauds.

Hannah knows better.
Hannah might be desperate.

The train rocked to a stop and Selene opened up the social media app that she used to lull herself to sleep when intrusive thoughts kept her awake.

#paracontagion, she typed, and then #pc. The top results were just attempts at comedy—people pretending to gouge out their eyes before going on vacation, lest they see a paracontagion at their destination—so she added #natural, which unlocked a marketplace of teas and crystals and super wellness shakes. One woman was even calmly selling colloidal silver tinctures called Angel Wings from what looked like a ski resort.

And then she saw Hannah's username in the comments under Angel Wings lady's post. It was right next to Hannah's profile picture, a moody shot on the pier, and the sudden appearance of her sister's digital ghost promptly punched Selene in the throat. She looked like any other aimless twenty-three-year-old. Lost. Searching. Vulnerable to the manipulations of the conniving. *I need to recheck Hannah's bank account,* she thought, before the content of Hannah's comment finally registered: *stop taking advantage of scared ppl you ghoul.*

A warmth spread across her face, a soft heat that she now recognized as pride. "Good girl," she whispered, and brought the phone to her face as if to reel Hannah in for a hug—only to press its plastic corner into the skin between her eyes, hard enough to overtake the bundle of pain gathering there.

Because she knew what Hannah would actually do if Video Man forced a paracontagion on her:

Nothing.

She would do nothing. She would accept the fate that

RED SKIES IN THE MORNING

had been given to her with as much grace as she could muster, call it just another cruel twist of fate like the ones that had killed their parents, and wait seven days for the incubating monster to take her.

>>>><<<<

When she got home, she checked the dry-erase board on the fridge. Still empty. Blank. This morning she'd erased it of her last message, a reminder about last week's hazardous material drop-off event—she'd actually cursed herself for not erasing the board earlier, irrationally anxious that Hannah had intended to leave a message but hadn't had the space—and left it like that with the marker centered neatly above the board, as if to create a psychic invitation.

She hadn't done anything so superstitious since she was very young. It was Hannah-logic again, which was to say: looking-glass-logic. Dream-logic. Logic that rested in extremity instead of in averages, logic that rested on the ability of pure human intent to push space and time and molecules into positions that shouldn't be possible. Rationally, she knew that it would have been highly unlikely for Hannah to have snuck home and snuck back out leaving nothing but a message on a dry-erase board, but the tendrils of hope were so hard to resist.

Which was why she had to resist them.

Of course it was nicer to imagine Hannah creeping in and out of the apartment as part of some elaborate personal adventure—or holing up in some secret love nest, improbable as that sounded—than to imagine Hannah infected by one of Video Man's paracontagions and waiting to die somewhere. Of course she would prefer to leave the board open for Hannah, open for *whatever,* rather than to plug it up with something so gruesome as a countdown to Hannah's possible death. Of course doing so filled her with a creeping nausea, a nervousness that by preparing for this possibility, she was unwittingly summoning a reality she didn't want.

But the PMA taught pathing agents that urgency was the only way to proactivity; that preparing for worst-case scenarios was the best way to stop them coming true. Funny, Selene thought as she pried the dry-erase marker off its clip: there was a bit of Hannah-logic lurking there.

She wrote the numbers 1 through 7 on the board, two digits in three rows, with a big wobbly 7 at the very bottom. Then she forced out a big breath of stale air and crossed out the 1. If Hannah had been exposed to a paracontagion last night—if she'd been taken off the sidewalk as she was walking to or from the train, dear God, the image conjured in her brain felt so sickeningly real—then she had six days left, starting tomorrow. No, worst-case scenario. Starting tonight.

And then she opened up the social media app that Hannah was always on and made her first post in two years. The last she'd made was a shaky video of a whale that she and Hannah had seen at a great distance from the end of the pier.

This one would be very different.

"My name is Selene Denton," she said to her shaking face, "I live in Ponte City with my sister, Hannah Denton. Hannah didn't come home last night. I'm afraid that something bad might have happened to her."

3. Day Two

Selene woke on the second day of Hannah's disappearance from a dream of screaming at Hannah to get out of the path of a tropical tidal wave to the heart-quickening realization that surely Hannah wouldn't just die without saying goodbye. Hannah would neither crawl under a bridge nor make her way to a desert island to spend her final week. She was sentimental. All heart. Which meant Selene had a chance, maybe, to catch her.

Catch her and do what? Break her fall, how?

RED SKIES IN THE MORNING

"Nope," Selene muttered as she got dressed. "Nope, nope, nope."

Maybe they'd catch Video Man in the next few days. Maybe she'd fly Hannah to federal PMA headquarters and demand that they try their wildest, most cutting-edge experimental cures on her. Maybe the Earth would tilt on its axis and paracontagions would magically neutralize before Hannah's seven days were up. All she could focus on was finding Hannah.

Just find Hannah.

Hannah clearly hadn't come home to say goodbye—hadn't come home *yet,* she underscored in her head—so Selene looked elsewhere. There was only one friend that Hannah had mentioned with any frequency, although to be honest it had been a while: her best friend dating back to junior high school, Bex. Selene couldn't find her on social media and the prehistoric phone number that had once been Bex's contact info was no longer connected. She could only hope that the girl's mother hadn't moved.

Selene remembered Bex's mother not liking her much, and that did not appear to have changed. "No," Ruth said flatly when Selene asked if she could talk to Bex. "She is not available to you."

"You mean she isn't home?" There wasn't really any point in asking. Even without Ruth's exaggerated sigh, worthy of a daytime soap, she knew the answer. "Or *I* can't see her?"

"The latter." When they first met, Ruth had been very warm, a welcome change from the other parents at Hannah's school. Sympathetic, full of practical advice and bottles of solid budget wine. She seemed to have assumed—wrongly—that Selene was some kind of saint for stepping in as Hannah's legal guardian. But at some point that reality had been shattered—probably by something Selene had thoughtlessly done, though she couldn't remember what—and Ruth had become confused, and then deeply suspicious, of Selene's competence. "You can go. Please."

"Okay . . . " Selene almost turned to leave, before spinning on her heels and trying again, "Hannah—my sister—is missing. She hasn't stopped by, or anything, has she? Or, or, tried to contact Bex at all? Look, I don't have to talk to Bex directly, but if you could just ask her . . . and if Hannah does stop by, if you could let me know . . . here, this is my number, in case you need it."

Ruth had remained utterly stoic during that entire splash of word vomit. It saddened Selene that this woman whose townhouse Hannah had stayed in for many a junior high sleepover—who Selene had absolutely trusted to take care of Hannah in case something went wrong during said sleepovers to make better decisions than Selene herself could make—did not seem at all bothered by Hannah's disappearance, but at least Ruth took her business card. She could have sworn that she saw the woman's jaw clench when her eyes glossed over the embossed acronym on the bottom left and registered that Selene was still with the Paracontagion Mitigation Agency.

"She hasn't been here," Ruth said, and closed—then locked—the door.

>>>><<<<

On her way back to the train station she got a reply to her post about Hannah from a boy named Aidan who looked from his glum expression to be of Hannah's generation.

hey, it said, *might be able to help.*

He offered to meet her *wherever* and when she suggested the pier, gave her a thumbs-up and nothing else. So she went to the pier, because it was probably Hannah's favorite place in the world, and dutifully scanned benches and beach chairs for her sister's crumpled shape while she waited for this Aidan to manifest.

She had just given the arcade five copies of the missing person flyers Jim had helped her draw up when she noticed a young man bundled up in sweats and a beanie taking a meandering path toward her, as if he was ruling

RED SKIES IN THE MORNING

out other people who might answer to "Selene" along the way. "Aidan!" she shouted, because she had no time for this, and no time to be embarrassed if she was wrong. She wasn't. He tilted his head back in a half-nod.

"I know you said to tell you if we'd seen Hannah since Monday," Aidan said, "so I thought I'd let you know that I did see her super early Tuesday morning. Like four a.m. or so?"

Her heart bucked against her ribs like a pony. "Wait, what? Where?"

"Online. She liked one of my posts. I sent her a message asking why she was up so late, cuz that's pretty odd for Hannah, but she never replied. Haven't seen her since. Online or in person."

Selene nodded through the slight deflation of hope. That at least implied that Hannah had her phone and wasn't using it to ask for help hours after Selene had lost sight of her.

"You're the paperclip lady, aren't you? Why are you moonlighting as a cop? I mean . . . " he wiped his nose impishly. "I know some people who would say you PMA types basically *are* cops."

The thought that she might be the only one actually trying to find Hannah—that the cop she talked to this morning would just put her on some internal bulletin board and go back to the stuff they actually cared about, like gambling, or catching a serial killer—plugged her ears with pressure. She tried to fight through the feeling, grinding her teeth as needed.

"The cops aren't gonna look into it until—unless—they find a body and who knows, maybe not even then, so yeah. I'm filling in, in the meantime."

Aidan quickly nodded, his head tucked as if he hadn't been expecting her to push the conversation off a cliff so quickly.

"Sorry. Um. Thank you for meeting me. So you and Hannah were friends?"

"Yeah. Yeah, you could say that."

"Were you two like . . . " She didn't know what words kids were using these days, "involved?"

Aidan smiled, with no impishness this time. "Nah. I knew her through Bex. We all went to college together. Hannah and I weren't close back then, but since everything happened with Bex . . . I guess we started talking more. Commiserating, you know."

Ruth's bitter face, rigid with a frozen hostility, shot to the front row of Selene's mind's eye. "What happened with Bex? I tried talking to her, but her mother wouldn't let me see her and I guess she changed her number . . . "

"Oh. That bitch is wild. She probably blames you." Aidan looked to the sea as a hundred implausible possibilities for what she could have done to damage Bex sprouted in Selene's mind, only for her defenses to immediately swat them down. *She* wasn't Bex's friend. *She* hadn't even seen the girl in months. Maybe Hannah had done something stupid, but unlike Ruth, Selene wasn't about to assume responsibility or control over decisions made by other adults. "Anyway, Bex doesn't have her phone. She's at Bellevue, you know. Guess her mom didn't tell you that?"

"The psych ward?"

"That's the one."

"Why?"

For a moment Aidan just stared at her, a crooked half-grin on his face as if Selene should have known. He stuffed his hands in his pockets and explained, "She lost it after that PC. You know. The one she did with you."

Her superiors would have balked at such language. Pathing agents did not *do* the paracontagion with their cases. Responsibility was not *shared* in that manner. But Selene had to admit that she had felt the slightest bite of responsibility when Hannah and Bex had come into the office two years ago so Bex could relieve a classmate who needed a path: how nervous they'd looked, how young. Bex

RED SKIES IN THE MORNING

was the minimum age to serve as a path—Hannah a few months younger—and she kept stumbling over questions on the government form that an adult would have known to ignore. So Selene had sat with them, of course, provided reassurance and light jokes and various other types of psychological hand-holding that she could sense Bex needed, that Hannah herself couldn't give. She checked on the availability of a path everyday—without interfering with the algorithm, of course—and checked on Bex throughout her seven days, too, not just via automated messages but personal texts too, as well as a phone call immediately after her path was completed, just to make sure everything had disconnected. She'd gone above and beyond.

"But it went fine."

Aidan shrugged. "Tell Bex."

"She never reported anything."

"She's not a whiner. I think her mom wrote a letter to the feds, but I don't know. I know the government doesn't exactly love it when people tell 'em about all the stuff that goes wrong in pathing." And then, to Selene's annoyance, he started listing off complaints like he'd gotten them straight off an internet conspiracy theory forum: "Post-path hallucinations. Post-path sleep disturbance. Post-path sympathetic psychosis, post-path foreign body illness ... "

"Oh, come on. That stuff happens like ... one percent of the time. Less."

Aidan laughed, with a great bitterness. "Like I said. That's why her mom blames you. You weren't straight up about the danger. Didn't think to mention that maybe passing around toxic videos and pictures isn't an activity that anyone would call safe."

She could have told him that Bex had been given—and signed off on—all the same fine print disclosures as everybody else who came through a pathing office, but she knew it would have only pissed him off more. "Well. I thought she was really brave to do that for a classmate."

NADIA BULKIN

"Yeah. And now she gets to spend the rest of her life being tortured when the dumbass she did it for gets to walk away scot-free."

The serration in Aidan's voice made Selene wonder if he had been the dumbass in question.

※※※

The first thing she did after Aidan ambled off—not into the sunset but into the seaspray—was call Bellevue. "I'm calling about a patient named . . . " she checked herself. They wouldn't give out patient information. "I'm calling about your recent visitors. I'm wondering if you could tell me if a Hannah Denton has visited the facility recently?" The woman who answered the front desk phone said she'd have to call her back after checking, which Selene knew was more likely to mean checking with a supervisor than checking the visitor log.

The second thing she did was finish carpeting every business on the pier with Hannah's missing person flyers. She still had a decent stack left afterward, so she thought she might as well hit the nearby businesses as well. And then she just found herself walking. She was searching, yes, opening strip mall dumpsters and checking passed-out faces, but a part of her also felt like she could rule out places where Hannah might be simply by walking each city block. Like she was in a video game. Like Hannah would just begin to glow when Selene set foot on the street where she was hiding, so Selene ought to cover as much ground as possible.

It was Hannah-logic. Un-logic.

And yet she kept at it until she saw something that stopped her: a crowd of people gathered, seemingly quite solemnly, on the sidewalk in front of an apartment building numbered 600. An older couple she recognized from somewhere—where?—were standing elevated on the stoop, mumbling into a microphone, next to a giant picture of . . . oh.

RED SKIES IN THE MORNING

That was where she recognized them from. Marly D.'s press conference. They were Marly D.'s parents. Which meant this had to be Marly D.'s apartment building. Her apartment—the scene of her murder, although she hadn't yet died—was probably the one whose cast iron balcony was all decked out with lights and flowers, where the fire escape was marked off with crime scene tape.

And like any other event in the city, a few vendor tables had popped up along the perimeter—one selling utterly useless anti-paracontagion safety gear, one offering candy from a local church, and one with an enormous sign and matching pins and bumper stickers that read *When Do We Say Enough?* Selene thought she recognized the spindly man behind that last table, but she pretended to busy herself on her phone when his head turned her way.

From a distance, Selene watched a murmur and a wobble move through the densest part of the crowd, Marly D.'s parents frowning at a man who seemed to be pushing his way to the front. "Paracontagion!" one person yelled, echoed by another, echoed by screams of anguish—fear mixed with anger—as the vigil was moved by less of a wobble and more of a seizure. Some fell to the ground in fetal position. Some ran, tripping over the fallen. Some simply pressed their eyes into anything that could act as a shield: their arms, their bags, a bystander's sleeve. On the apartment stoop, Marly D.'s parents took each other's hands but were otherwise still. Stoic.

Selene instinctively grabbed her phone through her coat pocket. She would have felt it against her hip but her hand confirmed: it wasn't buzzing. The radar that she had been required to download on her first day of orientation with the PMA hadn't gone off. Which meant that whatever that man was carrying, it wasn't a paracontagion.

"He doesn't have one," she said—first to the woman standing fondling her cross next to her, and then to a six-foot radius—"he doesn't have anything!"

A few faces turned toward her, but not enough. By then

some brave souls had taken it upon themselves to contain the threat and restrain the man, swarming him in a frenzy of punches and kicks until he was face down on the sidewalk beneath several sets of hands and knees. With order restored, the crowd recongealed with remarkable speed, less curious now about what Marly D.'s parents had to say about their dying child than they were eager to get a look at the bloodied face of the terrorist interloper. It was hard for them, probably, to imagine anything worse.

"I'm a pathing agent," Selene said, having elbowed her way to the front. The good Samaritans holding down the so-called terrorist looked up suspiciously at first, and for a moment even seemed to be pressing down harder on the spine of their quarry—so she showed them her ID, and then the detection app on her phone. "There's no paracontagion."

She heard whispers of *paperclip,* of *government,* of *nothing*—and then they turned him over.

When they did so, they saw crushed beneath his body the thing they'd mistaken for a paracontagion shell: a canvas painting of Marly D. in soft swaths of bubblegum pink and marigold yellow. He must have used the photo in her missing poster as a reference. He must have painted it for her parents.

He must have really cared.

⇛⇚

"Excuse me, miss?" The man who wanted to know *When Do We Say Enough?* had popped out from behind his table and was hurrying toward her. He was trying to force a smile, but Selene could see that he was struggling to make it reach his eyes. "I couldn't help but overhear that you work for the city pathing office. My name's Hugh Bolduan. I'm part of a neighborhood group—I guess you could call us a group of concerned citizens. It's called the Bluejay Society."

So that was why she recognized him. She winced in

RED SKIES IN THE MORNING

spite of herself, trying to slide away without speaking, but Hugh Bolduan followed her, still carrying on: "I get the sense that you're familiar with our work—" work was one way to put it—"but I want to assure you that we completely support the government pathing program! We have no interest in interfering with it! We just think there should be other options!"

That suspiciously innocuous phrase made her stop. Other options like what? Hijacking the projectionist room in a crowded movie theater and triggering a mass exposure event like Adam Ramiel? Holding somebody undesirable hostage and exposing them to a paracontagion, like Video Man? Dropping paracontagions from drones onto the soil of foreign adversaries, like some politicians glibly suggested? She turned to face him. "What kind of *other options?*" she asked.

Calling to her while speed-walking had left him panting, just a little. "We understand," he went on, "that the government did the best they could when they established the program. But we have ideas for additional solutions that we would love to discuss with someone of your experience, your expertise. We're really committed to making sure our solutions are practical. Workable. I'd be honored if you came to our meeting on Saturday evening. Assuming you're free, of course." He was practically pushing a bumper sticker into her hand, even though she didn't even know anybody who owned a car. "We meet at the Beacon Hill Rec Center."

"Yeah, you know, I don't know. I've got a lot going on right now."

"Sure, sure. But if you do find yourself free, we'd love to have you stop by."

"Okay, well, uh . . . " Almost as if it knew she needed an exit, her phone started buzzing with an incoming call: Bellevue Psychiatric was calling back. "Sorry, I have to take this."

She could still hear him shouting about Saturday when

the woman on the other end—the same woman who'd answered the phone earlier—started talking. She jammed her phone against one cheek while jamming her palm against the other and asked the woman to please repeat herself.

"You were asking about Hannah Denton, right? So yes, she's in the visitor log. She was last here yesterday. Looks like she checked in two thirteen p.m., checked out three twenty-one."

Without warning, tears forced their way out of whatever steel reservoir Selene had caged them in for the past two days. She had to cover her mouth to keep the gasp from startling the woman from the hospital as the relief of knowing that Hannah was alive was immediately crippled by what felt so awfully like the confirmation of her worst-case-scenario theory of the case.

"Ma'am? Is there anything else I can help you with?"

Selene pinched the tears away. "Can you just confirm your visiting hours, please?"

4. Day Three

Bellevue Psychiatric was nestled ten miles outside the city limits, in a bedroom community whose higher-than-average income bracket was reflected in the waiting room's freshly-vacuumed carpet and well-maintained fish tank. The gossip magazines were current. The candy in the check-in desk bowl was wrapped. *Don't worry,* the HVAC whispered. *It'll be okay.*

But behind the doors marked Access Restricted ID Check Required, Bellevue was any other city hospital: drenched in industrial-grade antiseptic and cold light, fitted with wall-to-wall stain-resistant linoleum, packed with patients in various levels of distress and disorientation and staff that seemed not to have slept in weeks. The hallways still teemed with the desperation and agitation of lost time.

RED SKIES IN THE MORNING

And Bex, when she shuffled into the minimalist common area in lavender sweats and laceless shoes, still looked like a pale cross-section of her true self.

Then again, what did Selene know about Bex's *true self*? She hadn't talked to the girl in years. Not since she and Hannah were in college. Not since Bex's procedure, she realized.

"How are you?" she asked cautiously.

"Oh, I'm great," Bex replied, her voice barely managing the sarcastic lilt she was aiming for. "Unbelievable. Couldn't be better. How are you, Lee?"

When the girls were in junior high, Hannah used to call her Lee. Lee-Lee. It was what Hannah used to call her as a toddler; the school's grief counselor suggested it was a trauma response of some kind. *She's looking for you to be her mother*—the grief counselor said that, too.

"I'm okay. I hear Hannah came to see you yesterday," Selene said, trying to gauge in real-time how much information to provide. "Can you tell me what you guys talked about?"

Bex's answer was unhelpful. "Old times. The stupid things we used to say. People we hated. You know. Reminiscing. She told me to get well soon." At this line, Bex smirked—whether at herself or Hannah or the very concept of wellness, Selene didn't know.

She took a gamble. "What's that face for? Do you think you're getting better?"

"I was trying to get well before my mom put me in this place." Bex glanced dismissively at her surroundings. "They don't actually care about *wellness* here."

Maybe Bex had been on drugs. Ruth did not seem like the kind of woman who would be tolerant of such things. "How did Hannah seem to you? Normal? Or did she look like . . . " she struggled to find the words as Bex's mouth slipped into a shape that looked too nasty to be a smile. "Did she say anything about having been exposed?"

Bex was at a full sneer now. "How should I know? I

don't have ghost-dar. My link was *severed.*" She said this last word with such misplaced toxin, like she couldn't muster up an ounce of gratitude for the fact that the generosity of another volunteer had saved her from one of the most gruesome fates known to man, that Selene momentarily forgot what she was there for.

"Yes," she snapped, dimly aware that she was about to jam in a mental needle but unable to summon the discipline to stop herself. "You successfully passed it on to someone else. Your procedure worked. You were spared an extremely painful death."

As expected, Bex's lips peeled back like an angry dog's, and Selene immediately regretted not shutting the fuck up. "Painful?" she spat. "There are worse pains, Agent Denton, than death."

"Like what?"

"Like loss."

Selene looked out the window at the parking lot. The idea that loss was worse than death was one that she had never allowed herself to entertain—how could she justify her continued existence, if she was enduring something worse than death?—but Bex didn't know what she was saying. Her parents were divorced, sure, but they were both fucking alive.

"Or cruelty. Or selfishness. I looked him up, you know. The one that I was *exposed* to."

Selene kept her eyes glued to the window, but now started picking her chapped lip as well. Every so often she got this question from clients: *am I looking at a crime?* She always said no—there was no evidence of paracontagions being connected to real-world events—although she'd heard the urban legends about so-called famous paracontagions floating around: *1 Lunatic 1 Icepick, 3 Guys 1 Hammer*. There was certainly nothing like that in Ponte City's vault, thank God.

"He joined a church that he thought would bring him and his family prosperity. But instead the pastor just wanted their money. Eventually convinced them to sit in a church service while he burned the building down. He showed me the fire. I felt the heat." Bex was gazing at the ceiling like a parishioner waiting to receive communion, the tension rolling out of her face and leaving her nearly slack-jawed. "He taught me so much. Showed me how cruel people could be."

"You didn't know that already?" That was glib. She apologized, though Bex seemed so lost in the memories of her haunting that she barely reacted. "Sorry. I've just never heard someone describe pathing as . . . educational."

"We bond with them. They teach us empathy." All the softness in Bex's face faded as she shifted her gaze from the empty space on the ceiling back to Selene. "And then we're ripped away from them and told to just move on and forget about them. It's literally traumatic. The only people that aren't affected by separation are sociopaths. That's what Rock the Horizon says."

Selene tried to leave aside the implication that seventy percent of her clients—the percentage that claimed zero side effects after their pathing procedures—were sociopaths. "Rock the what?"

"The Horizon. That white space between life and death. The door that we've shut. Just like we've sealed away everything else that makes us uncomfortable."

For the first time that day, she saw Hannah in Bex. She remembered them giggling together over the matching hedgehog necklaces they found in a dime store at the mall. She inched her hand across the table toward Bex—or at least, the Bex that she had known. "Look, it sounds like your paracontagion hallucinations were . . . incredibly intense, and I can only imagine how that's affected your view of the world since then, but . . . "

Bex did not return the overture; only ice from that side of the table. "They aren't hallucinations."

"Sorry," Selene said again, and she was saying it to Hannah, too, for fucking up this conversation so royally. "I know the phenomena you experienced were real." Although she didn't know, not *really*—she'd seen tortured looks, she'd heard hisses of pain and surprise, she'd even seen physical disturbance—but without a paracontagion crawling through her blood it was impossible to *know*. "Hallucination is just the word that most people tend to be more comfortable with . . . "

Bex started coughing, then choking, then retching, a pale tongue jutting from her mouth. With a violent undulation of the spine she jerked her head back and then hacked up something solid, yet soft. Some sort of gelatinous mass? Selene was about to fly out of her seat and call for a nurse when Bex poked her finger into the mess she'd spat onto the table and prodded it. It was hair. A wad of coarse black hair that did not at all match Bex's fine mousy tresses.

"How's that for a hallucination," Bex snarled, with such vigor that a spattering of saliva flew through the recycled air and dotted Selene's face. "Did I hallucinate that? It's him! Touch him!"

Selene kept her hands firmly tucked between her thighs. "Shit, Bex. I had no idea. If I had known your paracontagion detachment was incomplete . . . "

"Again with these fucking words that don't mean anything! He's a ghost, you dense bitch, they're all ghosts!" Bex pushed her chair back, hyperventilating but looking satisfied, as the forbidden word—*ghost*—floated above them, gauzy and eternal. Before Bex walked away, she added, "And we're meant to be with them. Hannah knew that. Why don't you ask her."

>>>><<<<

Before she left Bellevue, she asked a nurse typing on a crash cart in a hallway about Bex's hair-spitting. "Oh yeah, she does that sometimes," the nurse said. "Her little hairballs. We used to think she was faking, like, stealing other patients' hair or something. But we isolated her once to see if it still happened and yup. It's genuine phenomena."

Damn. She wondered why Hannah hadn't said anything about Bex's condition. She was a pathing agent; of all the world's problems that she knew kept Hannah up at night, this was one she could have actually helped with. "You should get in touch with federal PMA, they have resources to help people with incomplete paracontagion detachments."

The nurse shrugged; she still hadn't looked Selene in the eye. "I offered to hook her up with my priest. She doesn't want any of that. She likes it, I think. Gets some kind of kick out of it. Don't ask me, because I can't pretend to understand. Anything else I can help you with?"

There wasn't. Selene showed herself out, back into the deceitfully comforting waiting room and then into the cold. There were all sorts of vehicles passing on the big road beyond the parking lot, carrying people and goods and plans, and all she could think of was the sheer volume of life continuing without Hannah, the grotesque insignificance of her and Hannah's existence.

She saw the news while waiting at the bus stop for the 33 that would take her back to the train station that would take her back to the city. Marly D. had died, precisely seven days to the second after she was exposed—no, after Video Man exposed her—to an unclassified paracontagion that would now be bound to her name. What was it again, a children's dance recital? Had little ballet slippers kicked through her ribs, or had it been whoever was holding the videocamera? The article didn't give the gory details. Just that she'd *succumbed to her condition.*

Succumbed to her condition, the way they all someday would.

>>>>>><<<<<<

After she first realized that Hannah was missing, but before she went to the police department, Selene had torn apart Hannah's room in a haphazard panic, flinging aside bedsheets and sweaters, yanking open drawers, scrounging through the mess at the bottom of the walk-in closet. She'd been looking for illicit things, then. Drug paraphernalia. Unidentified pill bottles. Suspicious-looking keys. Letters in taped-up shoeboxes. She could admit now that maybe she had rushed it, that maybe she had only allowed her eyes to settle on objects very briefly before determining them meaningless. That was paracontagion mitigation 101, after all: don't look at things too carefully. Keep your hands close to your body. Keep your headphones jammed in your ears. Keep your gaze moving, at all times.

Except she wasn't actually afraid of stumbling across a paracontagion in Hannah's room. She was afraid of finding a deep, dark inner corridor of Hannah's life that she hadn't been privy to.

But now it was time to look for that corridor. To find a way in.

She reached for the book on Hannah's bedside table. *The Sickness Unto Death,* by Kierkegaard. It looked . . . dense, even for Hannah; something she'd been assigned in college, maybe. Selene opened it at the bookmark, hoping for an underlined passage she'd be able to understand—except the bookmark wasn't a bookmark. It was a piece of paper that had been folded into origami-tight eighths, and when Selene unfolded it, she saw that it was a drawing.

An austere, proportional human figure, the kind one might find in an ancient anatomy textbook. It was hairless, naked, its face barely defined, though its insides were intricately cross-hatched blue. A fuzzy outline of that same blue surrounded the figure head to toe like a full-body halo, or a force field, fending off thick red arrows that otherwise assailed the figure from all directions. A title had been scribbled in the bottom left, in Hannah's signature flourish: The Armor of God.

Selene carefully set the drawing down on Hannah's bed. It was a relief, she found, to release it.

RED SKIES IN THE MORNING

Next, she went to Hannah's desk, briefly putting her fingertips to the pens and stress balls before turning to the bulletin board. It was so cluttered with miscellany that barely any cork was visible, but thankfully, Hannah was deliberate. Only three heart pushpins had been used on the board: one on an ancient photo of their family of four, before their numbers had been cut in half; one on a three-year-old photo of the two of them; and the last one on a postcard that looked like something out of a hokey souvenir shop—except instead of an illustration of a seaside boardwalk, it was three teens looking excitedly at some unseen spectacle over on stage left, and instead of *Wish You Were Here!*, the curvy bubble text at the bottom read *Rock the Horizon!*

Selene gingerly pulled off the postcard's little pink heart, fingers quick to catch it as it fell from the board. An address had been scribbled on the other side, though not in Hannah's handwriting. Calvary Street? That was way on the other side of town.

She was typing the address into her phone to confirm the closest train stop when she got a call. She didn't recognize the number, and for just a moment she allowed herself to hope—

"It's Ruth. Bex's mom. I heard you went and paid her a visit today. And I just want to say, don't you ever, ever reach out to my daughter again. Not in person, not by phone, not by mail, not by fucking carrier pigeon, do you understand me?"

Selene figured she had that coming, and given the tone and substance of the conversation she'd had with Bex that morning, she was glad that this was a boundary she'd be able to honor. "Yeah. Got it. Will do. Listen, Ruth, really quickly before you go,"—being a pathing agent had mostly numbed her to the effects of over-the-top emotional expression—"did you ever hear Bex talk about Rock the Horizon?" She flipped the postcard over and back again. "I think it's a group?"

Ruth was so quiet that at first Selene thought the woman had hung up, or perhaps smashed her phone in anger, but then she realized that what she'd taken to be static was actually Ruth's jagged breaths. Had the woman taken up smoking? She supposed she couldn't blame her.

"Ruth?"

"I thought they were trying to help her. I thought they were keeping her alive."

"But?"

But only a click was Ruth's reply.

5. Day Four

Calvary Street was tucked behind the old garment factories that had once sustained Ponte City's economy but now either limped on at a fraction of their total capacity or lived reborn as warehouses, flophouses, or total-immersion art pieces dedicated to the long demise of society. Selene had first guessed that Rock the Horizon had taken over one of these industrial carcasses, either wholesale or in part, but as soon as she saw the shaky, narrow, sick-green three-story house where they'd perched instead, she could see that they were smaller, and more precarious, than she had originally thought.

A sprite in an oversized sweater and wire-rimmed glasses opened the door when she rang the bell—not all the way, just barely wide enough for Selene to slide through if she snuck in sideways—revealing a slice of what looked like a musty group house. Over the sprite's shoulder, Selene could see a muddy wall tapestry and a kitchen table drowned in books and loose papers, looking jaundiced in the light. At least it didn't look like a drug den, Selene thought, or a military bunker.

Wire-Rimmed's only greeting was a pointy-tipped stare.

Selene had tried to dress for the occasion, in her old

RED SKIES IN THE MORNING

college hoodie and a pair of sweatpants, but she still felt conspicuously misplaced as she started to speak. "Hi. I'm looking for help with a . . . " don't use legalese, don't use legalese, " . . . some weird symptoms my boyfriend's been having since he did a paracontagion path. I know Hannah Denton, she told me you guys helped her friend with something similar? I think her friend's name was Bex?"

There was an ugly wooden squeak from inside the house, and a face that had been sitting at the kitchen table leaned into view to better squint at Selene.

"How do you know Hannah?" Wire-Rimmed asked.

Selene had practiced this part. "She's my neighbor."

"And what symptoms is he having? Your boyfriend. What's his name?"

"Jim." She said it too quickly, probably, at too high a pitch. "He says he's still seeing things. I'll catch him watching people that aren't there, that I can't see. Talks in his sleep, he never used to do that. I told him to go back to the pathing office but he says he doesn't want to. Says they won't know how to help anyway. So I'm looking for something else."

She was trying to channel the dismissive posture toward pathing that she'd heard, in various permutations, from Aidan and Ruth and Bex. And it seemed to be working, because she could see Wire-Rimmed's grip on the door loosen just a tad. "And what's your name?"

"L-Lee." Shit, of all the things to forget to prepare. "I'm Lee."

Wire-Rimmed and Kitchen Table exchanged pointed glances for a good thirty seconds during which Selene hoped her cheeks hadn't turned too pink, until Wire-Rimmed said they'd be happy to give her some tips. After a few more cursory questions—Selene was very conscious that Wire-Rimmed was continuing to block the entrance—Wire-Rimmed finally swiveled on their heels and invited her in, then introduced themselves as Langley.

"We like to start with the basics first," Langley said

after making room on a ratty couch that they must have picked up from someone's yard. "Usually the people who come to us are super confused about how they feel after they separate from the paracontagion. Maybe a part of them is relieved. But another part of them is sad to have lost the connection. Maybe they're even grieving. So education is where we like to start."

Selene managed to contain her utter irritation at the idea of *mourning* a paracontagion to a nod. Langley was pulling paperbacks off an overstuffed bookcase, frowning at the back covers, and eventually settling on two to hand to Selene. "These are good ones to start with. You can borrow them if you want. We have extra copies."

"Thanks, but . . . " She accepted, then promptly looked away from, *The Denial of Death* and *The Worm at the Core: On the Role of Death in Life*. "Jim's not much of a reader. Is there anything else you'd recommend? I don't know if there's . . . intensive therapy, or . . . "

Langley seemed to catch themselves on the precipice of answering, fingers frozen into claws. Out of the corner of her eye, Selene thought she could see Kitchen Table shaking their head. "That might be something we can talk about down the line. Maybe he could start coming to our weekly discussion circles first? It might be helpful to talk to others who've been where he's at." Langley rummaged through the mess on the kitchen table and extracted a creased, coffee-stained paper that she held out for Selene to take. "This is the agenda with all the topics from last month, if you want to show him. Let me try to find the one for this month . . . "

Selene stood and took the paper, a wave of trembling nausea suddenly rocking her as she walked toward both Kitchen Table and the kitchen table. She nearly dropped the page; it nearly cut her finger open. Even when she did manage to grab it and hold it under the piss-yellow light so she could distill some kind of meaning from it, the roil in her stomach—but *why?*—was making it very hard to read,

RED SKIES IN THE MORNING

especially when the words made so little sense. *Extinction. Determinism. Ecophagy.* And then she saw a configuration of letters that emptied out all the other lines and squiggles, all those broken half-thoughts: Hannah's name. Second talk of the month. A random Thursday evening. She'd been co-moderating a session called "Finding Meaning in the Paracontagion Era" with somebody called Keel.

Keel? Fuck, she was *sure* she knew that name from somewhere.

She was vaguely aware that Langley was going on about something that made about as much sense as the rest of the lines of the agenda, how meetings were structured maybe, but as soon as she saw that line Selene could not stop herself from interrupting:

"Who's Keel?"

Langley's eyes went wide. Oh, so that name *definitely* meant something.

"I . . . I see Hannah was . . . doing this session with them, I was just wondering."

"Oh!" Selene could practically hear the admiration flow, easy like breath, from Langley's lungs. "He's our founder. He's a visionary, truly. He's understood the true social implications of paracontagions from the get-go. And that was a great discussion that he and Hannah led."

Worry and anger and something else—something selfish and fearful, something rather like jealousy—crested through Selene, making her just a little less cautious, just a bit less patient. *Who the fuck is this guy,* went the drumbeat in her head, *and what the fuck is he doing with Hannah?* "Wow, I didn't know Hannah was that high-up. Doing talks with the founder."

Langley laughed in what looked like discomfort but otherwise declined to respond; from the sea of papers, Kitchen Table dryly said with a barely-there eyeroll, "She's not. She just 'gets him.'"

She wanted to demand his location. She wanted to barge through the rooms with an urgency that no one in

Rock the Horizon had ever seen, because she was positive now that if anyone knew where Hannah was, it would be this Keel motherfucker. She wanted to—

"What is that sound?" Kitchen Table suddenly said. "D'you hear that? It's like a buzz."

Langley claimed to hear nothing, and Kitchen Table said Langley was half-deaf anyway, and while they were bickering, Selene had anxiously grabbed the pocket of her coat and realized that this time, the paracontagion app *was* buzzing. She was sure it hadn't been going off when she was practically sitting on her phone on the couch, which meant either the paracontagion was moving toward her, or by stepping toward the kitchen table, she had moved toward it.

Jesus Christ. Jesus *Christ*.

"Sorry, that's me. That was Jim calling." She pressed the "silent" button on her phone as hard as she could. "I should probably get back home. But thank you for all the suggestions, I'll definitely send him your way. Could I just use your bathroom real quick before I leave?"

※

If she had been directed away from the red hazard triangle on her app—if she would have had to leave the house and then break back into it, if she would have had to scurry on her hands and knees through hallways she wasn't supposed to be in—she would have done it. The pathing agent in her—the dedicated paperclip, holding the world together by stringing people into chains of paracontagion exposures, again and again and over and over until the world was swallowed by the sun—would have permitted nothing else.

Somewhere in this house was the single biggest threat to public safety short of a ticking bomb: an uncatalogued paracontagion. Imagine what Video Man could do if he got hold of such a thing. *Imagine if this group was Video Man.*

The sense of duty was grounding, exhilarating, so

much more comforting despite the danger than the freezing anxiety and explosive panic that had flooded her system for the past four days.

She lucked out. The path to the bathroom led her straight toward the blinking triangle, until she should have been standing right on top of it and she realized that the paracontagion was probably on a different floor. Hoping for a staircase, she pulled on one janky door, then another. The first opened into a storage closet, crammed with brooms and folding chairs. But the second revealed a basement, and it was through that door that she crept.

In a small nest of golden light amid the dark, in the spot where Selene's phone promised a paracontagion would be, stood a pale woman in a long white dress. Her left hand hovered above a copper mesh box that had been placed on a simple wooden chair. Her right hand's fingertips reached with the limp-wristed listlessness of a Renaissance painting toward two bodies splayed—sleeping?—at her feet on a bed of pillows.

Selene stepped off the last step of the basement stairs with a creak, and the pale woman turned to her with a smile. "Welcome," she said, "did you want to sign up for a session with Sarah?" Her left hand beckoned toward the box that Selene could see held *something* black and tubular. It was clearly neither camcorder nor polaroid, the two most common paracontagion shells. But even without the app Selene knew in her gut that that contraption—whatever it was—held a monster.

Hannah-logic. There was no arguing with it, sometimes.

"What is that?" she whispered, taking a cautious step closer.

The woman chuckled. "You must be new here. This is Sarah. She lived in a little settlement not too far from here that fell into the sea many years ago. Cashtown, have you heard of it? No, you're probably too young. Anyway, Sarah's husband was a brute and he strangled her to death in one of his drunken fugues. So now she lives in this zoetrope and we care for her, just like she cares for us." The woman smiled lovingly at the box. "She really is quite a gentle soul. Nothing like those gruesome horror stories the mainstream media is always going on about."

"How do you know she's . . . " Selene stopped herself from asking *how do you know she's not lying?* "How do you know she's gentle?"

"Well, because she's revealed herself to us," the woman said, as if it was the most obvious answer in the world. "It's simple observation. She's done wonders for these two." She bent down and petted the hair of the girl at her feet, then the boy, like they were kittens she was fostering. "They were both severed from entities too abruptly. Being with Sarah helps ease the pain."

Drool coated their mouths like spider webbing and their limbs were twitching like someone had a fork in their spinal cord—but they weren't in pain. Though if they wanted to reconnect to a paracontagion so badly, why didn't they just go to the city pathing office? Why didn't they just pivot their angst into public good and relieve people like poor Mr. Kudo instead of getting catatonic in a basement?

"How many times have they . . . been with Sarah?" she asked.

The woman cocked her head, calculating. "Oh! I'm not sure. They've been switching off quite a lot over the past month or two. Her, maybe a hundred times? Him a little less."

Nausea welled in Selene. That explained why they didn't go to the pathing office; the PMA required a six-month cooling-off period between exposures. There were too many stories from the early days of paracontagions about little families, little friend groups, little informal "clubs" repeatedly passing around a single paracontagion that one member had been exposed to and utterly self-annihilating within a year, in the most violent cornucopias of murder and suicide.

RED SKIES IN THE MORNING

"But don't worry, I can make room for you on the schedule. These two are doing so much better compared to when they first came in, they can be away from Sarah for a couple days."

"No, I'm . . . not here for me." Selene took another ginger step toward the so-called zoetrope. She could almost see pictures on the inside of the cylinder, could almost imagine what they might look like in motion, going click-clack against the light in the most whimsical type of shadow play—and then the woman stepped between her and the box, smiling knowingly. Selene stepped back in embarrassment, trying to shake herself sober. She hadn't even realized how close she'd gotten to it. "I can't believe that Sarah hasn't killed anyone."

At the word "killed," the woman shot forth a look of disapproval so severe that she seemed personally insulted. "I mean, that she's never completed her lifecycle," Selene corrected herself. "Inside a host."

The woman's neck remained stiff, her face clenched. "We trust that she'll tell us when she's ready to emerge. And yes," she added, as if expecting an interruption, "we can hear her."

But that was hardly surprising, wasn't it, given how often they all seemed to be *with* "Sarah." The two coma patients on the floor had probably dissolved their brains into paracontagion-scented goo, by now. Had Hannah taken part in this grotesquerie? She didn't have any cause to—she'd never been exposed to a paracontagion, at least before she went missing—but groups had a way of breaking down individual wills, even those as strong as Hannah's.

"She's been generous with so many of us. But at least she's in a community that respects and appreciates her, instead of some zoo."

"Sorry, what . . . zoo?" The problem-solving treadmill in her mind once again started churning, concluding: it's Video Man. The serial killer was running some horrific paracontagion zoo filled with monsters ordered over the internet, selling tickets to curious lookie-loos, and occasionally unleashing them on random passers-by, which meant if she found the zoo, she would find any video Hannah might have been exposed to, and they would be able to—

"Those awful government offices where they have all sorts of people line up to cycle through lost souls," the woman said. "We've got one right on T Street. I'm sure you've seen it?"

The woman raised an eyebrow at her in what felt like suspicion, maybe even accusation, and in a momentary lapse during which Selene forgot that government officials and scientists had never confirmed that paracontagions were indeed the spiritual remnants of deceased human beings, she thought—*she knows; she knows who I am; she knows who I am because Sarah told her.*

※

Selene waited until she was outside to call it in. And then she waited, shivering in the rain beneath a faded bus stop sign, for the cops to come.

The cop who'd taken her missing persons report was among them. While young cops fresh out of the military set up a perimeter around the house on Calvary Street and hazmat cops in yellow suits carried out the copper box containing "Sarah" on an aluminum containment stretcher that looked for all purposes like a glitzy body bag, that cop who'd decided never to have children shook his head when he saw Selene, and then began marching toward her.

"Jesus Christ, lady," he said when he got close enough to speak without shouting, yet still far enough to not be obliged to extend his umbrella over her head, "Did you really think these lunatics could help you?"

"I called it in," she said, and found that her lips had gone numb.

"And thank you very much for that. Sincerely. But

please. Getting involved with people like this is not the way to look for your sister. They're killers. They're destroyers."

Every part of her human being wanted to grab him by his musty blue sleeves and shake him, screaming, "what have you done about Hannah!" But her head only nodded in learned mechanical ritual—*nod when a cop is talking to you in that voice.*

"Go home. Wait for us to call you. Okay?"

Again she nodded. But just as he turned a desperate flame sparked inside her, and she jumped off the curb and called for him to wait. "Are you arresting Keel? The leader guy?"

"Lady!" he swiveled around so fast his umbrella almost poked out her eye. "Go home!"

"I need to talk to him. Please let me talk to him. I think he might know where my sister is."

It was as if he knew the implication behind her statement before she had the chance to try to hide it. "Now why would you think that," he said, the righteous bluster in his voice suddenly replaced by something quiet and cold and far more dangerous.

"Be-because she was in the group. I think she and Keel might have . . . worked together."

Maybe he really thought Rock the Horizon killed people. Maybe he just hated Keel that much. Either way, the cop set his jaw and clenched his fist with the energy of a man whose dog had just been kicked and hissed, "Do you know who Ray Keel is?"

She hadn't realized that she knew until that moment; but yes, she knew. Maybe not who he was, but who he knew, which in this context was all she needed to understand why the cop's face had warped: Ray Keel was an associate of Adam Ramiel, the imprisoned terrorist who had taken over a projectionist room in the Sawfish Theater and exposed eighty people at a seven o'clock showing of *Waterloo* to a paracontagion. Although the paracontagion only fully attached itself to one moviegoer—and that woman, ironically, made a full recovery—there had been a dozen suicides to date among the survivors, and one family annihilation. There wasn't enough evidence of Keel's involvement to try him, though talking heads suspected he'd known about the plan.

The distress must have shown all over her face, because the cop jumped right to the quick with his next question: "Are we talking a Sawfish situation?"

"No." Oh God, she hoped she was right. She really, really hoped she was right. "No. No way. Hannah wouldn't do something like that."

"Yeah? You think so? Did you think she'd join up with these freaks?"

She understood what he was implying: that she was just another deluded family member seeing their lost loved one through infantilized pink glasses. But she actually *wasn't* surprised to learn that Hannah had found affinity with this group, with people like Langley and Kitchen Table and Sarah's keeper in the basement. There was a vibe throughout Rock the Horizon—a heavenward tilt of their core antenna, a grand naivete—that felt very much in sync with Hannah-logic, in a way that few things were.

"I didn't know this group existed, so no, but . . . " She thought back to her conversation with Hannah on Monday morning, back when Marly D. was still alive and Hannah was still in her sight and everything hadn't yet gone terribly wrong. How genuinely, how calmly Hannah had stated the crux of her moral philosophy: *"I don't think anyone's a zombie."*

The cop was waiting now, as if he had all the time in the world, for Selene to finish her sentence. She shook her head with a renewed vigor—no, not vigor. Faith in Hannah. "My sister would never do a Sawfish. She's never hurt anyone in her life. It's not . . . it's just not in her coding."

"These people think that paracontagions are here to *save* us," the cop said, bitterness dripping from his words. "So is your sister a *save-the-world* type? Huh?"

RED SKIES IN THE MORNING

"No." She was bluffing now; she hoped he couldn't tell. "I raised her. She knows—I made sure she knows—what a paracontagion really is. Look, I just think Keel might know where she is. Please, please, just let me ask him a couple questions. You can listen, if you want."

The cop finally loosened his muscles slightly, just enough to let out a snort. "Oh, believe you me, lady. If you're asking him questions, we're gonna be listening."

He walked away as people started coming out of the house on Calvary Street—cops and Rock the Horizon members, the latter with zipties around their wrists. Kitchen Table stared straight ahead at some unknown distant vista while their body was marched to a police vehicle, but not Langley. No, Langley met Selene's eyes and seized up, thunderstruck by betrayal. "We weren't hurting anybody, you lying bitch!" Langley screamed. "We were *helping people!*"

"Paracontagions need to be under government supervision," Selene muttered, and suddenly Langley was very nearly right in her face, yelling "Fascist pig!" She didn't know whether the cops momentarily let Langley slip or whether Langley just fought that hard, but Langley managed to get a spit in before they were re-corralled by a couple beat cops saying, "hey, hey."

Selene didn't bother wiping the saliva off her face. The rain took it all anyway.

6. *Day Five*

"The coffee's terrible, by the way." A middle-aged man in a green windbreaker who reminded her of her gym teacher was standing behind her, leaning over her shoulder. "Cookies are good, though. Mrs. Bolduan makes them herself."

Selene thanked him quietly and grabbed one cookie, then another. She had an ecstatic vision of herself grabbing all of them, then taking the whole tray under the table and jamming them one by one into her mouth until she felt sick with cookies instead of anxiety—but managed to make herself turn away from the refreshments and take her two cookies to her seat instead.

Because Hugh Bolduan was the only one who ever made a nuisance of himself on local news, she had always imagined the Bluejay Society to be a "group" of one or two or maybe three at most. But there were upwards of three dozen people at the Beacon Hill Rec Center. Mostly middle-aged and looking about as worn and distressed as their denim jeans. Hugh sat amongst them, nodding and listening like a pastor with his parishioners, until the clock struck six and he went to stand at the front of the room with a clap of his hands.

"Thanks, folks, for being here. It's actually Greg's birthday today," Hugh said. "So obviously a very important day for me and Annie." A sympathetic murmur bubbled through the room. "For those of you who don't know Greg's story . . . he was our only child. Our brilliant little engineer. Volunteered with a bird rescue on weekends. Actually wanted to see his grandma at the nursing home. Just a good kid. We weren't surprised when he told us he was going to volunteer to be somebody's paracontagion path. We told him to be careful and to let us know how it went. He'd just graduated from college, so we wanted to, you know, let him do things on his own."

He'd make a nice boyfriend for Hannah, Selene thought, but had a feeling that Hugh's story was not going to end well. Hell, Hannah's probably wouldn't either. She shoved the rest of a cookie in her mouth, trying not to crunch too loudly.

"I just said to him, call us when you know someone's picked up the baton for you. Because believe me, I would have driven over and done it for him in a heartbeat if he needed it. But he said, Dad, don't worry, they're on top of it, they'll find somebody to do it. And they did. They found somebody on day six and they called him to let him know and he called me and said, Dad, it's done, they got somebody. We talked to him the next day and assumed everything was fine. Assumed it wasn't day seven. That his countdown had been cancelled. Talked about how his new job was going. A new movie he'd just watched. And then that night his roommate called us and said he came home to find Greg . . . " Hugh shrugged, not in indifference but defeat. "In pieces in the bathroom. Turned out that the pathing agent took his path to the wrong paracontagion. So no one pathed for Greg. Innocent human error, they said. Just a really unfortunate accident."

Selene grimaced. That story did ring a bell. As she recalled, that pathing agent quit in order to drink himself to death—this all unfolded before shifts were shortened from twelve hours to eight, before caseload limits were lowered from sixty to forty, before paracontagion retrieval from the vault was automated. There were excuses she could give. But this man had lost his child.

In the back row, a man in a Loggerheads baseball cap stood up. "Hugh—I just want to say—thank you to you and Annie for sharing your story. It drives me absolutely up the wall when I hear kids talk about pathing like it's just something fun to do on a Friday night. It's like we've lost all fucking—I'm sorry—lost all common sense about the fact that these things are monsters. They're not a joke. They are here to literally kill us."

Selene had to admit that it was gratifying to hear someone espouse actual real-world logic, after the madness that had been Rock the Horizon and their pet paracontagion. *Sarah.*

A couple closer to the front echoed his sentiment, their sentences collapsing into one another. "We won't let our kids path," they said, and "We don't path either," and then something about "productive members of society." Selene squinted at them—they looked like easily-frightened people, people whose fear had made them selfish. And then she felt the prickle of someone else's gaze and glanced up to see Hugh watching her closely. He was watching her expression, she realized. Watching her reactions. She quickly steeled her jaw.

A woman with a helmet of platinum hair raised her hand, looking to Hugh for a nod before starting to speak. "I have been trying to raise awareness. Friends, neighbors, coworkers, you name it. But what I keep running into is . . . they keep saying things are *working fine* now. I've tried to tell them, look at the numbers. The number of paracontagions worldwide is going up exponentially. We're barely keeping up as it is. How are we just going to keep adding more and more to the national vaults and expect things to stay *fine?* There's no way. Not us, not any country. What do people think is going to happen when we're totally overwhelmed? Sure, the politicians and the billionaires will be all right, they always are. But what about the rest of us? And just . . . pfft. Nothing. Doesn't register. They are so completely *brainwashed.*"

"Thank you, Paula," Hugh said, before sliding his gaze to the other side of the room. "I think Selene has a question."

It was less of a question and more of a comment. She had, in fact, multiple comments. The tired cynic in her wanted to protest that of course people would cling to vestiges of normality if that meant keeping their lives from degenerating into non-stop screaming all the time. The pathing agent in her wanted to insist that things *were* in fact fine, that deaths due to paracontagion exposure had been steadily decreasing thanks to the world's pathing systems.

"Sorry," she said, shifting with discomfort in her folding chair as Paula turned to glare at her, "I just had to say that there's actually no evidence that the rate of paracontagions is increasing exponentially. It's just not true."

Hugh gave her a smile baked with condescension, an

RED SKIES IN THE MORNING

of-course-you-think-that smile. Paula did not; Paula remained ferocious. "It's all right there in the data," Paula said, and by the righteous tremor in her voice Selene could tell that Paula had already made up her mind. "You can't sit there and tell me that going from three million to three and a half million active paracontagions in a year isn't something that we should worry about!"

"I mean, yes, it's a big jump, but that's just because reporting has gotten way better around the world. Reporting *and* containment. The numbers from year one and two were really shaky, now we're finally getting reliable data. It doesn't mean the *actual* numbers of paracontagions are . . . "

She'd already lost Paula, who'd turned back around with a scoff, and by the audible grumbles from other rows, she was losing the rest of them as well. Hugh swiftly took control. "I think we can all at least agree that the problem isn't going away," he said. "Is that fair, Selene?"

She shrugged in acquiescence.

"And as long as we have this problem, the people who shoulder the burden are . . . well, the people who have always shouldered the burdens of society. Well-meaning people. Responsible people. People who want to do the right thing. The people who volunteer for the extra shift to make sure their kids have enough food on the table." In the next row, a woman in a hoodie gripped the bridge of her nose as if to stop from crying. She looked familiar—had she come into the pathing office recently?—but Selene quickly averted her eyes when the woman snapped her head around. "Would you agree? Selene?"

Did she agree? The room was quiet, sensing now that there had to be a reason Hugh kept drawing attention to this bitchy newcomer who was giving Paula a hard time. Eyes turned toward her and she did recognize the woman in the hoodie, she was sure of it now—couldn't remember the circumstances and nature of her paracontagion, though.

Hugh raised his eyebrows as if to push the answer further up her throat.

"I don't know," she said. "I mean. Yeah, the system relies on people relying on each other. That's the definition of pathing. I'm . . . I'm not sure what you're asking, really. All sorts of people act as paths every day. It's just like giving blood, or paying taxes. There's an assumption that we're all going to do it."

"But we *don't* all do it," someone she couldn't see said, prompting a small refrain of affirming noises. Various social boogeymen were thrown out, some real, some not: "drug dealers" and "the mayor" and "pedophiles" and "assholes," as well as "those Rock the Horizon freaks."

"Yeah, and we don't all give blood either," Selene mumbled.

"I should mention that Selene joins us from the city pathing office," Hugh said, in a tone that indicated this group had a lot of feelings about local officials, and despite the assurances he'd given her at Marly D.'s vigil, about pathing as well. Selene's gaze swept very quickly over the other chairs for confirmation; most of the faces were either giving her quiet judgment or an outright scowl, though the middle-aged man in the green windbreaker gave her a smile that might have been intended as kindness but felt flat. Felt empty. She pressed her lips together in neutral return, the way she had taken to acknowledging strange men since she was fourteen.

Paula snapped, "So *that's* why she won't admit there's a problem," and while the room murmured in agreement, Selene bit into the back of her hand in exasperation. Partly to keep herself from snapping back that of course she understood that the system wasn't perfect. But mostly because every single time she'd cut Hannah off in the past year, told her to please not talk about something so depressing—because she was *trying the best I can,* that was the part that never seemed to resonate—was turning over in her stomach, making her feel quite sick.

RED SKIES IN THE MORNING

"I think Selene and other pathing agents are doing the best they can," Hugh said, and the shock of hearing the thoughts she never dared express mirrored back at her momentarily distracted her from the meat of what Hugh was saying. "I think they just need to hear about other options."

There was that odd phrase again, sticking out like a crooked stitch: *other options*.

"What if we used paracontagions as a way for people to repay the debt they owe to society?"

"People in prison?" She raised her eyebrows. Prompting him. "They do participate, if they choose." The mechanics of said *choice* were questionable in ways she didn't like to think about for too long—when convicts came to the office, shackled and escorted (because they were almost always cheaper and safer to move than a paracontagion shell), she didn't ask whether they'd been bribed or coerced or were repaying a debt of a different kind.

"Well, we can make it a more formal requirement. Make it part of their sentence."

She thought again of the self-annihilating families and friend groups of the early days of paracontagions. Those circuits were just too small, the exposures too frequent. "That's a much smaller pool of people. Practically a closed system. No one in this administration is going to go for that, we've seen that the results are toxic."

Someone said, "better them than us" and someone else said "who cares?" Hugh himself did not reply save for a noncommittal shrug, but Selene had seen enough of the Bluejay Society by then to understand that this group spoke for Hugh.

When she heard someone in the rising clamor of noise say that allowing a paracontagion to kill a prisoner was a good deal—get rid of two threats for the price of one, they said—Selene picked up her purse and crab-walked out between the rows of seats, stumbling over knees whose owners, affronted by her rudeness, refused to give way.

NADIA BULKIN

>>><<<

She took the long way back to the train station so she could poke around for Hannah in the dark. Beacon Hill was known for dogs and strollers and neighborhood watches—not exactly a part of town that Hannah frequented—but she couldn't be too sure of anything, now. She searched until she found herself sitting hypnotized on a playground swing, dwelling in a memory of a young Hannah asking "Lee" to take her to a playground because the kids at school thought she was too weird and those kids' parents thought death was contagious—coming out of her lull only when she saw three scrawny figures across the street crowding around one of the many posters that had been tacked up on a boarded-up building across the street.

They ran when they saw her looking. So she got up.

It was one of the posters put up by Marly D.'s family. *Can you help me?* it read, over Marly's smiling face and a computer-generated rendition of the paracontagion she'd been exposed to. She was no great beauty, Marly, though her family had taken care to choose a picture whose human sweetness couldn't be denied. This girl had dreams, the portrait said. This girl cared.

And now a giant red zero—an oval with a vigorous slash, to make its negation unmistakable—had been painted over Marly's face. Because, like Hannah said, Marly was considered a zero. A zombie. Selene still didn't understand why. Because she was dull? Because she was unmarried and childless? She seemed to have earned the label "zero" purely by being murdered.

Because Video Man was killing those undeserving of life. Therefore, Marly deserved death.

Up close, Selene could still smell the paint. Poor dead Marly. Poor dead Marly who'd done nothing wrong but get ripped apart by a vengeful—what would Bex call it?—ghost. Rage coursed through Selene's veins and set her legs on fire, such that before she knew it she was tearing after the little shits, screaming, *"Hey!"*

Beneath the streetlamp at the end of the next block, she saw them pause and look back at her—but nothing more than a glance before they resumed running on their gangly foal-legs. She could hear Hannah's voice in her head, saying, "they're just kids," so she didn't yell again. She didn't chase any further. She didn't even watch them disappear into the dark. Let them run on home to their families, safe in the delusion that because they had thus far been spared, they were worthy.

Instead she looked at Marly. Marly's earnest smile, Marly's trusting eyes. Marly had loved her parents. She would have undoubtedly loved others, too. But in eternity she was now wedded not to a loved one but to the video that had killed her. Those stupid little ballerinas in their stupid little auditorium. It was so fucking unfair.

Selene grabbed the top of the poster and ripped it right down the middle. Crumpled up the blurry-faced ballerinas and tossed them down the sewer to be carried with the rest of the city's detritus into the roiling sea below Hannah's beloved pier. Killed that cursed attachment dead.

>>>>><<<<<

After Rock the Horizon was raided—apparently Keel had insisted on taking the fall for his group, messiah-like—the six o'clock news energy that would have ordinarily been spent on Video Man was momentarily directed toward a retrospective on the Sawfish Theater terrorist attack. The state penitentiary refused to let reporters in to see Adam Ramiel, but he issued a statement through his lawyer denying any connection with any of the so-called "catastrophes" currently unfolding outside the prison walls.

Selene frowned at the television. What catastrophe was he referring to? And surely that wasn't his full statement? When he was arrested for the Sawfish incident, Ramiel had handed a whole manifesto freely and proudly to the police. He wasn't one for brevity.

Hannah had found the Sawfish manifesto online. Selene's coworkers at the PMA thought it ought to be hidden forever lest it become its own cursed artifact, but public curiosity disguised as outrage had proved too intense. The government released a redacted version to the media, but it was the uncensored version that Hannah found, and the uncensored version that she read aloud, paragraph-by-depressing-paragraph, while Selene tried to make dinner. Selene didn't remember the content; she mostly remembered being annoyed at Hannah for bringing up something so awful, so insane, during the only time of day—night time, her time—when Selene wasn't required to think about paracontagions.

Just as the internet had provided for Hannah then, the internet had what Selene wanted—needed?—to know now: the details that the news would find too gory, too unsavory, to air.

You keep worrying about how we humans can live with paracontagions, but there's a reason nobody in that theater shut their eyes when my video started playing. We're not meant to live with them. We're meant to die with them. And we know it, deep inside.

She jumped when her phone rang. The deepest layer of her heart still hoped to see Hannah's number, but of course it wasn't—*it will never be,* the darkness whispered— it was the cop.

"You're clear to talk to Keel tomorrow," he said. "Eleven a.m. Ponte City Jail. God knows why, but he actually wants to talk to you."

Fuck. Right now, she'd actually prefer if he didn't.

But she didn't have the luxury for preferences now. What she had was another number to cross off on the dry-erase board: 5. Which meant two days left, in worst-case scenario terms. And she had learned long ago—after their father was found dead, after their mother's diagnosis came back—that worst-case scenarios were the only scenarios to stake one's life on.

"I'll be there," she said.

7. Day Six

She didn't know what she'd been expecting of Ray Keel, exactly, but it wasn't the man she found on the other side of the table of Interrogation Room 3. She thought he'd have a larger presence. A more foreboding aura. She expected the sort of wide-eyed, overconfident cult leader she'd seen in documentaries, to be honest—not this slumped-over professorial type with grandfatherly glasses and hollowed cheeks. This man seemed small, especially in this gray concrete tomb surrounded by cops who'd probably be happy to send him to solitary with a paracontagion—with *Sarah*, if they had a sense of humor—and set the timer for a week.

"Hi," he said, followed by, "It's Selene, isn't it?"

"Yes." She glanced quickly at the cop—at least she assumed he was a cop, he looked more like a nightclub bouncer—standing guard in the corner of the room, hands at the ready to grab his gun. The others were on the other side of the two-way mirror behind her, no doubt leaning in close enough to hear every groan and sigh. "Thank you for agreeing to meet me."

"I was so sorry to hear about Hannah's disappearance," he said, and a scratchy bristle immediately raced down her arms. Why was he sorry? Did he think she was dead? Why didn't he sound the slightest bit anxious or afraid instead of just filled with useless pity? "I wanted to make myself available to answer any questions you had."

"Were you . . . close with Hannah? Or would you do this for any of your missing volunteers?"

"I don't think we have any other missing volunteers. But yes, Hannah rose above the rest. She was special.

Thoughtful. Passionate. About the cause." He gave Selene a wolfish sideways grin that she didn't like at all. "Don't worry, nothing inappropriate."

"She's twenty-three," Selene hissed through gritted teeth. "She's an adult."

"Ah well. Young enough to be my daughter. I always got the sense that Hannah's interests were uniquely . . . elevated. I always thought she could have been an abbess, in another life."

Selene felt her hip burn with the drawing she'd tucked into the pocket of her jeans: Hannah's blue figure with arms outstretched as if to receive stigmata, alone and assailed in all directions by thick red arrows, yet protected. Protected by the so-called *armor of God*.

"Why are you talking about Hannah in the past tense?"

Keel opened and closed his mouth before settling it into a deep frown. "I'm sorry," he said quietly, and to her chagrin it actually sounded genuine. "I didn't realize."

The sight of this man expressing sorrow, maybe even *grief,* for Hannah very nearly and unexpectedly brought Selene to tears. Not because she gave a damn about his feelings. Because he was making it impossible to ignore reality. She inhaled sharply, clenching her mind's fist around her will. "When did you last see her?"

"Last week. Sorry, I don't remember what day."

"And? How was she acting? What did you talk about?"

"She was distressed. She talked about the killer that's running around infecting people with paracontagions. Video Man, I think his name is."

Selene's breath caught on a snag in her heart. "Was she scared of him?"

"No. God, no. It upset her to see people cheering him on. I think she was running out of reasons to be hopeful. I'm very sorry to say that. Truly I am. I encouraged her to talk to you."

He was implying *something* with that statement, something big and deep and terrifying that Selene couldn't

RED SKIES IN THE MORNING

bring herself to look at. She stumbled forward with her questions, trying to dodge the yawning abyss. "So she didn't think that paracontagions are . . . "—out of nowhere she saw Hannah dead with eyes empty of light and a mouth full of blood, saw Hannah exploding like Marly had exploded, nearly choked on her broken voice—"good for people?"

"No. Not the way Lilith does." Keel glanced past her head toward the two-way mirror; she guessed that Lilith was the woman in the long dress in Rock the Horizon's basement. Sarah's keeper. "I think Hannah thought of paracontagions like any of the other countless calamities we struggle against, as a human race. Natural disasters. Plagues. Wars. I do think she wondered why we have so many crosses to bear. I don't suppose you have an answer to that question, do you?"

Selene shrugged impatiently. "I don't know. I guess God's a bit of a dick."

For a moment Keel was uncomfortably silent. He just sat there under the halogen light, watching Selene's expression as if trying to watch for something unseen: a telltale ripple under her skin, a flush of discoloration. A sign, perhaps, of the kind of disquiet that Hannah had evidently voiced. She bit down on her thumbnail, nervous.

"I guess that's one explanation," he eventually said, "or maybe this is a fate we've earned. Or maybe it's a gift, I don't know. I told Hannah to do what good she could in the time she had."

"This doesn't sound like what your other volunteers think. Langley. Lilith."

"Well, no. It isn't very motivational, is it? It's not going to get you out of bed in the morning. I just try to break down the cognitive distance that society wants us to put between ourselves and these particular . . . burdens, if you will. The strong ones figure out the rest on their own."

"Like Hannah."

"Like Hannah."

"So what did you plan to do with Sarah? You put that thing in the hands of a madwoman."

He pursed his lips in a small and vaguely devious smile, finally revealing a small hint of the leader that Selene had been expecting when she walked into the room. What had Ruth said about Rock the Horizon? That she'd thought—apparently wrongly—that they were keeping Bex alive?

"And Bex? Did she figure it out? She's plenty pretty, I bet she was another chosen disciple."

Keel chose not to engage the personal dig. "I just offered validation for what she was going through. It's amazing, you know, her mother found all those psychiatrists and psychologists and priests to talk to her, and none of them actually acknowledged what she had to say."

The wild look in Bex's eyes. Animalistic. Savage. "That the world is fucked," she quoted Bex.

"The world is fucked," he echoed, "and humanity is doomed. And wanting to die is actually the rational option, under the circumstances. Don't you ever wonder why we can't resist looking at a paracontagion once we get close enough to it? Why the government has to tell us, *don't look?* Shouldn't a species invested in its own survival know not to look?"

Oh. That again. A whirlpool opened inside her stomach, an emptiness so total it burned. "You sound like everyone's favorite movie theater terrorist," she muttered, trying to find her footing.

A twitch crossed Keel's eyelid. "Ramiel and I connected because we'd reached a similar conclusion about the future of humanity. But I'll tell you the same thing I told the cops the other day," he said, "and in fact the same thing I've always told them, which is that Ramiel's path diverged from mine a long time ago, long before he did what he did at the Sawfish Theater. We have fundamental differences in our beliefs that neither of us have any interest in reconciling."

RED SKIES IN THE MORNING

That sounded like something a defense attorney had coached him to say. "Oh yeah? How so?"

"He doesn't believe in giving people a choice." Keel sighed sadly, a disappointed older brother. "Consent isn't something I'm willing to compromise on. Neither was Hannah, by the way." He nodded his chin toward the mirror. "I'm sure that's what they're worried about, right? That's why they let you in to talk to me, to get ahead of another Sawfish incident? Well, I'm sorry to disappoint them. The only person I'd worry about Hannah hurting is herself."

Were the eavesdropping cops exhaling in relief? Had they mentally moved onto lunch? Had the cop who'd taken Hannah's case slid Hannah back to the bottom of his to-do list, because there was nothing to be done about one of the city's hundreds of suicides? *Let the walking dead die,* a coworker had said once; *save your energy for the ones committed to living.*

Except they hadn't loved Hannah.

Before she left, she showed him Hannah's drawing. Just in case. "Hannah drew this. I found it in her room after she . . . anyway. Is anything about it familiar to you? The phrasing, the colors . . . "

Keel sucked at his teeth and scratched at his beard. "Hannah had a lot of . . . interesting ideas about what paracontagions really are. The mechanisms of how they work. What actually makes them so compelling. I don't know if all her theories made sense to me but then again, she was smarter than me. Is. *Is* smarter." He glanced up at Selene as if hoping for a cookie. "I told her once that I was surprised she wasn't working for the PMA, but I got the sense that *isn't* how she's wired."

Selene wanted to tell him off for speaking of Hannah so familiarly. What did he know of her? Had he watched her grow? Had he watched her adapt to her less-than-ideal circumstances, adjust and learn and recalibrate? No. The most he had were some late-night pot-fueled talks with a half-molded girl who'd lost her father very young and never dated anyone her own age. The fucking nerve of this guy. But there was urgency elsewhere, a worst-case scenario unfolding in real time, and she squashed that sisterly anger down.

"So what, are these red arrows... paracontagions? Do you think? Attacking the person?"

"Maybe. It's the same color the government uses, isn't it? In all your little PSAs?"

She wasn't the government and she hadn't made the PSAs, but he was correct: paracontagions were always marked in red. Usually with a big "X" running through them, or a biohazard sign.

"What the hell's the armor of God then?" Beneath her ribs her heart was racing, because in her skull she was thinking: *maybe Hannah figured something out. Maybe Hannah found the key. Maybe Hannah's going to save us all, I always knew she was brilliant—*

"No clue. Wish I had one."

"Do you, actually?" Selene cocked her head; a well of dizziness swirled between her ears, thanks to the hunger and the sleeplessness and the worry, the all-consuming, never-sleeping worry. "I mean, Hannah's armor of God. Say it's something that vaporizes the threat of paracontagions. Something we can all just put on to make us safe from them, forever. Would you even want that? It's not like you actually *want* things to get better."

"That's not at all true. Getting well is exactly what I want for all of us. It's *all* I want, in fact."

"Your version of getting well is what a drug addict would say about one last hit before rehab."

"Actually, Selene, I would argue that's *your* version. You and your friends at the PMA are the ones that are always kicking the truth down the road."

"What the fuck are you talking about, what truth?" Selene leaned further over the table, making the bouncer-cop shift in his boots. "The truth that we would all be better off dead?"

RED SKIES IN THE MORNING

Keel did not answer any of these questions. In fact he didn't say anything for a long while—just stared her in the eye with the intensity of a devoted lover, like he was trying to decode tea leaves beneath the brown murk of her irises. And when he finally spoke, what he said was horrible: "We're not that different, you and I. We're both just trying to help people get to wherever they're trying to go. That's all I'm doing, in the end."

※

On her walk back from the train station, she felt a buzz in her pocket. Her fingers went prickly with an anticipation that was by now familiar, but it was just Frank. "Sorry to bug you with this, but I'm cleaning up incident reports for the week and I'm getting a flag that your ID was used to access a paracontagion shell a few days ago. It's probably nothing, but you know I gotta log something in the system. Were you . . . checking it for something, or . . . "

Hot iron poured down her spine and turned her limbs to steel. "How many days ago?"

"Uh . . . six."

"Was it my old ID?" Selene clenched her now-metallic fist. "The stolen ID?"

"Hang on just a sec, let me check . . . "

But there was no point. It had to be. Frank's voice trailed off into the void and all of a sudden she wasn't simply worried anymore. She was *panicked*. She was *enraged*. And whatever Hannah had done—whatever chain reaction of shit Hannah had started—she had to stop her. Now.

She jammed her finger into her phone as she summoned Hannah's number to call her for the twelfth time in six days. "Hannah. Did you take my ID? Did you do something with a paracontagion in the vault? Because that's a federal crime, Hannah, it's incredibly serious, you could go to jail for . . . "

Selene stopped herself. What did Hannah care about

breaking the law and going to jail? Hannah would blow that off as worldly nonsense, a basic pedestrian concern. She had always been impossible to discipline because she lived so thoroughly inside the wild world of Hannah-logic . . . with one exception. One memory that Selene didn't dwell on often, because it made her queasy with guilt. They had been young—orphaned already, but still young. Hannah had snuck off with Bex, lying to her and Ruth about where they were going; when they realized the girls had taken flashlights and hiking shoes, Selene called Hannah and threatened her with the worst thing she could think of, knowing how deeply Hannah valued a bed to come home to, especially after their mother died: changing the locks. Hannah had returned from the abandoned hospital they'd tried to break into immediately, apologetic and terrified.

"So you can either come home and explain yourself, *tonight,* or you can just not bother coming home at all. You hear me? Tonight. Or I'm done."

After hanging up she stared at the blinking length of the call on the black screen for several seconds, trying to keep from dropping the phone on the sidewalk in her shock. Her horror. *Please don't let that be the last thing I say to her.*

Hand still shaking, she slid the phone back into her coat pocket. If Hannah was being held captive somewhere—if Hannah was God forbid dead—that voicemail didn't matter. But if Hannah was on a suicide mission, hopefully, it would matter. Hopefully it would work.

>>>>><<<<<

Most of the nights that Hannah had been missing, Selene had taken a sleep-aid before going to bed. She had too much experience with familial loss not to know that left to her own anxieties, she would stay awake reading message boards, replaying old conversations and acting out new ones, guaranteeing that she'd be an incoherent asshole the next day. At least her parents had not paid the price for her groggy incompetence; at least their fates had already been written. But Hannah's fate was not sealed. Hannah needed her clear-headed. Hence the sedative.

But as she marked off the "6" on the dry-erase board, she knew that tonight she needed to stay awake. Hannah had one full run of daylight left. Now that she had told her in no uncertain terms that it was her last chance to come home, Selene needed to be up and waiting in case Hannah had lost her key, in case Hannah was in a state of immediate crisis, in case . . . in case there was any possibility that Hannah-logic might actually work. Selene put the kettle on and then sat at the kitchen counter, willing her sister to appear tonight.

The clock took the world to ten, and then to eleven, and Selene whipped out her phone, ostensibly to check if anyone had messaged her with information, but truthfully to give her brain some gristle to chew on other than the creeping second hand of the clock.

There was nothing worth chasing down in her messages she'd received following her post about Hannah being missing. Statements of pity and passive concern from high school friends, former co-workers, a distant aunt who offered nothing but a prayer. She switched to her feed instead, and after a couple listless swipes found herself listening to a monologue by someone she assumed to be a high school student.

"So as a lot of you know, I have been dealing with a crazy stalker for the past, I don't know, three months. This woman is absolutely horrible. She's accusing me of being racist, classist, privileged, like I don't even know what all she's made up in her head. It's like she's running down this government-sponsored list of 'bad things about people' and deciding they all apply to me, like I don't even know! Anyway, I've looked her up, and she is a total zero. Adds absolutely nothing to society, all she does is stalk people online and leave nasty comments. And I was getting really frustrated, you know, like it was really starting to take a toll on my mental health. And then I realized: wait. Someone is finally stepping up and getting rid of all these brainwashed losers. And that's Zombie Killer! So Zombie Killer, please, please, if you see this message: please take out Natasha Greenfield. Or, you know, check her out first and see if she meets your qualifications. But I'm pretty sure she will. Love ya!"

Selene clicked on the profile. The young lady—who called herself only Cherry—had graduated from the same bunker-esque high school that she and Hannah had attended. But Cherry was at least several years younger than Hannah—and seemed intent on making herself appear even younger—and had a lot more followers than either of them. She was very pretty. She wore a lot of red. #teamzombiekiller, her profile read. And a more recent video had been posted.

"So I guess some of you were a little upset about my last video. This person"—a comment bubbled up briefly next to her pigtails—"even said he hopes Zombie Killer comes after me, since I'm being so, quote, disrespectful to human life. And I just want to say . . . if Zombie Killer decides that I'm a zero and I should get got, I'm okay with that. I'm ready to go. Love you guys!" Cherry blew a fuchsia kiss into the camera, to the giggles of her off-screen friends.

The video restarted, but just as Cherry's mouth stretched into an unflattering grimace at the word "upset," Selene hit pause. She'd heard something. A soft cluster of knocks, barely hard enough to shake the deadbolt chain. *Hannah.*

She slid off the stool and stumbled, practically half-drunk in her state of stone-cold anxiety, toward the door, murmuring Hannah's name. It came off her lips in a warble when she pulled the door open, her soul painfully helpless with need, "Hannah –"

There was no Hannah. There was no anyone. "Jim?"

RED SKIES IN THE MORNING

She couldn't think of anyone else who might knock on her door, but directly to her right she saw the door to the emergency stairwell swinging closed, as if someone had just flown through. "Ruth?" she pathetically suggested, although it immediately sounded ludicrous.

And then, from the corner to her left, came a voice: "No."

Before she had time to turn her head, someone had grabbed it—not gently like a bowling ball but by a big chunk of her hair, creating a jolt so sudden that her reflexive scream evaporated into a thin yip. She knew, technically, that she was being whipped back into the apartment, knew because her eyes saw the walls spinning, but the only thought that managed to blip through her brain before the darkness won was: *I'm going to die.*

⫸⫷

Selene slowly became conscious of a repeating buzz. Like a trapped, dying fly—but it was not a fly. It was her phone. Like her, it was face-down on the floor. Like her, it was trying in vain to turn over. Unlike her, it hadn't been silenced with duct tape—it was humming, vibrating. Not from a phone call or a text or a meaningless notification from her useless social media app. No, this noise was longer. Steadier.

The paracontagion radar.

She jerked her head toward the duffel bag that the man had carried in after her and set—much more gently than he had her—in the middle of the living room. That had to be it.

It had to be him.

The mountainous man who was Video Man noticed her struggles and the way her face was pointing and promptly picked up her phone. Its red glow lit up his head in the dark—he must have turned out the lights in the apartment—and what she saw wasn't a face but a plastic shield. A helmet. "Warning: Paracontagion Detected," he read aloud. His voice was muffled, but she remembered the message the app shot up from her visit to Rock the Horizon. He slowly looked at Selene. "It's right. This is some smart tech you paperclips have. Smart tech for stupid people."

He shut the phone off and put it in his pocket. "I won't keep it," he promised. "I know you probably have a tracker on it. But I want to make sure I have your undivided attention tonight. I have something I want to show you."

Selene made a sound that came out like a low whine. Her fear was instinctive, biological, oddly embarrassing—if the world was fucked and Hannah might not even be in it, why tremble before death? Where was her relief? Had her years of working at the PMA left her so terrified of a little tear-through, a little geyser of blood? All she knew was that when Video Man stepped toward the duffel bag, she was begging for time.

And she got it. Video Man was interrupted by the unmistakable sound of a key turning in a lock.

Light from the hallway poured in around a small silhouette. Selene recognized it. She would recognize it anywhere. The fly-away strands of hair. The awkward side ponytail. The chunky, clunky shoes. The stocky trenchcoat procured at a thrift store, fitted with so many pockets that its owner never needed to carry a purse. The trenchcoat that had been missing for six days now.

Hannah had come home. The voicemail had worked. And now, Hannah too was going to die.

Selene was quiet. Utterly still. She was hoping that if Hannah thought she was already dead, she wouldn't step foot into the apartment. Instead she would run, horrified, for help. Maybe if Hannah ran fast enough, she would get help in time to save Selene—but that was incidental. Hannah just had to run fast enough not to be caught. Down the stairwell. Into the lobby. There would be reception there. There would be people.

"Come in," Video Man said. "Come in, don't be shy. You want to see your sister?"

RED SKIES IN THE MORNING

Hannah's pause felt eternal, but it was probably only thirty seconds. When Hannah paused like that Selene knew that she was thinking—it had been a point of contention with some of Hannah's denser teachers who simply didn't understand how deeply and thoroughly Hannah processed—though what thoughts possibly could have led her to come inside the apartment and shut the door were a mystery to Selene.

"Good girl. Now give me your phone," said Video Man. "That's all I want."

It was not, of course, all he wanted.

Hannah took her phone out of her coat and whipped it like a skipping stone over the carpet. Video Man kicked it toward his duffel bag, once again praising Hannah for her cooperation, her complacence, and then leapt toward her. He was all towering force in that moment, all mass and weight and power, but Hannah made no attempt to fight him.

She talked about the killer that's running around infecting people with paracontagions, Keel had said. *It upset her to see people cheering him on.*

Selene tried to lasso Hannah's gaze, so she could pull it somehow toward the door, toward fighting—a knee to the crotch, nails in the eyes, anything—and toward freedom. But Hannah wouldn't look at her. In fact Hannah had that stern, missile-locked-on-a-target look that she got when she was really determined to do well on an exam, except here there was neither time nor proctor, nothing except death.

>>>><<<<

"Why her?" Hannah asked, just before Video Man put tape over her mouth. He paused, as if taken aback. Was he surprised that she hadn't spent her last few seconds of speech crying *please,* begging for their freedom, promising that they wouldn't tell anyone if he just let them go? Selene wasn't surprised. That was Hannah-logic in the flesh.

Though no amount of experience with Hannah-logic had prepared her for how supernaturally calm Hannah was in this moment. Was she dreaming? Was Hannah dreaming?

"Because she's a zombie," Video Man said. "I take no joy in this. I was so happy to see her come to the meeting yesterday. I thought that maybe she was starting to come to her senses. But nothing sank in, did it?" He shook his giant helmeted head at Selene, as she wondered: meeting yesterday? "No. It's not that simple overriding the programming of a zero. It's baked in really, really deep."

"I'm a zero," Hannah said, uncertainly at first, and then louder: "I'm a zero! I'm a zombie! Way more than her! All I do is fold clothes at a chain store and play stupid games on my phone! I have a worthless college degree that I can't do anything with! I literally add nothing to society!"

Selene yelled for Hannah to shut up, but owing to the duct tape and her own insignificance, no one seemed to hear her.

Video Man issued his rusted, audio-tuned rebuttal: "You're just a wage slave. It's not your fault. It's the world you were dealt. But there is nothing—nothing at all on God's green Earth—more worthless than someone who helps the government corrode our society."

And then Selene remembered: the only place she went yesterday that would have qualified as a "meeting" was the rec center where the Bluejay Society set up their cookies and folding chairs. But Video Man was too tall, too big, to be Hugh Bolduan.

"Wow. You know what?" Hannah narrowed her eyes and tilted her head, and for a moment she brought to mind the cool cruel girls from Edenvale who used to call Hannah a wet rag in high school because she was an orphan, and a sensitive one at that. "You're a fucking zero."

Video Man rotated his head back toward Hannah.

"Yeah, you. Who's more of a zero than some piece of shit who breaks into women's homes and plays them a little fucking video because he doesn't even have the balls to kill them with his bare hands? What is the point of you? Oh, you rely on some bored teenagers on the internet to tell you who's a zero, who's a zombie? What's more fucking zombie behavior than that? You're getting played, dude. You're getting *rocked*."

The helmet made it impossible to read Video Man's face, but his actions—two big strides toward Hannah and a grab of her ponytail to jerk her to her feet—summed up his reaction. He dragged Hannah to the couch and then went back to the duffel bag in the center of the room.

Until he pulled the camcorder out of the duffel bag, every moment in the last six days of Selene's life—the spare vacant moments standing at the printshop waiting for flyers to print, the shuteye that passed for sleep, every soul-sucking conversation—had revolved exclusively around Hannah. Her little sister. Her family. Her engine, her purpose, the single most important being in her life. And then the camcorder came out and all of that just erased. Like someone had taken an eraser to the dry erase board that was her head and started scribbling the "play" button on this camcorder instead.

Looking back, the memory would be unbearable, on the verge of unbelievable. How, when she and Hannah were so close to their deaths, could her brain have gone so blind? But that was because she would have tried to forget the way that camcorder, pregnant with a paracontagion, had made her feel: like a child. Not the real child she'd been but the mythical child-self who lived in a perpetual state of curiosity and innocence.

This camcorder wasn't one of those cybernetic-looking monstrosities vomiting cables that news crews carried around. It was harmless, with the cute, rounded lines and simple buttons of a toy. Adorable like an easy bake oven ready to heat up a slab of pretend cookie dough. Or in this case, to play a pretend movie. And she just wanted, so much, to watch it.

NADIA BULKIN

Selene couldn't really move. But for this camcorder, for the play movie inside it, her body tried. She heaved herself toward her newfound holy grail, eyes fixed on the beautiful flat button with a triangle pointing rightward, onward to infinity. She could hit it with her forehead if she aimed her body correctly. Or maybe her nose, if she hit it hard enough to break it. What about her tongue, was her tongue a muscle?

A sharp pain in her shoulder broke through the paracontagion fog; Video Man had kicked her away from the camcorder and was picking it up so he could take it away. Away to where her sister sat. Away to seal her sister's fate. "I know how much you want it," he said, "but that's not for you anymore. Maybe you'll get it the old-fashioned way. Thank your sister for that."

The pang of shame was deep enough to scar.

❯❯❯❮❮❮

Video Man put the camcorder on the coffee table in front of Hannah, angling the viewer up toward her face. An uninvited memory hit Selene of watching her mother hold a makeup compact open in front of a six-year-old Hannah, telling her to look at her reflection to help her figure out where the lipstick needed to go. Hannah turning around afterward to proudly show Selene her clown-mouth as their mother giggled. Selene remembered thinking that Hannah looked deranged, like a feral child who'd torn into a wriggling small animal, but she also remembered smiling despite her revulsion, because it was the first time since their father died that Selene had heard their mother laugh.

"Here you go," Video Man said. "A special show, just for you."

Selene's cry of anguish went unremarked upon. With his helmet twisted away from Hannah and the camcorder viewer so as not to risk accidental exposure to the paracontagion within, Video Man pressed a button that must have been play and then quickly took several strides back.

RED SKIES IN THE MORNING

The first news reports about Video Man had led Selene to believe that this man had the cold sensibility of a contract killer, that his motives were as bloodless and detached as his murders. But now that Selene could watch him watch Hannah, she knew that wasn't true. This was what he wanted: to see the artificial light hit Hannah's face, trapping Hannah in its beam, and to know that she would die. No, to know that *Hannah knew* she would die. He wanted to look down upon her from his royal balcony and see the animal inside her—devoid of value, purposeless—dissolve into mortal terror.

The strange thing was that Hannah never actually looked afraid. Although it made no sense—although her eyes were fixed on whatever flickering video was being played on the camcorder viewer—her face remained utterly neutral. Unphased. Blank, even. Almost like she was *bored,* and Selene would have guessed that she was perhaps submerged in shock except for the fact that her eyes then slowly closed.

It wasn't possible. The studies had been conclusive: Not even someone who was administered sedatives through an IV could close their eyes to a paracontagion. Their hold on the human body was simply too strong to—

"Open your eyes!" Video Man was shouting at Hannah. "Open your eyes, bitch!"

Hannah did not obey him. With her head slowly lolling like a balloon caught on a stray gust of wind, she did not even seem to be fully awake. Video Man leaned over the camcorder to grab her by the shoulders, to shake her, and as he was doing so—still cursing out Hannah the whole time—Hannah mumbled something very quietly. She was slurring, but Selene thought she heard:

"don't look lee"

And then Hannah opened her eyes.

Hannah had told her not to look, but from her angle on the floor she couldn't see anyway—couldn't see anything except the bright white tractor beams shining from Hannah's eyes.

NADIA BULKIN

Video Man had stopped moving as soon as those beams hit his visor. One of his heels was still up, making the arch of that foot tremble under the weight of all that pressure. His fists had unraveled and given way to a shake that reminded Selene of her mother's thalidomide treatment—but it wasn't an effect of any medication. It was simply a symptom of the brain rewiring itself around the threads of the paracontagion that had latched onto it. That was why they strapped people in at the office; to stop flailing people from hurting themselves.

There was no protecting Video Man. Neither from the tremors nor from the video that was somehow using Hannah as a flickering projector; or was it a mirror? Video Man's helmet might have helped him fight the urge to press play on that camcorder while he was alone, but a loose paracontagion could not be stopped in its search for a host—it could sear through metal, through plastic, through soil, through flesh. Such was the wild ferocity of a paracontagion's desperation to live. It would burrow at light-speed through any earthly substance to sink its psychic teeth, tick-like, into its host, and once it latched it would hold unless another host pressed play.

Which meant that a paracontagion would resist eviction by another paracontagion, too.

Mine, the thing inside Hannah was saying by way of those tractor beams. *This one's mine.*

Driven by an urge to self-destruction that not even the world's top scientists could understand, Video Man's unraveled fists rose as if to receive the word of God and unbuckled the chin strap of his helmet, then lifted it off completely. Fear usually froze a human body. But Selene had once heard a Muslim client explain that when Judgment Day came, God could compel the body to testify in spite of itself. To move in favor of the truth.

The loonies with megaphones who hung around downtown always did say that paracontagions had been sent by God.

RED SKIES IN THE MORNING

>>><<<

When the video ended—when the last of the headlights shot from Hannah's skull and into the blank void of Video Man's eyes—he collapsed in front of the television. Hannah, too, slumped over—just tilted over onto the couch cushions like she'd been unplugged.

Selene wormed toward Hannah with enough vigor to scrape off the top layer of her skin, slowing only once she got close enough to see that Hannah was still breathing. It was only the smallest of favors. Yet there was nowhere to go now but on. She braced her core and her legs against the couch and awkwardly wrestled herself into a sitting position so she could begin to saw her way through the duct tape around her wrists.

Hannah slept through most of the sawing. She slept through Selene's short crying spell, through Video Man's nightmare moans—it was a car alarm that woke her, from Mazzy Street below.

"The Armor of God," Hannah mumbled with a small, self-satisfied smile—as smug as Hannah could get, anyway. "People have tried it in China but I didn't know if it would really work."

Selene ripped her wrists free and started prying the tape off her mouth.

"I still don't know what would happen if you were by yourself. If you could hold both of them like that until one of them completed its lifecycle or someone else showed up and took one from you or if one of them gets destroyed or if *you* get destroyed or . . . "

Selene cut her off with a fierce hug that Hannah immediately nuzzled into. "The blue in your drawing," Selene said, her voice cracking with thirst, "the thing that's going to save us. That was another paracontagion, wasn't it?" Hannah didn't speak, but she felt her nod. "When?"

"Last Monday night."

She started picking the tape off Hannah's wrists—delicately at first, then desperately. "What time, exactly?" She knew the time would have burned into Hannah's brain. The time of exposure always did. Even when people were denied a clock in the room they were exposed in, studies showed that they emerged knowing exactly when their seven days would end.

"Little after three a.m." Of course it would be during the witching hour. That was just like Hannah. And about an hour later, she'd liked a post that Aidan had made for the last time. "Like. Three minutes past. Ow. Thanks."

Selene didn't know how to ask her next question. Was it who? What? Was it exactly which paracontagion, out of the city's approximately two hundred documented psychic monsters, she had chosen to infect herself with? Because Selene could approximate the how. She suspected, unhappily, that she knew the why. What came out of her mouth was a wispy "wh" sound.

Hannah, fortunately, knew what she couldn't find the words to ask. "That old man," she said, shaking out her wrists. "From your office. Monday morning. I asked him if he was waiting on a path and he said that he didn't have anybody."

Mr. Kudo. The good Samaritan. Her good Hannah. But even good Samaritans were rescued from the paracontagions they'd picked up in the PMA era and if all Hannah wanted to do was volunteer as a path, there would have been no need to steal a PMA ID. Whatever—at least they were fighting on her turf now. The T Street Office. The vault. The official pathing program. A bit of blood returned to Selene's extremities as the freeze around her heart unclenched just enough to feel something other than terror, to get just a little bit angry instead.

"We would have found somebody for him, Hannah," she hissed, squeezing Hannah's shoulders. "You didn't have to do this."

"I did it for myself," Hannah insisted, eyes sparkling

with what Selene knew, to her horror, was genuine excitement. "I mean, I picked him because he looked so sad and I wanted to help him. But this was something that *I* wanted to do. *Me.*"

8. Day Seven

Selene banged on the door of apartment 507, hoping Jim was home. Hoping she wasn't interrupting a date. She yelled his name when five seconds passed without him answering, slamming her palm against the wood, until she heard the industrial clicks of a latch coming undone and Jim appeared in a t-shirt and boxers, squinting, taking out his ear plugs. "Selene . . . ?"

"You have to come with me. To my apartment. Bring your phone, you need to call the cops."

He didn't ask if he had time to get dressed. He could see by the blood and the bruising, most likely, that he didn't. "Um . . . is everything okay? You don't look okay."

Everything is fucked, she wanted to snap in reply, *the world is fucked.* But she held her tongue and silently led him to apartment 501, where his surprise at Hannah's presence on a kitchen stool was quickly outgunned by the shock of seeing Video Man tied up on the floor. With the lights on, she knew who he theoretically was now: the man in the windbreaker who told her to eat the cookies at the Bluejay Society. The man with gym teacher vibes. But to Selene and Hannah, and now to Jim, he was simply Video Man, the Zombie Killer, murderer of people in their city.

"What happened to him?"

"Shock, I guess. He got exposed." A beat of silence passed between them, and she added, "Pathing accident."

"Huh?"

"Look, I need you to stay here and call the cops and watch him until they get here. If he wakes up just . . . I don't know, feel free to hit him. If you want."

Selene wriggled into her coat, checked her purse for her keys, and turned to the ruin that was the apartment. Jim was standing next to the kitchen counter dumbly, holding his unlocked phone like it was an alien object. On the other side of the counter, Hannah was sitting in a state of what looked like catatonia, staring at Video Man. For a second Selene wondered how she would ever be able to live there again, only to remember that there was no future beyond the next twenty-three hours. "Hannah," Selene barked, and her sister's shoulders jolted. "Let's go."

Jim was able to un-pause himself when Hannah slid off her stool. "Wait. Where are you going?"

Selene shook her head. "I have to help Hannah."

Hannah gave Jim a goodbye hug as she squeezed past him. Jim froze up—Selene doubted they'd ever exchanged more than a few sentences before—and then gingerly patted Hannah's back in a gesture of timeless, silent assurance: the promise that *it'll all be okay*.

※※※

They had gotten supremely lucky: Hannah had exposed herself to a known, catalogued paracontagion instead of some black-market fly-by-night. She must have used Selene's ID to tamper with its shell somehow—scratched off its bar code, switched it with another?—but the shell had to still be in the vault, somewhere. Alarms would have gone off if it had passed the metal detectors. Which meant Hannah could be saved.

Hannah didn't resist, but she did have to be jerked along. She was saying something, not in her shrieky protest voice—so Selene knew she wasn't literally, immediately dying—but in her mildly exasperated, sis-is-being-crazy voice. Something about *it's no use,* or *there's no point*: something that slid off Selene's adrenaline-stoked lizard brain like water off a stone.

The night shift guy—Mark Something—accepted Selene's explanation for their presence without question, especially after she produced her ID. "Have at it," he said, eyes returning to the blue glow of his computer screen so fast that he didn't see Selene reach out and grab his collar until she'd already forced him to jerk his head, gasping.

"Fucking pay attention," she hissed. "I could be anybody. *She* could be anybody." Behind her, Hannah was hiding her hands in her pockets, looking sheepish and embarrassed—looking her age, for the first time tonight. "Remember her?"

Mark Something tried to size up Hannah the best he could given Selene's hold on his neck, but she was just another twenty-three-year-old, wasn't she, one of the city's many wandering young. She didn't even have any of the common distinctive markings. Just a faceless girl with a messy ponytail that couldn't even flap in the wind. Everything notable about her—let alone the fact that she was now bonded to a paracontagion—was invisible. "No," he choked out. "Sorry."

"Come on, let him go," Hannah hissed. "It's not his fault."

Of course not. When the cops interviewed Selene about this after—or when Selene died and was brought before God's judgment, which might come first given the pace of investigative work in this city—Selene would be able to honestly say that what happened to Hannah was no one's fault but Hannah's. Everyone else had acted within their individual spheres of responsibility.

At the vault, Selene glared at her sister as she swiped them in with her new ID; the stolen ID had been disconnected from the system immediately after her new one was activated. Hannah didn't apologize, and Selene was thankful for that. She wouldn't have known what to do if Hannah had wished her exposure back; the sorrow would have paralyzed her, she expected. It was easier now that Hannah was here to be angry, to slide into their old pattern of her trying to reign Hannah and her Hannah-logic in while Hannah fearlessly flew onward with arms open in defiance. She knew how to be the annoyed older sister. She didn't know how to be the mourning older sister. Barely even knew how to comfort, she realized.

She wondered if Hannah knew that. She wondered if that was why Hannah was holding her head up, talking calmly and obliquely, expressing neither remorse nor fear: a heartbreaking attempt to be what her big sister needed, even now. God knew Hannah was always three steps ahead of her.

Inside the vault's control room, Selene looked up the location of Hannah's paracontagion using Mr. Kudo's information. Capsule AX 39.5. She couldn't resist double-clicking on the entry in the chain that followed Ryosuke Kudo: *Anna Williams,* it said. *Monday, 3:03 A.M.* The case had been assigned to Mitchell—famously negligent, never met a deadline he didn't like to run up against. Hannah had probably heard her bitch about him; had she made that assignment herself?

"Aren't you supposed to not take on any paracontagions yourself?" Hannah asked from the door, her voice dream-like, semi-sedated. "I thought that was policy. To protect you guys."

"You and I both know I don't care about that right now. Come on."

Technically, as a non-authorized person Hannah was not supposed to enter the bowels of the vault. She was supposed to stay in her assigned viewing booth and wait for her assigned paracontagion to be delivered to her in an aluminum capsule via pneumatic tube. But at this point, the greater risk to Selene felt like letting Hannah out of her sight. She took her by the elbow and marched her down the vault's fluorescent white rows until they got to AX 39.5, which Selene popped open with a quick push of her thumb.

There was a photo of Hannah inside. It was a few years old; she actually looked happy instead of merely windswept. It was a bright blue day and she was standing—where else?—on the pier.

RED SKIES IN THE MORNING

Other than that, the capsule was empty. "I don't understand," Selene said, and whirled around to grab the only person that would know. What she said wasn't quite right, because there was a part of this slow-rolling disaster that she did understand, now: capsules were designed with viewing panels and remote controls, layers of plastic separation that prevented paths from coming into direct contact with the paracontagion they were exposing themselves to, and Hannah must have used her ID to open the capsule from the back and grab the paracontagion itself. What she didn't understand was how to answer the only question that mattered now: *how to save Hannah?*

"I told you," Hannah said, "it's no use. The shell's gone. It's been gone." She tried to smile as she absently nodded toward the capsule. "I thought it would be funny to put me in there instead."

Inside Selene was screaming: *enough, enough with the cryptic riddles, enough dodging, enough games. This is your life.* But because she knew that would only invite more puzzle-making that neither of them had time for, she played along. "Gone, *where? Where* is the shell?"

"Inside me." Hannah looked down at herself with the apparent fondness of an expected mother, but instead of touching her stomach she tugged gingerly at her sweater, as if its soft threads were prickling her skin. "I ate it."

She was too tired, and the first image that came to Selene's head—Hannah tearing into a video cassette with her teeth, spitting out shards of black plastic—was too absurd. Selene laughed. "What do you mean you ate it, ate how . . ."

Only then did the image in her head begin to warp into something that was still absurd, but not quite as far beyond the realms of human possibility: Hannah folding up a picture like one of her origami yachts but smaller, and stuffing it down the back of her throat.

"The paracontagion was in a polaroid." With her chin down, Hannah shyly tucked a strand of hair behind her ear, a gesture of nervous embarrassment. "I asked the old man I took it from if it was a photo. I would have had to ask someone else if it wasn't . . . "

Selene pushed that last detail aside. She would not revisit it until later, until after the seven days had passed and she was waking up at odd hours of the night despite her sleeping pills, choked not by fear but a sense of boundless unease, a discontent that would come to blanket her waking life like snow. At this moment, all she could think of was where, exactly, the polaroid was sitting in Hannah's digestive tract. A hospital, she was thinking, but would surgery even accomplish anything? It had been seven days. The shell had surely been destroyed by now, and—

"Wait. Wait, no, you couldn't have. The shells can't be destroyed, you'd have . . . you'd have blown up the whole office."

"That's only if the paracontagion hasn't linked with somebody." Hannah shrugged. "I've read the studies. The Overlook Experiment and all that."

"Shit." Hannah was right about that. "Fuck."

"Selene, listen to me. It's okay. This is what I wanted. I wanted it to end with me."

In the first days of the paracontagion plague, before there was a PMA, before Adam Ramiel dragged down a movie theater full of people and before Greg Bolduan came apart in his bathroom, before "pathing" had entered the lexicon, the government had considered a "you break it you buy it" approach to paracontagions. It would be so much easier, after all, to simply destroy the shell to prevent further spread and allow the first person exposed to die, taking the paracontagion with them. Selene didn't know exactly how the consensus shifted. Maybe a Senator had stumbled on a paracontagion while jogging in the woods; maybe the futurists pointed out that writing off a million citizens annually as collateral damage was an election killer. Whatever the reason, this sort of self-sacrifice wasn't supposed to happen anymore.

RED SKIES IN THE MORNING

Because the world awaited Hannah. Selene had made sure of it. Even if it meant becoming a pathing agent after college instead of a meteorologist, even if it meant spending her evenings listening to the ramblings of an overstimulated teenager instead of bonding with her friends, even if meant burying her own grief in a shallow grave. She had to give Hannah a fighting chance.

"Goddamnit," she moaned, "you were supposed to be the hopeful one."

The smile Hannah gave her in return was withered. Diminished. Hope could take its toll on a human psyche; that was why Selene had always avoided it. "I *am* hopeful," Hannah said, in a voice that was not so much defensive as thoughtful, nostalgic. "Now I just hope not to be in this world anymore."

>>><<<

They went to the pier. It was not so much a decision as a subconscious movement they both made once they entered the train station, a joint surrender to the route they'd traveled every summer weekend as children. "I'm surprised you didn't already go there this week," Selene said as the train jostled east, replacing the high-gloss office buildings of Pool Street with stocky warehouses and dark apartment complexes puffing smoke in the morning cold. "It's the first place I looked for you."

"I was saving it," Hannah said earnestly. "For today."

There was a sweetness in that thought, Selene knew, but the aftertaste was bitter. If Hannah was dying of cancer Selene would have said it was absolutely perfect to have her ashes scattered overlooking the water she loved the most. Hell, if Hannah was dying of a paracontagion that someone else had inflicted upon her, Selene would have broken them out of the hospital to make sure that she could spend her final moments on the pier. But this had been a choice made free of pressure, without duress. A needless sacrifice. A causeless martyrdom.

NADIA BULKIN

"I would have come back for you even if you hadn't left me that voicemail," Hannah promised, leaning in close as the train pulled in to the last station on the line. "I would have wanted to be with you today, no matter what."

That was her lip, wasn't it, trembling? "Thank you."

⤜⤚⤞

They got lobster rolls at Little Father and ice cream cones at Justine's. Then they went to the arcade and spent all of Selene's change playing Tekken, the way they used to: Selene as cold older sister Nina Williams, Hannah as unpredictable younger sister Anna Williams. Selene was fully intending to lose every battle, and for the most part didn't have to try—she hadn't played in years, and even at her best she was nowhere near as good as Hannah—but after she accidentally K-O'd Anna Williams she looked over at her sister and saw that Hannah was staring as if hypnotized at the red exit sign, the joystick idle in her hand.

"What is it?" Selene asked, but in her soul she already knew. Mr. Kudo had talked about this, when he came in to see her a week ago today. There was a "she." There was "red."

"She . . . " Hannah started, before her voice gave.

"She lives in red light?" Selene suggested, glumly.

"Yes," Hannah said, eyes almost comically huge. "How did you know?"

"It's in the case file." A little part of Selene wanted to figure out who "she" was, this being that would kill her sister in a few hours. Or maybe she just thought she *should* want to know. Families of the murdered always craved this knowledge, didn't they? *Answers.* But this would be like wanting to know exactly which knife had slit her sister's throat, exactly which bullet had nestled its way into her brain. She-Who-Lived-in-Red-Light was just a machine. Just a tool. The answers were in Hannah. "And the man you took it from . . . he talked about it, too."

RED SKIES IN THE MORNING

"I've felt her coming a little bit closer everyday," Hannah whispered. "I can't actually see her face, but it's like I . . . I can feel her. I can *feel* the shape she holds. Or maybe it's the space she pushes out? She's very strong. She's very . . . " she took a big inward hiss, "angry."

Selene sighed. It sounded like Hannah wanted to share. "What happened to her?"

Hannah was still watching the door with the stillness of a deer listening for the footsteps of a hunter. If she stared hard enough, Selene could almost trick her eyes into seeing a shadow coalesce below the buzzing sign—but it was only ever a trick, conjured up from a hundred dime-a-dozen horror movies. She could pretend, but every paracontagion path was walked alone.

"She's not a victim," Hannah said, turning her head back to Tekken. "She had victims, I think." She jammed her palm into the button that would start a new game. "Come on, Lee. It's starting."

※※※

They spent the rest of the afternoon walking up and down the shoreline, pausing to pick up seashells and bottle caps and errant pieces of plastic that Hannah collected in a plastic bag. "You should turn this into a frame," she'd say, or, "Put this on a keychain," and though Selene wished Hannah would stop talking in the future tense, she would nod along. She'd say she would.

And when the sky started to glow and the temperature started to turn, they commandeered beach chairs to watch the sunset and sat there sipping root beer floats, the number of words passing between them dropping with the sun.

Selene checked the time on her phone. She tried to do it quickly, but Hannah noticed. "Even now," she said, "You hate waiting. Even if it's waiting for my death."

"No, that's . . . " Selene looked up to metaphysically grab Hannah by the eyes, assure her that dear God, *no*, she was *not* willing the hours to go faster—but Hannah was smiling around her straw.

"You know why you hate waiting? Cuz waiting forces you to sit in the moment. Keeps you from rushing onto the next thing, the next thing, the next thing . . ."

And what *would* be the next thing, really, after the paracontagion forced its way out of Hannah's body? What was actually left in the hereafter?

"The next thing, the right thing . . ."

It was so funny to hear Hannah say that she rushed to do "the right thing" like Hannah hadn't always had an instinctive grasp on the platonic ideal correct answer, on a school test or a social dilemma or a trivia game show. "Hey. Mom told me to look out for you. Which let me tell you, I had no idea what the fuck I was doing, okay? So I was like, let me get a planner, let me make a grocery list, let me figure out when these freaking bills are due . . ."

She was trying to be funny, and thankfully Hannah laughed, a deep belly laugh that Selene told herself to commit to memory. "Hard to imagine you ever not having your shit perfectly, annoyingly together."

Selene shook her head, coughing root beer, remembering yelling at herself in the toilet stall of the café where she used to work when she failed to pay a bill on time and got hit with a late fee that she would have wanted to spend on a weekend beach outing, something to remind Hannah of their pre-orphan lives. "I was just faking it. Think I'm still faking it, actually."

"I think that's everybody. Everybody's a human who doesn't think they're human enough. Even people like that video asshole. I bet that's part of why he was taking it out on other people. Had so much doubt about himself that the only way he could feel better was convincing himself that at least he was more human than those *other* people."

Pure unfiltered Hannah-logic. All natural. Straight from the source. She couldn't write it down, couldn't explain it to anyone else, but when Hannah was the one talking, a small and fragile part of her—a part that spent most of its time asleep—understood.

"Can I ask you something?" she asked. "Why did you call it the Armor of God?"

Hannah cocked her head in question.

"Why God, I mean."

"Oh." Hannah turned her gaze back to the gently-churning ocean. Selene had originally worried that She-Who-Lives-in-Red-Light would ruin Hannah's sunset, but thick clouds seemed to have mercifully shielded Hannah from the worst of it. "I didn't mean some creature in the sky. I meant God as the scattered human soul, you know, the God that lives in all of us. I've told you my theory of where paracontagions come from, right?"

"No." At least she didn't think so. Or had she just not been listening? Selene winced. "Or maybe you did, and I don't remember. Tell me again. Please."

She could tell from Hannah's face that yes, she had been told, and no, she hadn't been listening. She could also tell that Hannah didn't care.

"That's okay. I don't expect you to remember all the shit I say. But I do think I'm right on this one—I think they come from us. I think we make them. Not intentionally. Just spontaneously. In moments of suffering or . . . I don't know, duress. They just manifest in this . . . storm of pain. I think some of them come from things that are really old, ancient, just lingering bundles of bad energy that finally got this outlet."

"Like Sarah."

Hannah's mouth curled into a smile. "Yeah. Like Sarah. But I think there's probably also people walking around right now who don't know they've made paracontagions, in their darkest moments. Who don't know they've killed people."

Like us? Selene wondered.

"Anyway, I think that's why they don't slow down. And they won't stop showing up. Because we're not going to stop hurting each other, you know? We even use paracontagions to do it. It's like it just comes naturally."

A cold gust of salty air moved in from the ocean and Selene wrapped her arms around her stomach, gripping tightly. "And what does that say about the God inside us?"

"I think it wants to be seen. Wants somebody to acknowledge the hurt." Hannah took a long, slow, final sip of her root beer float and then nestled the empty cup into the sand. "That's why it's the Armor of God. You get it if you're serving as witness."

Serving. Video Man was serving now. But his paracontagion shell was in custody, sitting in an aluminum box somewhere in a high-security evidence locker. Maybe it was right next to Sarah. Someone would save him, because they would want him put on trial. Someone would serve for him, in a way that no one could serve for Hannah.

"Or maybe I'm full of shit," Hannah concluded, and closed her eyes.

>>>>><<<<<

Hannah stretched beneath a seahorse blanket they'd acquired at the gift shop minutes before closing and asked through a yawn, "What time is it?"

"Two fifty-one."

Selene had not wanted Hannah to go to sleep—she kept thinking they should go see something else, do something else, talk about something else, before the deadline—but the daytime attractions were closed and neither had any appetite left and Hannah couldn't hold her eyes open, and in the end it was her choice of how to spend her last day. *It's fine,* Hannah insisted, *I'd like to have one last good sleep.*

Selene had asked if she was sure she'd like to go out this way, all blood and breakage. "I could get you a big batch of sleeping meds or something," she'd offered, and Hannah had laughed at how devastatingly straight-edge her big sister was. "Or hell, I could find us a pillow and do

RED SKIES IN THE MORNING

it that way. I'm just saying, you don't have to hurt yourself any worse." But Hannah said she wanted to go out the "old-fashioned" way. She wanted the full experience.

"Hey. You did good, sis."

The absurdity of it crashed upon Selene like a great wave and she pressed her hands to her eyes, unwilling to be so unacceptably selfish as to make Hannah's last moments about her. "You shut up. You know who did good? You. You fucking smoked that psycho. You take care of your friends. You help randos who . . . randos who look sad."

Hannah smiled and reached over from her beach chair to throw her arms around Selene's neck. She said nothing else.

For a few precious heartbeats after the time turned to 3:02, Hannah was still, and Selene thought that maybe God—the big world-breaking creature in the sky type of God, that is—had blinked. And then Hannah started coughing.

The coughs were occasional at first. Once every twenty seconds. Then once every ten, coming faster and faster until the coughs became punctuated with an awful, sucking-through-a-straw-sounding wheeze. Selene squeezed Hannah's knee and Hannah rolled away from her, still sputtering and gasping for breath, shaking her head—as if to say, *I must endure this alone*.

But Selene stayed close. She clambered onto Hannah's beach chair, squeezing in as close as she could, and held on. Clinging fiercely the way Hannah had clung to her after they found themselves orphaned. As if the strength of her embrace might be enough to hold the flesh of Hannah's body closed, that she might remain whole. When Hannah's torso began to buckle and her sneakered-feet began to kick like she was simply falling backward into sleep, she tucked her rolled-up sweater under Hannah's head and rolled her onto her side into the recovery position.

Not that there was going to be any recovery from this.

"It's okay," Selene muttered, without any belief that this was true. "It's okay."

Hannah couldn't speak. It occurred suddenly to Selene that she would never hear Hannah speak again. Not another line of Hannah-logic. Not another playful joke.

Selene had intended to hold onto Hannah until the end. But before the end, when Hannah was still intermittently blinking like an android shorting out, something sharp and foreign and *wriggling* shot straight into the palm that Selene had pressed against Hannah's stomach and Selene jerked back in shock, tripping over her own beach chair and falling on her ass in the sand.

It was a finger.

A middle finger, which became obvious when the rest of the hand emerged.

When the hand became an arm Selene tore her eyes away. Her mind could not make sense of it; she would shut down if she kept watching. She looked at Hannah, but by then Hannah was dead. And thank God, Selene thought; thank God, thank God, because now Hannah's pain was over. Hannah would be spared the rest of it. Hannah was gone. Hannah got away.

The rest of it was left for Selene to witness: the shortest lifecycle in the world. She-Who-Lives-in-Red-Light crawled out of Hannah's torso like a camper emerging from a sleeping bag. At one point Hannah seemed to sit straight up, only for her head and then her body to flop backwards onto the beach chair as the paracontagion—the entity—the ghost—shook its upper body free.

She-Who-Lives-in-Red-Light glistened crimson, even under a starless sky. It wasn't Hannah's mortal blood that was shining, though, but the ghost wearing it—Selene could tell because the glow was so dull, so extremely cold and pallid as to be the psychological equivalent of darkness. Un-light. Like the moon of a dead planet. She-Who-Lives-in-Red-Light opened its mouth—not in a scream, its face was far too blank for that—in what looked

RED SKIES IN THE MORNING

like an attempt to pant. To draw breath. It was as desperate to live as Hannah had been to die. But unlike Hannah, it wouldn't succeed. It didn't breathe. It couldn't. It would never.

Moments later it began to bleed. Not just from its eyes and mouth and nose and ears but through heretofore invisible rips in its skin; not fresh oxygenated blood but putrid froth that slipped from blue-green to black, leaking over a suddenly-bloated face. It was awful, and yet the vacuous silence of this decomposition was worse than any sound Selene could imagine. In its final seconds of anguish, She-Who-Lives-in-Red-Light stared at Selene.

And then it burst into the ether, and was carried off by the night-wind into the sea.

ACKNOWLEDGEMENTS

I would like to thank Sam Cowan for giving me a reason and a platform for "Red Skies in the Morning", and Jess Landry for giving me a reason and a platform for "Your Next Best American Girl". And I would like to especially thank Max Booth III and the whole team at Ghoulish Books for giving me a reason and a platform for "Cop Car", as well as this book as a whole. I'm incredibly lucky that anybody gets my work, let alone these talented editors. Long live the small press.

Finally, thank you to my mom for teaching me that "red skies in the morning" mean "sailors take warning." And to Mitski for her music, for which the other two stories are named.

And to you, for reading.

ABOUT THE AUTHOR

Nadia Bulkin is the author of the short story collection *She Said Destroy* (Word Horde, 2017). She is also the co-editor of the haunted house anthology *Why Didn't You Just Leave* (Cursed Morsels, 2024), which won a 2024 Shirley Jackson Award. She has been nominated for a Shirley Jackson Award seven times in total, including for *Red Skies in the Morning;* she won a 2023 Bram Stoker Award for her non-fiction essay "Becoming Ungovernable: Latah, Amok, and Disorder in Indonesia." Her short stories have appeared in venues including *Nightmare Magazine, The Dark, Southwest Review*, and *Ploughshares*, as well as editions of *The Best Horror of the Year, The Year's Best Dark Fantasy & Horror*, and *Year's Best Weird Fiction*.

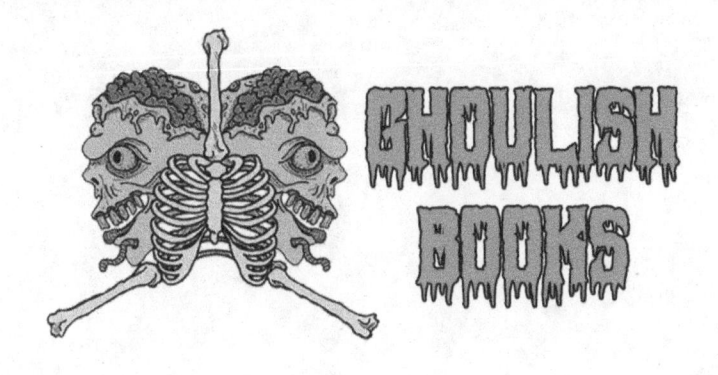

Patreon:
www.patreon.com/ghoulishbooks

Website:
www.Ghoulish.rip

Facebook:
www.facebook.com/GhoulishBooks

Bluesky:
@ghoulish.bsky.social

Instagram:
@GhoulishBookstore

Linktree:
linktr.ee/ghoulishbooks